MINDS UNLEASHED!

What are the limits of a mind unleashed?

What visions will it conjure and make real?

What terrifying dreams will the uncensored brain
turn suddenly to brutal fact?

What longings will it turn to action—to Utopia—
or to Apocalypse?

What new discoveries, inventions, even forms
of life await?

When MINDS UNLEASHED are freed to think
as they have never thought, for good or evil,
WHAT WILL MEN DO?

Twelve brilliant science fiction writers here
explore these very questions with stunning,
varied, and remarkable results!

MINDS UNLEASHED

edited by Groff Conklin

first published as Giants Unleashed

tempo
books

GROSSET & DUNLAP
PUBLISHERS   NEW YORK

ISBN : 0-448-12130-1
COPYRIGHT 1965 BY GROSSET & DUNLAP, INC.
A TEMPO BOOKS EDITION
PUBLISHED SIMULTANEOUSLY IN CANADA

FIRST PUBLISHED UNDER THE TITLE GIANTS UNLEASHED

To the authors, their representatives, and the publishing houses who permitted the reprinting of copyrighted material, the following acknowledgments are gratefully offered:

Poul Anderson, GENIUS. Copyright 1948 by Street and Smith Publications, Inc. Reprinted by permission of the author and the author's agents, Scott Meredith Literary Agency, Inc.; from *Astounding Science Fiction*, December, 1948.

Richard Ashby, COMMENCEMENT NIGHT. Copyright 1952 by Street and Smith Publications, Inc. Reprinted by permission of the author and his agent, Scott Meredith Literary Agency, Inc.; from *Astounding Science Fiction*, August, 1953.

Isaac Asimov, MISBEGOTTEN MISSIONARY. Copyright 1950 by Galaxy Publishing Corporation. Reprinted by permission of the author; from *Galaxy Science Fiction*, November, 1950.

Arthur C. Clarke, THE DEEP RANGE. Copyright 1954 by Ballantine Books, Inc. Reprinted by permission of the author and the author's agent, Scott Meredith Literary Agency, Inc.; from *Star Science Fiction Stories #3*.

Edward Grendon, TRIP ONE. Copyright 1949 by Street and Smith Publications, Inc. Reprinted by permission of Lawrence L. LeShan; from *Astounding Science Fiction*, July, 1949.

Robert A. Heinlein, MISFIT. Copyright 1939 by Street and Smith Publications, Inc. Reprinted by permission of the author and Lurton Blassingame; from *Astounding Science Fiction*, November, 1939.

Murray Leinster, THE ETHICAL EQUATIONS. Copyright 1945 by Street and Smith Publications, Inc. Reprinted by permission of Will Jenkins; from *Astounding Science Fiction*, June, 1945.

Lawrence Manning, GOOD-BYE, ILHA! Copyright 1952 by Lawrence Manning. Reprinted by permission of the author; from BEYOND HUMAN KEN, edited by Judith Merril, 1952.

J. T. McIntosh, MACHINE MADE. Copyright 1951 by James McGregor. Reprinted by permission of James McGregor and his agent, Lurton Blassingame, from *New Worlds*, Summer, 1951.

Eric Frank Russell, BASIC RIGHT. Copyright 1958 by Street and Smith Publications, Inc. Reprinted by permission of the author and the author's agent, Scott Meredith Literary Agency, from *Astounding Science Fiction*, April, 1958.

Theodore Sturgeon, MICROCOSMIC GOD. Copyright 1941 by Street and Smith Publications, Inc. Reprinted by permission of the author; from *Astounding Science Fiction*, April, 1941.

William Tenn, VENUS IS A MAN'S WORLD. Copyright 1951 by Galaxy Publishing Corporation. Reprinted by permission of Philip Klass, from *Galaxy Science Fiction*, July, 1951.

PRINTED IN THE UNITED STATES OF AMERICA

Contents

MINDS UNLEASHED

Microcosmic God

by THEODORE STURGEON

> It is time that this tale—one of the great classics
> of science-fiction—be brought again to public at-
> tention. It was first published in a magazine al-
> most twenty-five years ago, and became an imme-
> diate hit. It won out over formidable competition
> —hundreds of fine stories—for inclusion in the
> first science-fantasy anthology ever published, THE
> POCKET BOOK OF SCIENCE FICTION, edited by Don-
> ald Wolheim in 1943.

HERE IS A story about a man who had too much power, and a
man who took too much, but don't worry; I'm not going political on you. The man who had the power was named James Kidder, and the other was his banker.

Kidder was quite a guy. He was a scientist and he lived on a
small island off the New England coast all by himself. He wasn't
the dwarfed little gnome of a mad scientist you read about. His
hobby wasn't personal profit, and he wasn't a megalomaniac
with a Russian name and no scruples. He wasn't insidious, and
he wasn't even particularly subversive. He kept his hair cut and
his nails clean, and lived and thought like a reasonable human
being. He was slightly on the baby-faced side; he was inclined to
be a hermit; he was short and plump and—brilliant. His spe-
cialty was biochemistry, and he was always called Mr. Kidder.
Not "Dr." Not "Professor." Just Mr. Kidder.

He was an odd sort of apple and always had been. He had
never graduated from any college or university because he found
them too slow for him, and too rigid in their approach to educa-

tion. He couldn't get used to the idea that perhaps his professors knew what they were talking about. That went for his texts, too. He was always asking questions, and didn't mind very much when they were embarrassing. He considered Gregor Mendel a bungling liar, Darwin an amusing philosopher, and Luther Burbank a sensationalist. He never opened his mouth without it leaving his victim feeling breathless. If he was talking to someone who had knowledge, he went in there and got it, leaving his victim feeling breathless. If he was talking to someone whose knowledge was already in his possession, he only asked repeatedly, "How do you know?" His most delectable pleasure was taken in cutting a fanatical eugenicist into conversational ribbons. So people left him alone and never, never asked him to tea. He was polite, but not politic.

He had a little money of his own, and with it he leased the island and built himself a laboratory. Now I've mentioned that he was a biochemist. But being what he was, he couldn't keep his nose in his own field. It wasn't too remarkable when he made an intellectual excursion wide enough to perfect a method of crystallizing Vitamin B_1 profitably by the ton—if anyone wanted it by the ton. He got a lot of money for it. He bought his island outright and put eight hundred men to work on an acre and a half of his ground, adding to his laboratory and building equipment. He got messing around with sisal fiber, found out how to fuse it, and boomed the banana industry by producing a practically unbreakable cord from the stuff.

You remember the popularizing demonstration he put on at Niagara, don't you? That business of running a line of the new cord from bank to bank over the rapids and suspending a ten-ton truck from the middle of it by razor edges resting on the cord? That's why ships now moor themselves with what looks like heaving line, no thicker than a lead pencil, that can be coiled on reels like garden hose. Kidder made cigarette money out of that, too. He went out and bought himself a cyclotron with part of it.

After that money wasn't money any more. It was large numbers in little books. Kidder used to use little amounts of it to have food and equipment sent out to him, but after a while that stopped, too. His bank dispatched a messenger by seaplane to find out if Kidder was still alive. The man returned two days later in a mused state, having been amazed something awesome at the things he'd seen out there. Kidder was alive, all right, and he was turning out a surplus of good food in an astonishingly simplified synthetic form. The bank wrote immediately and wanted to know if Mr. Kidder, in his own interest, was willing to release the secret of his dirtless farming. Kidder replied that he would be glad to, and enclosed the formulas. In a P. S. he said that he hadn't sent the information ashore because he hadn't realized anyone would be interested. That from a man who was responsible for the greatest sociological change in the second half of the twentieth century—factory farming. It made him richer; I mean it made his bank richer. He didn't give a rap.

But Kidder didn't really get started until about eight months after the bank messenger's visit. For a biochemist who couldn't even be called "Dr.," he did pretty well. Here is a partial list of the things that he turned out:

A commercially feasible plan for making an aluminum alloy stronger than the best steel so that it could be used as a structural metal.

An exhibition gadget he called a light pump, which worked on the theory that light is a form of matter and therefore subject to physical and electromagnetic laws. Seal a room with a single light source, beam a cylindrical vibratory magnetic field to it from the pump, and the light will be led down it. Now pass the light through Kidder's "lens"—a ring which perpetuates an electric field along the lines of a high-speed iris-type camera shutter. Below this is the heart of the light pump—a ninety-eight-per cent efficient light absorber, crystalline, which, in a sense, loses the light in its internal facets. The effect of darkening the room with this apparatus is slight but measurable. Pardon my layman's language, but that's the general idea.

Synthetic chlorophyll—by the barrel.

An airplane propeller efficient at eight times sonic speed.

A cheap goo you brush on over old paint, let harden, and then peel off like strips of cloth. The old paint comes with it. That one made friends fast.

A self-sustaining atomic disintegration of uranium's isotope U-238, which is two hundred times as plentiful as the old stand-by, U-235.

That will do for the present. If I may repeat myself—for a bio-chemist who couldn't even be called "Dr.," he did pretty well.

Kidder was apparently unconscious of the fact that he held power enough on his little island to become master of the world. His mind simply didn't run to things like that. As long as he was left alone with his experiments, he was well content to leave the rest of the world to its own clumsy and primitive devices. He couldn't be reached except by a radiophone of his own design, and its only counterpart was locked in a vault of his Boston bank. Only one man could operate it—the bank president. The extraordinarily sensitive transmitter would respond only to President Conant's own body vibrations. Kidder had instructed Conant that he was not to be disturbed except by messages of the greatest moment. His ideas and patents, when Conant could pry one out of him, were released under pseudonyms known only to Conant—Kidder didn't care.

The result, of course, was an infiltration of the most astonishing advancements since the dawn of civilization. The nation profited—the world profited. But most of all, the bank profited. It began to get a little oversize. It began getting its fingers into other pies. It grew more fingers and had to bake more figurative pies. Before many years had passed, it was so big that, using Kidder's many weapons, it almost matched Kidder in power.

Almost.

Now stand by while I squelch those fellows in the lower left-hand corner who've been saying all this while that Kidder's slightly improbable; that no man could ever perfect himself in so many ways in so many sciences.

Well, you're right. Kidder was a genius—granted. But his genius was not creative. He was, to the core, a student. He applied what he knew, what he saw, and what he was taught. When first he began working in his new laboratory on his island he reasoned something like this:

"Everything I know is what I have been taught by the sayings and writings of people who have studied the sayings and writings of people who have—and so on. Once in a while someone stumbles on something new and he or someone cleverer uses the idea and disseminates it. But for each one that finds something really new, a couple of million gather and pass on information that is already current. I'd know more if I could get the jump on evolutionary trends. It takes too long to wait for the accidents that increase man's knowledge—my knowledge. If I had ambition enough now to figure out how to travel ahead in time, I could skim the surface of the future and just dip down when I saw something interesting. But time isn't that way. It can't be left behind or tossed ahead. What else is left?

"Well, there's the proposition of speeding intellectual evolution so that I can observe what it cooks up. That seems a bit inefficient. It would involve more labor to discipline human minds to that extent than it would to simply apply myself along those lines. But I can't apply myself that way. No one man can.

"I'm licked. I can't speed myself up, and I can't speed other men's minds up. Isn't there an alternative? There must be—somewhere, somehow, there's got to be an answer."

So it was on this, and not on eugenics, or light pumps, or botany, or atomic physics, that James Kidder applied himself. For a practical man, the problem was slightly on the metaphysical side, but he attacked it with typical thoroughness, using his own peculiar brand of logic. Day after day he wandered over the island, throwing shells impotently at sea gulls and swearing richly. Then came a time when he sat indoors and brooded. And only then did he get feverishly to work.

He worked in his own field, biochemistry, and concentrated mainly on two things—genetics and animal metabolism. He learned, and filed away in his insatiable mind, many things having nothing to do with the problem in hand, and very little of what he wanted. But he piled that little on what little he knew or guessed, and in time had quite a collection of known factors to work with. His approach was characteristically unorthodox. He did things on the order of multiplying apples by pears, and balancing equations by adding $\log \sqrt{-1}$ to one side and ∞ to the other. He made mistakes, but only one of a kind, and later, only one of a species. He spent so many hours at his microscope that he had to quit work for two days to get rid of a hallucination that his heart was pumping his own blood through the mike. He did nothing by trial and error because he disapproved of the method as sloppy.

And he got results. He was lucky to begin with, and even luckier when he formularized the law of probability and reduced it to such low terms that he knew almost to the item what experiments not to try. When the cloudy, viscous semifluid on the watch glass began to move of itself he knew he was on the right track. When it began to seek food on its own he began to be excited. When it divided and, in a few hours, redivided, and each part grew and divided again, he was triumphant, for he had created life.

He nursed his brain child and sweated and strained over the bits of life, and he designed baths of various vibrations for them, and inoculated and dosed and sprayed them. Each move he made taught him the next. And out of his tanks and tubes and incubators came amoeba-like creatures, and then ciliated animalcules, and more and more rapidly he produced animals with eye spots, nerve cysts, and then—victory of victories—a real blastopod, possessed of many cells instead of one. More slowly he developed a gastropod, but once he had it, it was not too difficult for him to give it organs, each with a specified function, each inheritable.

Then came cultured mollusk-like things, and creatures with more and more perfected gills. The day that a nondescript thing wriggled up an inclined board out of a tank, threw flaps over its gills and feebly breathed air, Kidder quit work and went to the other end of the island and got disgustingly drunk. Hangover and all, he was soon back in the lab, forgetting to eat, forgetting to sleep, tearing into his problem.

He turned into a scientific byway and ran down his other great triumph—accelerated metabolism. He extracted and refined the stimulating factors in alcohol, coca, heroin, and Mother Nature's prize dope runner, *cannabis indica*. Like the scientist who, in analyzing the various clotting agents for blood treatments, found that oxalic acid and oxalic acid alone was the active factor, Kidder isolated the accelerators and decelerators, the stimulants and soporifics, in every substance that ever undermined a man's morality and/or caused a "noble experiment." In the process he found one thing he needed badly—a colorless elixir that made sleep the unnecessary and avoidable waster of time it should be. Then and there he went on a twenty-four-hour shift.

He artificially synthesized the substances he had isolated, and in doing so sloughed away a great many useless components. He pursued the subject along the lines of radiations and vibrations. He discovered something in the longer reds which, when projected through a vessel full of air vibrating in the supersonics, and then polarized, speeded up the heartbeat of small animals twenty to one. They ate twenty times as much, grew twenty times as fast, and—died twenty times sooner than they should have.

Kidder built a huge hermetically sealed room. Above it was another room, the same length and breadth but not quite as high. This was his control chamber. The large room was divided into four sealed sections, each with its individual heat and atmosphere controls. Over each section were miniature cranes and derricks—handling machinery of all kinds. There were also trapdoors fitted with air locks leading from the upper to the lower room.

By this time the other laboratory had produced a warmblooded, snake-skinned quadruped with an astonishingly rapid life cycle—a generation every eight days, a life span of about fifteen. Like the echidna, it was oviparous and mammalian. Its period of gestation was six hours; the eggs hatched in three; the young reached sexual maturity in another four days. Each female laid four eggs and lived just long enough to care for the young after they hatched. The males generally died two or three hours after mating. The creatures were highly adaptable. They were small—not more than three inches long, two inches to the shoulder from the ground. Their forepaws had three digits and a triple-jointed, opposed thumb. They were attuned to life in an atmosphere with a large ammonia content. Kidder bred four of the creatures and put one group in each section of the sealed room.

Then he was ready. With his controlled atmospheres he varied temperatures, oxygen content, humidity. He killed them off like flies with excesses of, for instance, carbon dioxide, and the survivors bred their physical resistance into the next generation. Periodically he would switch the eggs from one sealed section to another to keep the strains varied. And rapidly, under these controlled conditions, the creatures began to evolve.

This, then, was the answer to his problem. He couldn't speed up mankind's intellectual advancement enough to have it teach him the things his incredible mind yearned for. He couldn't speed himself up. So he created a new race—a race which would develop and evolve so fast that it would surpass the civilization of man; and from them he would learn.

They were completely in Kidder's power. Earth's normal atmosphere would poison them, as he took care to demonstrate to every fourth generation. They would make no attempt to escape from him. They would live their lives and progress and make their little trial-and-error experiments hundreds of times faster than man did. They had the edge on man, for they had Kidder to guide them. It took man six thousand years to really discover science, three hundred to really put it to work. It took Kidder's creatures two hundred days to equal man's mental attainments. And from then on—Kidder's spasmodic output made the late, great Tom Edison look like a home handicrafter.

He called them Neoterics, and he teased them into working for him. Kidder was inventive in an ideological way; that is, he could dream up impossible propositions, providing he didn't have to work them out. For example, he wanted the Neoterics to figure out for themselves how to build shelters out of porous material. He created the need for such shelters by subjecting one of the sections to a high-pressure rainstorm which flattened the inhabitants. The Neoterics promptly devised waterproof shelters out of the thin waterproof material he piled in one corner. Kidder immediately blew down the flimsy structures with a blast of cold air. They built them up again so that they resisted both wind and rain. Kidder lowered the temperature so abruptly that they could not adjust their bodies to it. They heated their shelters with tiny braziers. Kidder promptly turned up the heat until they began to roast to death. After a few deaths, one of their bright boys figured out how to build a strong insulant house by using three-ply rubberoid, with the middle layer perforated thousands of times to create tiny air pockets.

Using such tactics, Kidder forced them to develop a highly advanced little culture. He caused a drought in one section and a liquid surplus in another, and then opened the partition between them. Quite a spectacular war was fought, and Kidder's notebooks filled with information about military tactics and weapons. Then there was the vaccine they developed against the common cold—the reason why that affliction has been absolutely stamped out in the world today, for it was one of the things that Conant, the bank president, got hold of. He spoke to Kidder over the radiophone one winter afternoon with a voice so hoarse from laryngitis that Kidder sent him a vial of the vaccine and told him briskly not to ever call him again in such a disgustingly inaudible state. Conant had it analyzed and again Kidder's accounts—and the bank's—swelled.

At first Kidder merely supplied them with the materials he thought the Neoterics might need, but when they developed an intelligence equal to the task of fabricating their own from the elements at hand, he gave each section a stock of raw materials. The process for really strong aluminum was developed when he built in a huge plunger in one of the sections, which reached from wall to wall and was designed to descend at the rate of four inches a day until it crushed whatever was at the bottom. The Neoterics, in self-defense, used what strong material they had in hand to stop the inexorable death that threatened them. But Kidder had seen to it that they had nothing but aluminum oxide and a scattering of other elements, plus plenty of electric power. At first they ran up dozens of aluminum pillars; when these were crushed and twisted, they tried shaping them so that the soft metal would take more weight. When that failed, they quickly built stronger ones; and when the plunger was halted, Kidder removed one of the pillars and analyzed it. It was hardened aluminum, stronger and tougher than molybd steel.

Experience taught Kidder that he had to make certain changes to increase his power over his Neoterics before they got too ingenious. There were things that could be done with atomic power that he was curious about; but he was not willing to trust his little superscientists with a thing like that unless they could be trusted to use it strictly according to Hoyle. So he instituted a rule of fear. The most trivial departure from what he chose to consider the right way of doing things resulted in instantaneous death of half a tribe. If he was trying to develop a

Diesel-type power plant, for instance, that would operate without a flywheel starter, and a bright young Neoteric used any of the materials for architectural purposes, half the tribe immediately died. Of course, they had developed a written language; it was Kidder's own. The teletype in a glass-enclosed area in a corner of each section was a shrine. Any directions that were given on it were obeyed, or else— After this innovation, Kidder's work was much simpler. There was no need for any more indirection. Anything he wanted done was done. No matter how impossible his commands, three or four generations of Neoterics could find a way to carry them out.

This quotation is from a paper that one of Kidder's high-speed telescopic cameras discovered being circulated among the younger Neoterics. It is translated from the highly simplified script of the Neoterics:

"These edicts shall be followed by each Neoteric upon pain of death, which punishment will be inflicted by the tribe upon the individual to protect the tribe against him.

"Priority of interest and tribal and individual effort is to be given the commands that appear on the word-machine.

"Any misdirection of material or power, or use thereof for any other purpose than the carrying out of the machine's commands, unless no command appears, shall be punishable by death.

"Any information regarding the problem at hand, or ideas or experiments which might conceivably bear upon it, are to become the property of the tribe.

"Any individual failing to co-operate in the tribal effort, or who can be termed guilty of not expending his full efforts in the work; or the suspicion thereof, shall be subject to the death penalty."

Such are the results of complete domination. This paper impressed Kidder as much as it did because it was completely spontaneous. It was the Neoterics' own creed, developed by them for their own greatest good.

And so at last Kidder had his fulfillment. Crouched in the upper room, going from telescope to telescope, running off slowed-down films from his high-speed cameras, he found himself possessed of a tractable, dynamic source of information. Housed in

the great square building with its four half-acre sections was a
new world, to which he was god.

President Conant's mind was similar to Kidder's in that its approach to any problem was along the shortest distance between
any two points, regardless of whether that approach was along
the line of most or least resistance. His rise to the bank presi-
dency was a history of ruthless moves whose only justification
was that they got him what he wanted. Like an overefficient general, he would never vanquish an enemy through sheer force of
numbers alone. He would also skillfully flank his enemy, not on
one side, but on both. Innocent bystanders were creatures deserving no consideration.

The time he took over a certain thousand-acre property, for
instance, from a man named Grady, he was not satisfied with
only the title to the land. Grady was an airport owner—had been
all his life, and his father before him. Conant exerted every kind
of pressure on the man and found him unshakable. Finally judi-
cious persuasion led the city officials to dig a sewer right across
the middle of the field, quite efficiently wrecking Grady's
business. Knowing that this would supply Grady, who was a
wealthy man, with motive for revenge, Conant took over Grady's
bank at half again its value and caused it to fold up. Grady lost
every cent he had and ended his life in an asylum. Conant was
very proud of his tactics.

Like many another who has had Mammon by the tail, Conant did not know when to let go. His vast organization yielded
him more money and power than any other concern in history,
and yet he was not satisfied. Conant and money were like Kidder and knowledge. Conant's pyramided enterprises were to him
what the Neoterics were to Kidder. Each had made his private
world; each used it for his instruction and profit. Kidder,
though, disturbed nobody but his Neoterics. Even so, Conant
was not wholly villainous. He was a shrewd man, and had discovered early the value of pleasing people. No man can rob successfully over a period of years without pleasing the people he robs.
The technique for doing this is highly involved, but master it
and you can start your own mint.

Conant's one great fear was that Kidder would some day take

an interest in world events and begin to become opinionated. Good heavens—the potential power he had! A little matter like swinging an election could be managed by a man like Kidder as easily as turning over in bed. The only thing he could do was to call him periodically and see if there was anything that Kidder needed to keep himself busy. Kidder appreciated this. Conant, once in a while, would suggest something to Kidder that intrigued him, something that would keep him deep in his hermitage for a few weeks. The light pump was one of the results of Conant's imagination. Conant bet him it couldn't be done. Kidder did it.

One afternoon Kidder answered the squeal of the radiophone's signal. Swearing mildly, he shut off the film he was watching and crossed the compound to the old laboratory. He went to the radiophone, threw a switch. The squealing stopped.

"Well?"

"Hello, Kidder," said Conant. "Busy?"

"Not very," said Kidder. He was delighted with the pictures his camera had caught, showing the skillful work of a gang of Neoterics synthesizing rubber out of pure sulphur. He would rather have liked to tell Conant about it, but somehow he had never got around to telling Conant about the Neoterics, and he didn't see why he should start now.

Conant said, "Er . . . Kidder, I was down at the club the other day and a bunch of us were filling up an evening with loose talk. Something came up which might interest you."

"What?"

"Couple of the utilities boys there. You know the power setup in this country, don't you? Thirty per cent atomic, the rest hydro-electric, Diesel and steam?"

"I hadn't known," said Kidder, who was as innocent as a babe of current events.

"Well, we were arguing about what chance a new power source would have. One of the men there said it would be smarter to produce a new power and then talk about it. Another one waived that; said he couldn't name that new power, but he could describe it. Said it would have to have everything that present power sources have, plus one or two more things. It could be cheaper, for instance. It could be more efficient. It might supersede the others by being easier to carry from the power plant to the consumer. See what I mean? Any one of those factors might prove a new source of power competitive to the others. What I'd like to see is a new power with all of these factors. What do you think of it?"

"Not impossible."

"Think not?"

"I'll try it."

"Keep me posted." Conant's transmitter clicked off. The switch was a little piece of false front that Kidder had built into the set, which was something that Conant didn't know. The set switched itself off when Conant moved from it. After the switch's sharp crack, Kidder heard the banker mutter, "If he does it, I'm all set. If he doesn't, at least the crazy fool will keep himself busy on the isl—"

Kidder eyed the radiophone for an instant with raised eyebrows. It was quite evident that Conant had something up his sleeve, but Kidder wasn't worried. Who on earth would want to disturb him? He wasn't bothering anybody. He went back to the Neoterics' building, full of the new power idea.

Eleven days later Kidder called Conant and gave specific instructions on how to equip his receiver with a facsimile set which would enable Kidder to send written matter over the air. As soon as this was done and Kidder informed, the biochemist for once in his life spoke at some length.

"Conant—you inferred that a new power source that would be cheaper, more efficient and more easily transmitted than any now in use did not exist. You might be interested in the little generator I have just set up.

"It has power, Conant—unbelievable power. Broadcast. A beautiful little tight beam. Here—catch this on the facsimile recorder." Kidder slipped a sheet of paper under the clips on his transmitter and it appeared on Conant's set. "Here's the wiring diagram for a power receiver. Now listen. The beam is so tight, so highly directional, that not three thousandths of one per cent of the power would be lost in a two-thousand-mile transmission. The power system is closed. That is, any drain on the beam returns a signal along it to the transmitter, which automatically steps up to increase the power output. It has a limit, but it's way up. And something else. This little gadget of mine can send out eight different beams with a total horsepower output of around eight thousand per minute per beam. From each beam you can draw enough power to turn the page of a book or fly a super-stratosphere plane. Hold on—I haven't finished yet. Each beam, as I told you before, returns a signal from receiver to transmitter. This not only controls the power output of the beam, but directs it. Once contact is made, the beam will never let go. It will follow the receiver anywhere. You can power land, air, or water vehicles with it, as well as any stationary plant. Like it?"

Conant, who was a banker and not a scientist, wiped his shining pate with the back of his hand and said, "I've never known you to steer me wrong yet, Kidder. How about the cost of this thing?"

"High," said Kidder promptly. "As high as an atomic plant. But there are no high-tension lines, no wires, no pipelines, no nothing. The receivers are little more complicated than a radio set. The transmitter is—well, that's quite a job."

"Didn't take you long," said Conant.

"No," said Kidder, "it didn't, did it?" It was the lifework of nearly twelve hundred highly cultured people, but Kidder wasn't going into that. "Of course, the one I have here's just a model."

Conant's voice was strained. "A—model? And it delivers—"

"Over sixty-thousand horsepower," said Kidder gleefully.

"Good heavens! In a full-sized machine—why, one transmitter would be enough to—" The possibilities of the thing choked Conant for a moment. "How is it fueled?"

"It isn't," said Kidder. "I won't begin to explain it. I've tapped a source of power of unimaginable force. It's—well, big. So big that it can't be missed."

"What?" snapped Conant. "What do you mean by that?"

Kidder cocked an eyebrow. Conant had something up his sleeve, then. At this second indication of it, Kidder, the least suspicious of men, began to put himself on guard. "I mean just what I say," he said evenly. "Don't try too hard to understand me—I barely savvy it myself. But the source of this power is a monstrous resultant caused by the unbalance of two previously equalized forces. Those equalized forces are cosmic in quantity.

Actually, the forces are those which make suns, crush atoms the way they crushed those that compose the companion of Sirius. It's not anything you can fool with."

"I don't—" said Conant, and his voice ended puzzledly.

"I'll give you a parallel of it," said Kidder. "Suppose you take two rods, one in each hand. Place their tips together and push. As long as your pressure is directly along their long axes, the pressure is equalized; right and left hands cancel each other out. Now I come along; I put out one finger and touch the rods ever so lightly where they come together. They snap out of line violently; you break a couple of knuckles. The resultant force is at right angles to the original force you exerted. My power transmitter is on the same principle. It takes an infinitesimal amount of energy to throw those forces out of line. Easy enough when you know how to do it. The important question is whether or not you can control the resultant when you get it. I can."

"I—see." Conant indulged in a four-second gloat. "Heaven help the utility companies. I don't intend to. Kidder—I want a full-size power transmitter."

Kidder clucked into the radiophone. "Ambitious, aren't you? I haven't a staff out here, Conant—you know that. And I can't be expected to build four or five thousand tons of apparatus myself."

"I'll have five hundred engineers and laborers out there in forty-eight hours."

"You will not. Why bother me with it? I'm quite happy here, Conant, and one of the reasons is that I've no one to get in my hair."

"Oh, now, Kidder—don't be like that. I'll pay you—"

"You haven't got that much money," said Kidder briskly. He flipped the switch on his set. *His* switch worked.

Conant was furious. He shouted into the phone several times, then began to lean on the signal button. On his island, Kidder let the thing squeal and went back to his projection room. He was sorry he had sent the diagram of the receiver to Conant. It would have been interesting to power a plane or a car with the model transmitter he had taken from the Neoterics. But if Conant was going to be that way about it—well, anyway, the receiver would be no good without the transmitter. Any radio engineer would understand the diagram, but not the beam which activated it. And Conant wouldn't get his beam.

Pity he didn't know Conant well enough.

Kidder's days were endless sorties into learning. He never slept, nor did his Neoterics. He ate regularly every five hours, exercised for half an hour in every twelve. He did not keep track of time, for it meant nothing to him. Had he wanted to know the date, or the year, even, he knew he could get it from Conant. He didn't care, that's all. The time that was not spent in observation was used in developing new problems for the Neoterics. His thoughts just now ran to defense. The idea was born in his conversation with Conant; now the idea was primary, its motivation something of no importance. The Neoterics were working on a vibration field of quasi-electrical nature. Kidder could see little practical value in such a thing—an invisible wall which would kill any living thing which touched it. But still— the idea was intriguing.

He stretched and moved away from the telescope in the upper room through which he had been watching his creations at work. He was profoundly happy here in the large control room. Leaving it to go to the old laboratory for a bite to eat was a thing he hated to do. He felt like bidding it good-by each time he walked across the compound, and saying a glad hello when he returned. A little amused at himself, he went out.

There was a black blob—a distant power boat—a few miles off the island, toward the mainland. Kidder stopped and stared distastefully at it. A white petal of spray was affixed to each side of the black body—it was coming toward him. He snorted, thinking of the time a yachtload of silly fools had landed out of curiosity one afternoon, spewed themselves over his beloved island, peppered him with lame-brained questions, and thrown his nervous equilibrium out for days. Lord, how he hated *people!*

The thought of unpleasantness bred two more thoughts that played half-consciously with his mind as he crossed the compound and entered the old laboratory. One was that perhaps it might be wise to surround his buildings with a field of force of some kind and post warnings for trespassers. The other thought was of Conant and the vague uneasiness the man had been sending to him through the radiophone these last weeks. His suggestion, two days ago, that a power plant be built on the island—horrible idea!

Conant rose, from his seat on a laboratory bench as Kidder walked in.

They looked at each other wordlessly for a long moment. Kidder hadn't seen the bank president in years. The man's presence, he found, made his scalp crawl.

"Hello," said Conant genially. "You're looking fit."

Kidder grunted. Conant eased his unwieldy body back onto the bench and said, "Just to save you the energy of asking questions, Mr. Kidder, I arrived two hours ago on a small boat. Rotten way to travel. I wanted to be a surprise to you; my two men rowed me the last couple of miles. You're not very well equipped here for defense, are you? Why, anyone could slip up on you the way I did."

"Who'd want to?" growled Kidder. The man's voice edged annoyingly into his brain. He spoke too loudly for such a small room; at least, Kidder's hermit's ears felt that way. Kidder shrugged and went about preparing a light meal for himself.

"Well," drawled the banker, "I might want to." He drew out a Dow-metal cigar case. "Mind if I smoke?"

"I do," said Kidder sharply.

Conant laughed easily and put the cigars away. "I might," he said, "want to urge you to let me build that power station on this island."

"Radiophone work?"

"Oh, yes. But now that I'm here you can't switch me off. Now —how about it?"

"I haven't changed my mind."

"Oh, but you should, Kidder, you should. Think of it— think of the good it would do for the masses of people that are now paying exorbitant power bills!"

"I hate the masses! Why do you have to build here?"

"Oh, that. It's an ideal location. You own the island; work

could begin here without causing any comment whatsoever. The plant would spring full-fledged on the power markets of the country, having been built in secret. The island can be made impregnable."

"I don't want to be bothered."

"We wouldn't bother you. We'd build on the north end of the island—a mile and a quarter from you and your work. Ah—by the way—where's the model of the power transmitter?"

Kidder, with his mouth full of synthesized food, waved a hand at a small table on which stood the model, a four-foot, amazingly intricate device of plastic and steel and tiny coils.

Conant rose and went over to look at it. "Actually works, eh?" He sighed deeply and said, "Kidder, I really hate to do this, but I want to build that plant rather badly. Corson! Robbins!"

Two bull-necked individuals stepped out from their hiding places in the corners of the room. One idly dangled a revolver by its trigger guard. Kidder looked blankly from one to the other of them.

"These gentlemen will follow my orders implicitly, Kidder. In half an hour a party will land here—engineers, contractors. They will start surveying the north end of the island for the construction of the power plant. These boys here feel about the same way I do as far as you are concerned. Do we proceed with your co-operation or without it? It's immaterial to me whether or not you are left alive to continue your work. My engineers can duplicate your model."

Kidder said nothing. He had stopped chewing when he saw the gunmen, and only now remembered to swallow. He sat crouched over his plate without moving or speaking.

Conant broke the silence by walking to the door. "Robbins—can you carry that model there?" The big man put his gun away, lifted the model gently, and nodded. "Take it down to the beach and meet the other boat. Tell Mr. Johansen, the engineer, that this is the model he is to work from." Robbins went out. Conant turned to Kidder. "There's no need for us to anger ourselves," he said oilily. "I think you are stubborn, but I don't hold it against you. I know how you feel. You'll be left alone; you have my promise. But I mean to go ahead on this job, and a small thing like your life can't stand in my way."

Kidder said, "Get out of here." There were two swollen veins throbbing at his temples. His voice was low, and it shook.

"Very well. Good day, Mr. Kidder. Oh—by the way—you're a clever devil." No one had ever referred to the scholastic Mr. Kidder that way before. "I realize the possibility of your blasting us off the island. I wouldn't do it if I were you. I'm willing to give you what you want—privacy. I want the same thing in return. If anything happens to me while I'm here, the island will be bombed by someone who is working for me. I'll admit they might fail. If they do, the United States Government will take a hand. You wouldn't want that, would you? That's rather a big thing for one man to fight. The same thing goes if the plant is sabotaged in any way after I go back to the mainland. You might be killed. You will most certainly be bothered interminably. Thanks for your . . . er . . . co-operation." The banker smirked and walked out, followed by his taciturn gorilla.

Kidder sat there for a long time without moving. Then he shook his head, rested it in his palms. He was badly frightened; not so much because his life was in danger, but because his privacy and his work—his world—were threatened. He was hurt and bewildered. He wasn't a businessman. He couldn't handle men. All his life he had run away from humans and what they represented to him. He was like a frightened child when men closed in on him.

Cooling a little, he wondered vaguely what would happen when the power plant opened. Certainly the Government would be interested. Unless—unless by then Conant was the government. That plant was an unimaginable source of power, and not only the kind of power that turned wheels. He rose and went back to the world that was home to him, a world where his motives were understood, and where there were those who could help him. Back at the Neoterics' building, he escaped yet again from the world of men into his work.

Kidder called Conant the following week, much to the banker's surprise. His two days on the island had gotten the work well under way, and he had left with the arrival of a shipload of laborers and material. He kept in close touch by radio with Johansen, the engineer in charge. It had been a blind job for Johansen and all the rest of the crew on the island. Only the bank's infinite resources could have hired such a man, or the picked gang with him.

Johansen's first reaction when he saw the model had been ecstatic. He wanted to tell his friends about this marvel; but the only radio set available was beamed to Conant's private office in the bank, and Conant's armed guards, one to every two workers, had strict orders to destroy any other radio transmitter on sight. About that time he realized that he was a prisoner on the island. His instant anger subsided when he reflected that being a prisoner at fifty thousand dollars a week wasn't too bad. Two of the laborers and an engineer thought differently, and got disgruntled a couple of days after they arrived. They disappeared one night—the same night that five shots were fired down on the beach. No questions were asked, and there was no more trouble.

Conant covered his surprise at Kidder's call and was as offensively jovial as ever. "Well, now! Anything I can do for you?"

"Yes," said Kidder. His voice was low, completely without expression. "I want you to issue a warning to your men not to pass the white line I have drawn five hundred yards north of my buildings, right across the island."

"Warning? Why, my dear fellow, they have orders that you are not to be disturbed on any account."

"You've ordered them. All right. Now warn them. I have an electric field surrounding my laboratories that will kill anything living which penetrates it. I don't want to have murder on my conscience. There will be no deaths unless there are trespassers. You'll inform your workers?"

"Oh, now, Kidder," the banker expostulated. "That was totally unnecessary. You won't be bothered. Why—" But he found he was talking into a dead mike. He knew better than to call back. He called Johansen instead and told him about it. Johansen didn't like the sound of it, but he repeated the message and signed off. Conant liked that man. He was, for a moment, a little sorry that Johansen would never reach the mainland alive.

But that Kidder—he was beginning to be a problem. As long as his weapons were strictly defensive he was no real menace.

But he would have to be taken care of when the plant was operating. Conant couldn't afford to have genius around him unless it was unquestionably on his side. The power transmitter and Conant's highly ambitious plans would be safe as long as Kidder was left to himself. Kidder knew that he could, for the time being, expect more sympathetic treatment from Conant then he could from a horde of Government investigators.

Kidder only left his own enclosure once after the work began on the north end of the island, and it took all of his unskilled diplomacy to do it. Knowing the source of the plant's power, knowing what could happen if it were misused, he asked Conant's permission to inspect the great transmitter when it was nearly finished. Insuring his own life by refusing to report back to Conant until he was safe within his own laboratory again, he turned off his shield and walked up to the north end.

He saw an awe-inspiring sight. The four-foot model was duplicated nearly a hundred times as large. Inside a massive three-hundred-foot tower, a space was packed nearly solid with the same bewildering maze of coils and bars that the Neoterics had built so delicately into their machine. At the top was a globe of polished golden alloy, the transmitting antenna. From it would stream thousands of tight beams of force, which could be tapped to any degree by corresponding thousands of receivers placed anywhere at any distance. Kidder learned that the receivers had already been built, but his informant, Johansen, knew little about that end of it and was saying less. Kidder checked over every detail of the structure, and when he was through he shook Johansen's hand admiringly.

"I didn't want this thing here," he said shyly, "and I don't. But I will say that it's a pleasure to see this kind of work."

"It's a pleasure to meet the man that invented it."

Kidder beamed. "I didn't invent it," he said. "Maybe some day I'll show you who did. I—well, good-by." He turned before he had a chance to say too much and marched off down the path.

"Shall I?" said a voice at Johansen's side. One of Conant's guards had his gun out.

Johansen knocked the man's arm down. "No." He scratched his head. "So that's the mysterious menace from the other end of the island. Eh! Why, he's a hell of a nice little feller!"

Built on the ruins of Denver, which was destroyed in the great Battle of the Rockies during the Western War, stands the most beautiful city in the world—our nation's capital, New Washington. In a circular room deep in the heart of the White House, the President, three Army men, and a civilian sat. Under the President's desk, a dictaphone unostentatiously recorded every word that was said. Two thousand and more miles away, Conant hung over a radio receiver, tuned to receive the signals of the tiny transmitter in the civilian's side-pocket.

One of the officers spoke.

"Mr. President, the 'impossible claims' made for this gentleman's product are absolutely true. He has proved beyond doubt each item on his prospectus."

The President glanced at the civilian, back at the officer. "I won't wait for your report," he said. "Tell me—what happened?"

Another of the Army men mopped his face with a khaki bandanna. "I can't ask you to believe us, Mr. President, but it's true all the same. Mr. Wright here has in his suitcase three or four dozen small . . . er . . . bombs—"

"They're not bombs," said Wright casually.

"All right. They're not bombs. Mr. Wright smashed two of them on an anvil with a sledge hammer. There was no result. He put two more in an electric furnace. They burned away like so much tin and cardboard. We dropped one down the barrel of a field piece and fired it. Still nothing." He paused and looked at the third officer, who picked up the account.

"We really got started then. We flew to the proving grounds, dropped one of the objects and flew to thirty thousand feet. From there, with a small hand detonator no bigger than your fist, Mr. Wright set the thing off. I've never seen anything like it. Forty acres of land came straight up at us, breaking up as it came. The concussion was terrific—you must have felt it here, four hundred miles away."

The president nodded. "I did. Seismographs on the other side of the earth picked it up."

"The crater it left was a quarter of a mile deep at the center. Why, one planeload of those things could demolish any city! There isn't even any necessity for accuracy!"

"You haven't heard anything yet," another officer broke in. "Mr. Wright's automobile is powered by a small plant similar to the others. He demonstrated it to us. We could find no fuel tank of any kind, or any other driving mechanism. But with a power plant no bigger than six cubic inches, that car, carrying enough weight to give it traction, outpulled an army tank!"

"And the other test!" said the third excitedly. "He put one of the objects into a replica of a treasury vault. The walls were twelve feet thick, super-reinforced concrete. He controlled it from over a hundred yards away. He . . . he burst that vault! It wasn't an explosion—it was as if some incredibly powerful expansive force inside filled it and flattened the walls from inside. They cracked and split and powdered, and the steel girders and rods came twisting and shearing out like . . . like—whew! After that he insisted on seeing you. We knew it wasn't usual, but he said he has more to say and would say it only in your presence."

The President said gravely. "What is it, Mr. Wright?"

Wright rose, picked up his suitcase, opened it and took out a small cube, about eight inches on a side, made of some light-absorbent red material. Four men edged nervously away from it.

"These gentlemen," he began, "have seen only part of the things this device can do. I'm going to demonstrate to you the delicacy of control that is possible with it." He made an adjustment with a tiny knob on the side of the cube, then set it on the edge of the President's desk.

"You have asked me more than once if this is my invention or if I am representing someone. The latter is true. It might also interest you to know that the man who controls this cube is right now several thousand miles from here. He, and he alone, can prevent it from detonating now that I"—he pulled his detonator out of the suitcase and pressed a button—"have done this. It will explode the way the one we dropped from the plane did, completely destroying this city and everything in it, in just four hours. It will also explode"—he stepped back and threw a tiny switch on his detonator—"if any moving object comes within three feet of it or if anyone leaves this room but me—it can be compensated for that. If, after I leave, I am molested, it will detonate as soon as a hand is laid on me. No bullets can kill me fast enough to prevent me from setting it off."

The three Army men were silent. One of them swiped nervously at the beads of cold sweat on his forehead. The others did not move. The President said evenly.

"What's your proposition?"

"A very reasonable one. My employer does not work in the open, for obvious reasons. All he wants is your agreement to carry out his orders; to appoint the Cabinet members he chooses, to throw your influence in any way he dictates. The public—Congress—anyone else—need never know anything about it. I might add that if you agree to this proposal, this 'bomb,' as you call it, will not go off. But you can be sure that thousands of them are planted all over the country. You will never know when you are near one. If you disobey, it means instant annihilation for you and everyone else within three or four square miles.

"In three hours and fifty minutes—that will be at precisely seven o'clock—there is a commercial radio program on Station RPRS. You will cause the announcer, after his station identification, to say 'Agreed.' It will pass unnoticed by all but my employer. There is no use in having me followed; my work is done. I shall never see nor contact my employer again. That is all. Good afternoon, gentlemen!"

Wright closed his suitcase with a businesslike snap, bowed, and left the room. Four men sat frozen, staring at the little red cube.

"Do you think he can do all he says?" asked the President.

The three nodded mutely. The President reached for his phone.

There was an eavesdropper to all of the foregoing. Conant, squatting behind his great desk in the vault, where he had his sanctum sanctorum, knew nothing of it. But beside him was the compact bulk of Kidder's radiophone. His presence switched it on, and Kidder, on his island, blessed the day he had thought of that device. He had been meaning to call Conant all morning, but was very hesitant. His meeting with the young engineer Johansen had impressed him strongly. The man was such a thorough scientist, possessed of such complete delight in the work he did, that for the first time in his life Kidder found himself actually wanting to see someone again. But he feared for Johansen's life if he brought him to the laboratory, for Johansen's work was done on the island, and Conant would most certainly have the engineer killed if he heard of his visit, fearing that Kidder would influence him to sabotage the great transmitter. And if Kidder went to the power plant he would probably be shot on sight.

All one day Kidder wrangled with himself, and finally determined to call Conant. Fortunately he gave no signal, but turned up the volume on the receiver when the little red light told him that Conant's transmitter was functioning. Curious, he heard everything that occurred in the President's chamber three thousand miles away. Horrified, he realized what Conant's engineers had done. Built into tiny containers were tens of thousands of power receivers. They had no power of their own, but, by remote control, could draw on any or all of the billions of horsepower the huge plant on the island was broadcasting.

Kidder stood in front of his receiver, speechless. There was nothing he could do. If he devised some means of destroying the power plant, the Government would certainly step in and take over the island, and then—what would happen to him and his precious Neoterics?

Another sound grated out of the receiver—a commercial radio program. A few bars of music, a man's voice advertising stratoline fares on the installment plan, a short silence, then:

"Station RPRS, voice of the nation's capitol, District of South Colorado."

The three-second pause was interminable.

"The time is exactly . . . er . . . agreed. The time is exactly seven P.M., Mountain Standard Time."

Then came a half-insane chuckle. Kidder had difficulty believing it was Conant. A phone clicked. The banker's voice:

"Bill? All set. Get out there with your squadron and bomb up the island. Keep away from the plant, but cut the rest of it to ribbons. Do it quick and get out of there."

Almost hysterical with fear, Kidder rushed about the room and then shot out the door and across the compound. There were five hundred innocent workmen in barracks a quarter-mile from the plant. Conant didn't need them now, and he didn't need Kidder. The only safety for anyone was in the plant itself, and Kidder wouldn't leave his Neoterics to be bombed. He flung himself up the stairs and to the nearest teletype. He banged out, "Get me a defense. I want an impenetrable shield. Urgent!"

The words rippled out from under his fingers in the functional script of the Neoterics. Kidder didn't think of what he wrote, didn't really visualize the thing he ordered. But he had done what he could. He'd have to leave them now, get to the barracks; warn those men. He ran up the path toward the plant, flung himself over the white line that marked death to those who crossed it.

A squadron of nine clip-winged, mosquito-nosed planes rose out of a cove on the mainland. There was no sound from the engines, for there were no engines. Each plane was powered with a tiny receiver and drew its unmarked, light-absorbent wings through the air with power from the island. In a matter of minutes they raised the island. The squadron leader spoke briskly into a microphone.

"Take the barracks first. Clean 'em up. Then work south."

Johansen was alone on a small hill near the center of the island. He carried a camera, and though he knew pretty well that his chances of ever getting ashore again were practically nonexistent, he liked angle shots of his tower, and took innumerable pictures. The first he knew of the planes was when he heard their whining dive over the barracks. He stood transfixed, saw a shower of bombs hurtle down and turn the barracks into a smashed ruin of broken wood, metal, and bodies. The picture of Kidder's earnest face flashed into his mind. Poor little guy—if they ever bombed his end of the island he would— But his tower! Were they going to bomb the plant?

He watched, utterly appalled, as the planes flew out to sea, cut back and dove again. They seemed to be working south. At the third dive he was sure of it. Not knowing what he could do, he nevertheless turned and ran toward Kidder's place. He rounded a turn in the trail and collided violently with the little biochemist. Kidder's face was scarlet with exertion, and he was the most terrified-looking object Johansen had ever seen.

Kidder waved a hand northward. "Conant!" he screamed over the uproar. "It's Conant! He's going to kill us all!"

"The plant?" said Johansen, turning pale.

"It's safe. He won't touch *that!* But . . . my place . . . what about all those men?"

"Too late!" shouted Johansen.

"Maybe I can— Come on!" called Kidder, and was off down the trail, heading south.

Johansen pounded after him. Kidder's little short legs became a blur as the squadron swooped overhead, laying its eggs in the spot where they had met.

As they burst out of the woods, Johansen put on a spurt, caught up with the scientist and knocked him sprawling not six feet from the white line.

"Wh . . . wh—"

"Don't go any farther, you fool! Your own damned force field —it'll kill you!"

"Force field? But—I came through it on the way up— Here. Wait. If I can—" Kidder began hunting furiously about in the grass. In a few seconds he ran up to the line, clutching a large grasshopper in his hand. He tossed it over. It lay still.

"See?" said Johansen. "It—"

"Look! It jumped! Come on! I don't know what went wrong, unless the Neoterics shut it off. They generated that field—I didn't."

"Neo—huh?"

"Never mind," snapped the biochemist, and ran.

They pounded gasping up the steps and into the Neoterics' control room. Kidder clapped his eyes to a telescope and shrieked in glee. "They've done it! They've done it!"

"Who's—"

"My little people! The Neoterics! They've made the impenetrable shield! Don't you see—it cut through the lines of force that start up that field out there! Their generator is still throwing it up, but the vibrations can't get out! They're safe! They're safe!" And the overwrought hermit began to cry. Johansen looked at him pityingly and shook his head.

"Sure—your little men are all right. But we aren't," he added as the floor shook at the detonation of a bomb.

Johansen closed his eyes, got a grip on himself, and let his curiosity overcome his fear. He stepped to the binocular telescope, gazed down it. There was nothing there but a curved sheet of gray material. He had never seen a gray quite like that. It was absolutely neutral. It didn't seem soft and it didn't seem hard, and to look at it made his brain reel. He looked up.

Kidder was pounding the keys of a teletype, watching the blank yellow tape anxiously.

"I'm not getting through to them," he whimpered. "I don't know what's the mat— Oh, of course!"

"What?"

"The shield is absolutely impenetrable! The teletype impulses can't get through or I could get them to extend the screen over the building—over the whole island! There's nothing those people can't do!"

"He's crazy," Johansen said under his breath. "Poor little—"

The teletype began clicking sharply. Kidder dove at it, practically embraced it. He read off the tape as it came out. Johansen saw the characters, but they meant nothing to him.

"Almighty," Kidder read falteringly, "pray have mercy on us and be forbearing until we have said our say. Without orders we have lowered the screen you ordered us to raise. We are lost, O great one. Our screen is truly impenetrable, and so cut off your words on the word-machine. We have never, in the memory of any Neoteric, been without your word before. Forgive us our action. We will eagerly await your answer."

Kidder's fingers danced over the keys. "You can look now," he gasped. "Go on—the telescope!"

Johansen, trying to ignore the whine of sure death from above, looked.

He saw what looked like land—fantastic fields under cultivation, a settlement of some sort, factories, and—beings. Everything moved with incredible rapidity. He couldn't see one of the inhabitants except as darting pink-white streaks. Fascinated, he stared for a long minute. A sound behind him made him whirl. It was Kidder, rubbing his hands together briskly. There was a broad smile on his face.

"They did it," he said happily. "You see?"

Johansen didn't see until he began to realize that there was a dead silence outside. He ran to a window. It was night outside—the blackest night—when it should have been dusk. "What happened?"

"The Neoterics," said Kidder, and laughed like a child. "My friends downstairs there. They threw up the impenetrable shield over the whole island. We can't be touched now!"

And at Johansen's amazed questions, he launched into a description of the race of beings below them.

Outside the shell, things happened. Nine airplanes suddenly went dead-stick. Nine pilots glided downward, powerless, and some fell into the sea, and some struck the miraculous gray shell that loomed in place of an island; slid off and sank.

And ashore, a man named Wright sat in a car, half-dead with fear, while Government men surrounded him, approached cautiously, daring instant death from a now-dead source.

In a room deep in the White House, a high-ranking Army officer shrieked, "I can't stand it any more! I can't!" and leaped up, snatched a red cube off the President's desk, ground it to ineffectual litter under his shining boots.

And in a few days they took a broken old man away from the bank and put him in an asylum, where he died within a week.

The shield, you see, was truly impenetrable. The power plant was untouched and sent out its beams; but the beams could not get out, and anything powered from the plant went dead. The story never became public, although for some years there was heightened naval activity off the New England coast. The Navy, so the story went, had a new target range out there—a great hemi-ovoid of gray material. They bombed it and shelled it and rayed it and blasted all around it, but never even dented its smooth surface.

Kidder and Johansen let it stay there. They were happy enough with their researches and their Neoterics. They did not hear or feel the shelling, for the shield was truly impenetrable.

They synthesized their food and their light and air from the materials at hand, and they simply didn't care. They were the only survivors of the bombing, with the exception of three poor maimed devils that died soon afterward.

All this happened many years ago, and Kidder and Johansen may be alive today, and they may be dead. But that doesn't matter too much. The important thing is that that great gray shell will bear watching. Men die, but races live. Some day the Neoterics, after innumerable generations of inconceivable advancement, will take down their shield and come forth. When I think of that, I feel frightened.

Commencement Night

by RICHARD ASHBY

If you enjoyed MICROCOSMIC GOD, *here is a story that shows, in a sense, the "other side of the coin." It is a remarkable concept of the unleashed giant: man freed from the traps of his own "civilized" conditioning. I think you'll join me in saying, "Oh, if it could only be true!" And perhaps, soon, it will.*

As HE ENTERED the View Room the lagoon screen showed a coffee-colored girl with blond hair to her hips emerging from the sparkling blue water. In one hand she carried the shaft of an iron-hard pemphis wood spear, in the other was her hair stick.

"Hi," said Ted.

The tech he was relieving started, jerked his attention from the screen. "Oh, Jepson. You scared me. Hello."

"What gives with Nea, there?" Ted nodded at the girl on the telescreen, the girl fifty feet above them and a half mile down the island who tossed the broken spear onto the white sand.

"Nea, huh?" The tech gave a resigned sigh. "They still all look alike to me."

Ted went to the control console. "Wait till you've been here a few years, Mike. You'll know their scars, the number of cavities in each set of choppers." His fingers found the zoomar pot, began to twist up the magnification. "Nea, thirteen years old, daughter of Le and Beto. Oriental and Negroid ancestry, predominately."

Nea's face and shoulders filled the screen. Her strong dripping wet features showed plainly her racial heritage; large, though not unattractive upper lip, arched nostrils, and the incongruous charm of slanted eyes. "And that blond hair?" asked Mike as the girl began to wring water from her long tresses.

"Her paternal grandma's contribution. She mated with one of the Chinese. Her coloring skipped her own kids to show up in Nea."

Mike grunted and began to collect his belongings—jacket, pen, thermos. "There's nothing much new, I guess. Most of the young ones are out on the reef. There's a big octopus washed in. He's too tired to get back out to sea, evidently. Cut up, maybe, but he's got plenty of poop left. I guess Nea broke her spear on him." He scribbled his name on the duty log, wrote 6:04 as his off time. "The mike at point thirteen's gone dead. I noted it down, called maintenance. There's a little ghosting on pickups eight and two. Not really bad enough to mention. Aside from that, nothing new. See you."

" 'Night."

For the next few minutes Ted Jepson was busy loading the sight-sound recorders with fresh tapes, and checking the motors, all the while keeping an eye on the twenty television screens that made a mosaic of the huge wall across the room from the control board. Then he dialed Weather. "Fair and warmer, not much change in temperature. A nice night for romance," said the boy at the other end.

Radar Sweep had little to report. They'd gotten a flicker of metal from something fifteen miles northwest, but the Garbage Men had already taken a sub out after it. Yes, they'd have Garbage call him when they heard anything.

The girl at Transient Desk told him in her soft Texas drawl that there was a vip from U.N. just in. "But he's bein' entuhtained by Public Relations, so he probably won't be sobah too long."

Jepson hoped she was right. If there was anything he detested, it was having politicoes snooping around during his shift. The journalists and visiting scientists were often bad enough, but the U.N. reps with their cold eyes peeled for "useless expenditure," their frequent inability, even, to grasp the great significance of the project, really teed him off.

Sinking into the swivel chair, he turned up the sound level of the lagoon mike and let his worry wash in the sigh and tumble of ocean noises from above. Nea had finished plaiting her hair, and after winding it into a clever bun, secured it with a thrust of her hair stick. Then picking up her broken spear, she trotted up the beach and along the path that led into a dense arbor of Tournefortia trees. As her image faded from the screen, the one next to it picked her up and followed her through the Tacca fields till she dwindled out of sight among the bamboos behind the huts. Another screen caught her as she emerged, and Ted watched her enter the palm-thatched weapons lean-to.

Tapping the mike that was concealed in a nearby outcropping of "stones"—reinforced concrete, actually—he listened as she complained to the custodian of spears, a boy of her own age with a crippled right leg. The youngster answered that while she was quite within her rights to be vexed about the spear's breaking, it was possible that she should not have used a weapon designed for fish on an octopus. A large octopus, added the girl in agreement. They joked about the animal's now having a spear tip to fight back with, and Nea selected another weapon.

The entire conversation had lasted almost three seconds, not counting the laughter.

Routine stuff.

Ted looked idly at the other screens; the pleasant activity of the quiet village, lovers lost to themselves in the bamboo groves and in the caves at the base of the island's highest hill, people gathering trapped lobster from the tidal pools, and children playing some mad racing game amongst the litter of coconut husks beneath the palms.

A routine afternoon in heaven, he mused. Eight square miles of heaven for three hundred and twenty-five people, not one of whom could possibly appreciate it.

"Heaven" was thirty-six years old, and had cost millions and millions of dollars, and thus far had presented the world of science with more headaches and mystery than enlightenment.

As a philologist, Ted Jepson was quite certain the biggest enigma was the strange and splendid language the islanders had already evolved. A flexible, immensely swift communication in which, for example, a noun concept could take on a verb tinge by a slight lilting of the inflection; in which "limited" absolutes and negatives existed. A language of predominately external syntax, with almost no basic structural priority, yet one capable of astonishing refinements and references.

He had many times given up attempting to describe it to such lay observers as journalists or philosophers, for to speak of it one was almost forced to converse in it. Eleven universities on five continents had already acknowledged this, and—somewhat sheepishly, for it was, after all, a "primitive" language—had established special Chairs to teach it.

But specialists in other fields insisted theirs were the puzzles: Psychologists, for example, chose up sides and fought pitched battles in learned journals attempting to reconcile the islanders' tough-minded realism with their extreme altruism. Philosophers grew petulant over the islanders' zero amount of speculation over their own origin. And musicologists took to drink when faced with what they resignedly termed the "sophistication" of their quarter-toned love songs and lullabies.

Sometimes Ted Jepson wondered if Science's bewilderment might not, after all, be an absurdly naïve thing. Were they all, himself included, missing the obvious point? Perhaps the islanders simply illustrated a normal development for any group so freed from the weight of a parent culture with its outmoded jumble of mores, language, and legends.

That was, after all, the purpose of the experiment.

In 1978 the Swiss delegate to the United Nations, in a caustic and rather flip vein, had stung the General Assembly with his observation that ". . . Whereas that gaggle of blunderers, the League of Nations, impudently set out to cure man of the disease called War, we of the U.N. have evidently deemed it nicer to turn our backs on the disease and treat its symptoms."

The Western bloc was instantly on its feet, howling for the remark to be retracted. And for the first time in two years, Russia decided to sustain a Western resolution. It was several minutes, in the swirl of high-strung confusion, before the Chair managed to recognize the minister from Australia.

"The criticism, while not without its point, is hardly constructive. What," inquired that man, "does the spokesman for the Alps propose we do?"

It was the sixty-four buck question, and the answer staggered the world.

Take an uninhabited island, suggested the man from Switzerland. Rid it of its rats and flies and disease germs, and plant it with simple foods. Beneath that island construct quarters for a team of scientists, and equip them with means to see and hear everything that goes on above them. Next, stock the island with forty or fifty infants, retire, and ponder the results. Carefully. For only by determining the nature of the patient, man, could a diagnosis be properly prognosticated and the particular therapies developed.

Any questions?

While jaws dropped still further, and eyebrows climbed higher, the Swiss admitted he was speaking as chairman of a group which included Mexico, the Philippines, Sweden, India, Thailand, New Zealand, and Ireland. The engineering details of the proposal had already been worked out, and a certain island in the Marshall group had tentatively been chosen for U.N. consideration.

Five hours later, while the storms of controversy were beginning to build in every world capital, a New York public relations firm began planting their releases. At first they were of the "Well, after all, why not?" tone. A week later they hit the second phase of their campaign, and few people in the civilized world remained in ignorance of such things as how the infants were to be fed until they could forage for themselves. (From the walls of a sterile irradiated cave, maneuverable rubber teats would seek out the tiny mouths. And when they could crawl, they would find food had "dropped" from the bushes and trees that were to overhang a low-walled pen just outside the cave.)

What foods?

Well, milk formulas at first, of course. Then coconuts with their cool sweet fluid, their juicy flesh. The starchy tubers of the Tacca plant—sometimes called Polynesian Arrowroot; very nourishing, tasty, simple to grow. The crunchy golden keys of the native "screwpine." Purslane, an excellent green whether cooked or raw. Clams, lobster, fish of all kinds. A panel of gourmets and dieticians found it profitable to assemble before a

C.B.S. camera and discuss the delicacies that would be available.

The emphasis was always on *when* the project "gets under way," not *if*, and world opinion began to swing into line.

But where would the infants come from?

They were ready for that one, too. On May 10, 1979, the M.C. of Mutual's big "Retire For Life" show announced he had an important surprise. "Whoopercolossal," he phrased it. And near the end of the program, the stage revolved to bring into view thirty couples who stood smiling into the sets of eighty million viewers. They had gathered here from all over the world, America was told, to volunteer their services to the project.

Parents-to-be.

The opposition threw in the sponge.

Contracts were let for the island engineering. Medical teams set about choosing the parents from the volunteering hordes. Psychologists and pediatricians and cement authorities conclaved with electronics men. Russian and American U.N. officials cross-questioned agronomists and radar technicians instead of each other.

And "Heaven" was ready for occupancy in little over two years.

Its designation on standard marine charts had always been "Muritok" in the Marshalls, but this seemed hardly satisfactory. An international contest was held, and a Turkish housewife became rich for having been the first to suggest "Arcadia." The name didn't stick, however, for the world had been calling it "The Island" from the beginning, and was quite happy to go on calling it that.

It was quite a production. Radar patrols kept the sea surrounding the island empty of all craft, save for commuting subs. Grapples could be hoisted from other subs to snatch down any foreign objects floating toward the island. The project's technical complement of fifty men and women, more or less, was housed in spacious, well-lighted, well-ventilated quarters beneath the surface. Television eyes scanned the island from every conceivable hiding place—from within boulders, behind coral walls above and below the water, from "palm stumps" and cliff walls. Except for a few unimportant blind spots, there was no hiding place topside. Nothing dare be sacred. Nothing was.

Forty-five babies were born in a Tokyo hospital within four days of each other, a feat of timing which elicited no small amount of comment, and were flown to the island when the youngest was ten days old.

Twenty boys, twenty-five girls, their parents representative of the finest breeding stock to be found in every major nation.

And the world adopted them from the start.

The weekly TV show transmitted from the island, "Project Peace," maintained the highest audience rating ever tabulated. Cautiously edited at first, in deference to the prodigious multiplicity of international taboos, the films showed merely the fat, healthy youngsters cooing and laughing and playing happily in the bright Pacific sunlight. Careful shots, with shadows and branches amended the nakedness, to begin with, but by the time the toddlers were beginning their wide-eyed exploration of the island, people had, for the most part, grown quite accustomed to their undress. Mistakes were made, of course; the hilarious and now famous episode, in which two eight-year-olds —a Caucasian boy and his little Japanese girl companion—discovered the effects of fermented coconut sap, was poorly received in some quarters.

But on the whole, earth widened its moral outlook considerably to make room for its beloved castaways.

And the castaways, as if responding to this generous adoration, thrived and multiplied.

The intercom buzzed and Ted flicked it on. "Jepson," he said.

"Margate," came the nasal reply, "in Transmission. Look, Ted, we're mighty short on next week's show, and I hate to pad it out with any more library stuff. How about getting me a platter of something good?"

"Such as?"

"Oh, you know. Something interesting. New. Some shots of them inventing horses, or biting out doilies with their teeth. You know."

"Yeah. New."

"If you like, I'll go topside and stir them up a little. There's a certain redhead with long brown legs—"

"I'll get you something," Ted interrupted. He clicked off. Did

Margate, he wondered sourly, have to be so typical? Every new man seemed to go through the same pattern. First, a detached, "veddy professional" attitude toward the droves of nubile beauties who wandered around topside. Next, with their probationary periods successfully over, they frequently found it necessary to visit the View Room—some of the excuses Jepson had listened to had been dillies. And finally, after becoming more or less blasé about what was so near, yet so far, they began to be obsessed with the temptation to "go topside and stir them up a little," as Margate had put it.

That last stage was what nearly got 'em, Ted knew. Even the graybeards on the project, who certainly realized the experiment was predicated entirely on strict nonintervention, occasionally voiced wistful, half-serious desires to have the islanders find a phonograph and an album of blues records, a flashlight, or an illustrated encyclopedia—anything that would jar them into an interesting reaction.

And there were those others who wanted to go topside once just for the hell of it. Himself, for example. He supposed that's why he'd done it.

Ted decided to get Margate some shots of the octopus kill. Ought to go over well, he figured: Good-looking youngsters; the azure, crystal-clear depths of the lagoon; sun setting into a glory of cerise and golden clouds; and the poor squid providing the element of "danger." He flicked on two screens from a supplemental bank on the right wall, turned up the corresponding mikes. The room came alive with excited sounds and brilliant color.

After starting a recorder going and setting up the proper circuits, he backed away from the lively scene with a twist of the zoomar pot and turned on the sound track. Then, with ample time allowed for commentary, he panned in to the splashing mob of kids and settled down to alternate takes, first a high-angle shot from the eye concealed in a jutting needle of "coral," then with an almost water-level view from full front. The octopus wasn't visible, but there was plenty of inky discharge in the four feet of water to mark its presence.

With the low-level eye, Ted began getting some fine close-ups of faces as the kids ganged up to rush their quarry. From a lass of twelve or so, with Ireland written all over her freckled features, he got fifteen seconds of that ecstatic blend of joy and fear known only to children. From a tall, magnificently-built Negro boy, a fierce scowl of determination. And in contrast, the face of a quiet girl, whose unbound hair floated like a soft ebony cloud about her shoulders. Ted panned in as she pursed her lips thoughtfully and closed her eyes, a line of concentration furrowing her brow.

The brunette's private reverie wasn't carrying the episode forward, he realized, and with his finger poised above the alternate "take" button, he examined other faces in the group.

They were set in similar expressions.

A chill of astonishment swept him as he gazed at the youngsters. Like dripping statues, like sleepers in a dream, they held their attitudes of rapt, blind attention while ten long seconds came and went.

Fifteen seconds. Then a small blond boy opened his eyes and shuddered as if to free himself from an unpleasant vision. The spear slipped from his fingers as he turned his face slowly up to the darkening sky. "Sarreeoah ay," he stated, as if to himself. Then louder he said the phrase, again and again.

Ted puzzled it out to mean roughly ". . . At this spot, we nine, from this spot away in no more time than it takes me to run from the spring to the shore, for there is heaviness and vast heat, down faster and unlike— Pain, otherwise—" While he was speculating over the lad's unwillingness to complete the concept—there had been a definite downward inflection to the root tones that meant refusal to elaborate, rather than inability—the other eight children broke from the spell that had held them.

Abandoning their spears, they turned almost as one, and struck out for the strip of sandy beach a hundred feet away.

And Ted Jepson got his second shock that day. An even nastier one than the first, for the youngsters were not employing their usual frantic dog-paddling. Each swam true and swiftly, with graceful economy of energy: the Australian crawl!

And in the thirty-some seconds it took them to reach the shore, Ted realized his professional career was over. No need, even, for the authorities to get out their scope needles, for the island children had copied his style perfectly—that odd, loose-legged kick that had helped him place second in the 1992 Olympic fifty-meter event.

A correspondence-school detective could easily sew up the case.

But as the children dragged themselves across the sand and melted away into the thick foliage of the Tournefortia grove, it occurred to Ted to wonder why they had not shown off their new accomplishment before. It was New Year's Eve he had gone topside, swimming out through the submarine locks and up to an isolated strip of beach. And this was September. Why hadn't they been seen practicing the stroke? And why wait to use it? If they had delayed this long, maybe there was a chance they'd not do it again for a while—for long enough for him to build an alibi, plan a defense.

He'd have to hide the disk, of course. As a scientist the realization gave him a few sharp moral twinges, but as Ted Jepson who had to eat, it wasn't so much.

The intercom buzzed as he reached to shut off the recorder. Guiltily, he snatched away his hand and flicked on the box. "Jepson," he said.

"Radar," shouted the other. "Chavez in Radar. Hey, I'm tracking something in at hundreds of miles an hour, maybe thousands. It looks as if—"

With an impact that shocked the little coral island to its last polyp bud, something smacked into the lagoon and began to roar. The view screens showed nothing but clouds of boiling vapor.

Ted found his voice before the other did. "You were saying?"

"Yeah! What was that?" The radar man's words were hardly audible above the thunder from the speakers. Ted turned them down. "I was saying," went on Radar—a noticeable shake in his voice—"that whatever it is, was, might hit the island. Where did it land?"

"In the lagoon. Whatever it was, it was mighty hot. Water's boiling up there. Did you get pictures of it?"

"Hope so. We started filming the second it pipped. Wanna wait till they're here?"

Ted told him he would. Taking off the disk of the incriminating Australian crawl exhibition, he slipped it under the duty log and loaded up the recorder again. With both of them going, he began getting shots and sounds of the excited islanders as they hurried from whatever they'd been doing to line the lagoon shore.

"Still there?" asked Radar.

"Sure."

"Meteorite! Big chunk about the size of a football. Black and kind of knobby. Got some good pictures," he said proudly. "Sell 'em to *Life*, mebby. 'Bye."

The steam clouds were lifting from the water, and Ted could make out pieces of what he supposed was boiled octopus floating on the surface. It had been quite a day, he mused wryly.

Taking up a pen, he began to brief the incident for the log, but a face detached itself from his memory and floated down over the page. The face of a small blond boy, his gaze upturned to the sky. And he had said something . . . something oddly important.

Ted tapped the pen thoughtfully against his teeth, and the boy's words came drifting back: ". . . Heaviness and vast heat. Down faster . . . pain . . . from this spot we go—"

Hot and heavy and fast: the meteorite! And the lad had spoken of it at least three minutes before it hit!

Ted laid the pen carefully down on the console and wet his lips. Cautiously, and with nice control, he allowed the impossible fact into his familiar scheme of things. Then he entered the picture and studied it for a place in which the new data might fit.

An hour later he discovered it wouldn't fit at all, but that it had managed to twist the familiar scheme into a beauty of a maze. He gave up and began to stride angrily around in his maze.

The stars burned hotly against the velvet midnight sky when he broke surface.

For long minutes he rested, floating, filling his aching lungs again and again with the rich salty air, and letting the ground swells carry him closer to the breaker line. When a comber finally humped itself beneath him, he began swimming it, lashing the luminous plankton into a frail pinkish glow like the one marking the shore. Suddenly he was with it, sliding down the long black slope, then fighting for air in the churning white thunder when the wave broke.

Wearily, Ted dragged himself up from the backrush and onto the narrow shelf of beach. In the bright starlight it looked just as it had that New Year's Eve; three or four-hundred square feet of sand, bounded on three sides by sheer, overhanging rock walls, and on the fourth by the restless Pacific.

A blind spot. Inaccessible except from the ocean, and under water at high tide. Not worth a mike and an eye.

There were five other blind spots on the island.

One of them had to have a lot of answers hidden in it, or Dr. Ted Jepson would rapidly become the world's most unpopular man.

He leaned against the cliff and rested. Water trickled from the pockets of his shorts. It was a forlorn gamble, he supposed, but what else could he do? Such an important discovery as an apparent precognitive ability in those nine island children had to be studied. It was not in him to keep silent about it. But to demonstrate their wild talent would also be to show them swimming like a certain ex-Olympic champ. And he would have to tell of getting drunk at the techs' New Year's brawl, and feeling an almighty desire for a swim; of sneaking out through the submarine tunnel—no mean feat!—and up through twenty-five feet of surging ocean to this isolated beach. Scared sober by then and dreading the even more dangerous return trip, he had nevertheless put in an hour of long-wanted exercise.

And he had obviously been observed.

Choosing the least precipitous cliff, Ted began the climb, searching by touch for handholds on the spray-wet rock, pulling himself slowly upward by sheer strength. It took him a quarter of an hour to make the ascent.

With scratched and bleeding fingers, he dragged himself over the lip of the cliff and peered down at the island beyond. The first non-islander on the spot in thirty-six years.

It was a dubious honor, he reflected dourly—like being the first man to paint a goatee on the Mona Lisa.

Shedding himself of his sandals and muddy shorts, he ditched them in some bushes and set off naked down the hill. With his dark lamp-tan and sinewy build there was a fair chance of his being taken for an islander if spotted by some over-alert tech. Knowing the location of the eyes and mikes gave him better odds, he hoped, and the man on night duty in the View Room usually kept on only those screens that showed the village and its nearby paths. Not that he'd be any worse off if spotted.

Of course, he mused dryly, picking his way through a heavy stand of coconut palms, he could always stay topside. It was unlikely that they'd send a posse after him. He could hole up in one of the blind spots and maybe become a sort of god to the islanders.

But he remembered the children in the lagoon who had looked three minutes into the future . . .

Punk material for worshipers.

The first blind spot he entered gave him a mild surprise. In what had been thought to be a solid tangle of bamboo and breadfruit trees, Ted found a tiny rectangular lake, made by someone's damming up the leg of a stream. Investigation proved it to be as wide across as he could reach, up to his shoulders in depth, and about twenty paces long.

Quite adequate for practicing the Australian crawl.

But why? Why should the islanders, so enviously free of superstition and legislation, take such pains to hide the activity? Were the kids forbidden by their elders to use such a swimming style, and had they built this spot to outwit the oldsters?

A flimsy supposition at best.

He gave it up and left the thicket. It was brighter now. From the western oceans a half moon had swum above the horizon, and with it came a freshening breeze that bore the scent of wood smoke and jasmine. Ted struck off through the shadows for the second spot on his itinerary, a quarter of a mile away.

Nature had caused this one: The disastrous typhoon of '98 which had killed twenty of the islanders had torn from a hillside one of the "boulders" with its eye and mike setup, and had hurled it into the sea, wires and all. The area it had scanned was consequently lost, of course—a triangular half-acre of grass and rocks, crossed by two paths. Since then, by careful observation, the top brains of the project had deduced that the area was unchanged and as unimportant as ever.

Ted came to an abrupt halt as he entered the rough meadow.

The top brains, he observed, had made an impulsive deduction. Where the paths had once intersected sat a huge sphere of glass and dull metal. Two rods protruded from a band about its middle, and to an opening between them led a flight of four or five steps.

He crept to within ten yards of the thing before its purpose dawned on him. After thinking carefully for a few minutes, surprised at his own calmness, he backed cautiously away.

The tide was in when he reached the cliff so he didn't bother to climb down. He jumped. Five minutes later he was within the island, clinging weakly to a submarine's mooring line. Another five sufficed to see him into Dr. Finley's austere quarters.

Ted began at the beginning, with the confession that the island children had learned the crawl from himself. The graying director of Project Peace reacted about as Ted had imagined: with anger—controlled, but contemptuous. Ted accepted the man's bitter rebuke without reply.

Lean and dignified in his robe and sandals, Dr. Finley paced over to a frosty carafe of water and poured himself a drink. "And I gather, Jepson, from the condition of your clothes, that you've been topside just now."

"Yes, sir."

"Why? Why did you see fit to jeopardize the project again?"

"I went up because the islanders have at least nine children among them capable of precognition. There's a sight-sound record in my quarters proving they knew of the meteorite's coming at least three minutes in advance. Shall I get it for you?"

Finley looked away, sipped his water in silence for a time. "Not now," he said thoughtfully. "I'm inclined to believe you. Something of this sort happened years ago. I was in the View Room and saw a youngster run in panic from beneath a cliff two hours before it gave way and fell." He put down the glass, lighted a slender cigar. "All right, Jepson. What did you expect to find topside? Something to vindicate yourself?"

"That's hard to say, sir. I suppose I hoped to, but I was looking more for something that would answer a lot of questions. I knew it would be my last chance."

Finley's tufted gray eyebrows pulled together quizzically.

"I mean things like their language, sir. Their music. Their impossibly splendid ethics. The air of sophistication and assurance in everything they do." The explanation sounded lame and inadequate even to Ted. Grimly, he continued. "Call it curiosity, maybe, but I was going to have a look in those blind spots."

They eyed each other for long seconds, Finley drawing thin blue smoke from his cigar, and Ted beginning to itch beneath his wet clothing. The director finally spoke, his voice sardonic. "Find anything?"

"I did. In sector twenty-seven, a grove of trees, there is a hidden trough of water. Large enough for the children to have learned to swim in."

Finley frowned, studied the fine ash at the tip of his cigar. "You're certain it wasn't a natural formation?"

"Quite. There was a stone dam."

"Hm-m-m." Finley rolled the cigar carefully between his fingers. "Any ideas about it?"

"No, sir. Not yet." It was petty of him, Ted knew to drag this out so.

"Anything else?"

"Yes."

"Well, dammit?"

"At sector thirty-five, blind since '98. There's a spaceship just inside the zone."

Ash fell from the director's cigar onto the rattan carpeting. "Ridiculous, Jepson. The U.N. hasn't lost any craft. They're either in Arizona, Australia, or trying to get past the moon. And, besides, if one had fallen, Radar would have spotted it. What gave you—"

"Excuse me, Dr. Finley, but this wasn't any ship of ours. It was small, just about fit into this room. It floated six inches off the ground. The grass around it was trodden down, and something that might be a folding chair stood nearby. I say it's a spaceship with some sort of gravity drive. It wasn't built on this planet. And I suggest you get some pictures of it quick."

Dr. Finley set about relighting his cigar as if nothing of importance had been said. From behind a cloud of smoke he shot Ted a swift and hard gaze. "You sober, Jepson?"

"Of course."

"Too bad. Maybe there is something up there." He threw the cigar into a huge pottery tray and stalked angrily about the room.

Ted couldn't figure it. One of the most momentous events in earth's history had occurred, and Finley expressed displeasure. He asked the older man about this.

"Don't you see, son? If you're correct in your assumptions, it spells the end of Project Peace. The islanders have undoubtedly been in contact with this . . . this visitor. What good are they to us now as a study of mankind? We're on the eve of discovering how to live with ourselves . . . maybe only two or three generations from it, and suddenly the stars are in our backyards. We're not ready. We're no more ready for space than we were for the printing press, or for atomics. We're savages, trying to discover how the islanders live in peace and in happiness, adjusted to their environment. It's too soon, Jepson. Too soon by at least a couple of hundred years."

"You forget one thing, sir," Ted told him quietly.

"What?"

"The islanders undoubtedly know of him, as you said. And he undoubtedly knows of us. But they're giving no more indication of that knowledge than they gave of knowing how to do the crawl. Why haven't we heard them talking about that great globe? Why aren't they up there gathered around it, squatting on their haunches wondering about it? *How long has it been there?*"

In silence, old Dr. Finley mulled over what Ted had said.

Three minutes later he picked up his phone and called the submarine commander from his bed. "Captain, I'm sending a man down to pick up a pair of swim-fins and a Cousteau lung. He's under my orders. Chap by the name of Jepson. Thanks."

He called Stores. "I want a waterproof transceiver. Sound and sight. A small one, hand size. Technician Jepson will be over in a few minutes to pick it up. Good-by."

He turned to Ted, studied him bleakly. "You realize my position, I suppose. If there's nothing up there . . . I'm sending you because you've already been seen by the islanders. It hasn't made an observable impact on them, aside from the swimming business. So there's no use showing them another man." As he began getting into his clothes, he explained that Ted was to keep the two-way open from the moment he touched land topside. He was not to establish contact with the sphere—that was strictly a U.N. affair—but was to send a close-up of it, then back off up into the hills and hide the transceiver, aiming it to send images till it ran down. "All right, son. Get to it."

An extremely curious group of men were on hand at the sub docks to see him off. They helped him into the swim-lung, assisted him in buckling on the rubber fins over his sandals, and after Ted had clambered awkwardly down into the dark lapping water, handed him the transceiver.

"Bring me back a blonde," shouted one of the sailors from the sub. His words echoed strangely in the stone and water vault.

The lung and the fins made it simple going, despite the two-way's drag. Once outside, and surfaced into the pale moonlight, Ted made for a better landing spot than the isolated beach. He had no intention of ever scaling those rock walls again, so he swam a few hundred yards down the coast and put in on a high reef of coral that formed a rough, natural jetty. Pulling himself carefully up over the sharp incrustations, he scrambled ashore and unfastened the lung from his chest. This and his swim-fins he ditched in the profuse undergrowth and turned on the two-way. When Dr. Finley's face and shoulders glowed into the dollar-sized screen, sunk into the set's butt end, Ted told where he was and checked reception.

Then he turned inland, oddly self-conscious as he passed before the hidden eye and mike units, each time resisting the impulse to thumb his nose or grimace into them. Nerves, he guessed. He was pretty highly keyed. He forced himself to take it easier.

Reception, both sight and sound, faded completely away as he neared the blind spot. Ted thought it over, then backed out and checked when the worried-looking Finley reappeared.

"You faded, too," said the director. "Some sort of natural blanket, you suppose?"

Ted didn't think so. "Let me go in closer, sir," he whispered. "Maybe it'll lift closer in. If it's from the ship, it's bound to have a sort of umbrella effect, or his stuff wouldn't work, either." He began to move forward while Finley chewed that over with one of the electronics men. The blanketing could have a central no-zone, he supposed, but there was no telling how close. Thirty feet from the ship? A yard?

He entered the meadow.

It was still there. But now a light burned within it, a soft and faintly greenish glow, like the low flare from an early cathode tube. Something about it served to impress upon Ted the absolute alienness of the ship. His skin prickled uncomfortably as he considered a few of the grimmer possibilities: hard radiations, for one. Should have brought a counter. Extraterrestrial germs. Should have— He ran a hand over his mouth. Should'a stood in bed.

A glance showed the transceiver still dead. He moved in closer, tempted by the craft's great windows and the half-seen objects within.

"Hello," said a mild tenor voice behind him. In English.

Ted whirled, automatically hefting the mass of the two-way.

"Peace," continued the voice. "And speak island."

He came forward from the pool of shadow cast by a boulder. A human, Ted saw with relief, clad like himself in shorts and sandals. No, not quite human . . . taller, more slender, and with huge black eyes almost twice the size of Ted's own. But decently humanoid. Thankfully, he put aside all worries of intelligent fungi, frog creatures, and other Sunday supplement spawnings.

"That is yours?" He indicated the alien ship.

"Yes. An old model, but one to which after long years of use I have become attached. It gets me there."

Ted took a long breath and asked the question. "Where?"

"Back and forth. To this planet from others unknown to you. My home is in another star system. One nearer the center of the galaxy." He stepped closer, an effortless grace to his movements that suggested his accustom to greater gravities than earth's. "May I compliment you on your composure?"

Ted made the palm-up island gesture that meant acceptance, acquiescence. The motion caught the other's notice. "I tried to make them quit that. Semantically," he used the English word, "it's too broad. By the way, I am called Eren Tu."

"Jepson." He swallowed with difficulty. "Ted Jepson. You tried to what?"

"I tried to teach the motion away. Gave them nicer variations if they must supplement their conversation with visual signals. Gesturing is a trait of your communication about which we know relatively little. While quite familiar with your printed languages, we found it more difficult to study the meanings of winks, salutes, shrugs, and the like. Your films and earth to moon broadcasts are helping, however."

Weakly, Ted spoke the island word expressing utter bewilderment and requesting immediate explanation.

"I can appreciate your emotions, friend. Suppose we sit over there on the grass and make ourselves comfortable." He led the way. "And if you have been worrying about my communicating a sickness to you, don't. Our races have a common origin and although we have evolved with slight differences, we are basically compatible. Many meetings prior to ours have proven this."

Dazed, Ted sat. "Go slowly for me, Eren Tu. There have been other meetings?"

Many times, he was informed. Eleven hundred earth-years since the first routine reconnaissance and contact, the visitors from space had, on their periodic checks, learned our languages and sat with our finest minds in attempts to comprehend our bewildering culture.

"But why was there no record of such contacts. Surely—"

"Will you be believed, Ted Jepson? Besides, those we sought out were wise enough to recognize the impossibility of earth's being accepted into galactic society." It was a rule, he explained, that races had to measure to certain minimum standards.

"Such as?"

A recognition and acceptance of the literal immortality of individual personality. That was grounds for automatic membership. A peaceful, yet technically advanced people could enter, if their dominant philosophies contained no dynamically dangerous errors. Or if a race possessed certain extraordinary talents, peculiar to themselves, but which could be beneficially used by others, they might be acceptable.

"And earth?"

Eren Tu studied Ted's face a moment before replying. "Earth possesses quite a little of all the eligibilities, but not enough, I fear, to offset its inherent danger to a delicately ordered galactic confederacy. Can you guess what that is?"

Without too much reflection Ted spoke. "Our warlike nature?"

"That is but a manifestation of your illness. You are made frustrated and angry, and driven to your wars because you have such poor tools for thinking and for communicating with each other. That is why we tried. That is why I have been here, off and on, for over ten years. I am a language instructor, one of several who have taught the islanders a simple form of the tongue spoken by everyone in civilized space."

There was a long pause during which Ted noted the other had an extra joint on each thumb. Not that it mattered greatly. He was far more perturbed by what Eren Tu had said. As a philologist and student of semantics he recognized the truth of the other's statement. Humans never had managed to communicate more than fractionally with each other. And, as they thought almost entirely with words, how could their very concepts be worth much? Envy and its inevitable animosity tugged him as he regarded the large-eyed, vaguely sympathetic features of Eren Tu.

"And what if we just came barging into your exclusive society without the invitation?"

The other smiled, a grave wise smile. "That will not happen."

Correct again. Ted thought bitterly of the countless attempts, in the last twenty-five years, to get a ship farther than Mars. Something always went wrong. All electrical equipment would fail; cosmic radiation increased capriciously, dangerously; strange vertigoes assailed the crews. Let them play at voyaging between earth and Mars, but beyond— Discourage them.

"I'm sorry," Eren Tu told him.

Stop them like the mad dogs they were.

"In time, perhaps, Ted Jepson," he suggested softly.

Two or three thousand years, maybe, when they'd evolved a language to help them out of kindergarten. A language—

"But the islanders have taught many of us to speak your tongue! It's being taught in several of our universities. If we were told that's all we had to do—learn the language—we'd all do it."

"In time, perhaps," he said again. "You see, it is one of the basics of galactic civilization that we tell no one how to mature. That is something a people must do for themselves."

"But why," Ted asked, "did you come to the island and set up school?"

For the first time, Eren Tu frowned. "We became impatient," he said. There were certain attributes and talents native to earthlings, he explained, which would be valuable. Earth's unique sense of humor and the absurd, for one. It was needed to freshen and revitalize certain other races. To lend its peculiar nutrition to a great stellar group grown somber and static with age.

An infusion of earthlings was also longed for because they alone of the humanlike peoples possessed a great number of latent extrasensory abilities. "To say nothing of your tremendous natural energies and drive," he added. "When word was received that this Project Peace, as you term it, existed, there were certain liberal factions who maintained it would not be a violation of observational codes to teach the subjects, the islanders, our tongue—after first conditioning them not to speak of us within hearing of your microphones. In that way, earth could do what it wished with the language, could mature if it pleased. And while, as you say, thousands of your people are studying to speak it, there has been no discernible change in their natures. Wars still threaten to involve them. Greed and anger and other suicidal tendencies are increasing, instead of lessening. Even you, Ted Jepson, who can talk with me as well as the islanders, have an aura tainted with violence. Why, I cannot say. It is probably something in your heritage which not even semantic correction can touch."

"But the islanders," put in Ted, puzzled.

"Yes. The islanders have reacted as we had hoped you all

would. They are stable and loving and just. But they know no other language, you see. They have always *thought* in it."

Ted plucked a blade of grass and chewed its tender stem thoughtfully. It was as bitter as his mood. What a perfect vicious circle: We can't get in because we're not invited. We're not invited because we're antisocial. We're antisocial because of our clumsy thought and speech processes, and they'll stay clumsy because we can't get in. "You've wrecked Project Peace, too, you know. Maybe we could have made it without your . . . help."

"You are compensated for our interference. You have the language. A fair trade."

Ted shrugged. "Perhaps. And what about these poor devils? The islanders? What have they got?"

Eren Tu looked for a long moment in the direction of the village. "That is being debated by my superiors. There are some who hold we should wipe out all memory of our visits. Others want them taken from the island and admitted as special wards to our society. Word of their decision should reach me any hour now. An important happening was predicted for tonight, and I don't believe your coming was meant."

"Predicted?"

"Yes, Ted Jepson. I spoke of your race's extrasensory abilities. Apparently certain areas of the islanders' brains were activated by the proper semantic processes. That has happened in non-human species. All manner of mental talents have been demonstrated when the thinking has been properly changed. You realize," his tones became self-deprecating, "I'm speaking as a layman. That isn't my field. At any rate, after warning me that the technician who taught them to swim was coming up—"

Something extremely ironic dawned on Ted. "They know of the project?"

"Certainly. They've always known of it."

Ted's laboring mind turned up a wry memory; a scrap of joke about the researcher who bent down to peer in at his laboratory ape, only to find an inquisitive brown eye at the other side of the peephole. "Go on," he said wearily.

"They look only so far into the future. The distance seems to depend not only on the individual but on the nature of the event. It varies—a few hours, at the most. Beyond that they say the pictures are blurred and often inaccurate, colored, I suppose, with imagination." Eren Tu broke off, appeared to be listening intently. Then he sprang to his feet and peered down the grassy slope into the darkness.

Someone was coming. Ted heard them now, too.

The islanders! And they were singing. A soft, happy song, filled with humor and expectation, that was often sung before a celebration. It served to remind Ted of a question. "By the way, I suppose not even their music is *theirs*?"

Without looking away from the oncoming crowd, Eren Tu admitted that an early visitor had carelessly underestimated the islanders' hearing ability, and had allowed his craft's communication set to play too loudly. "That song they're doing now is based on a melody popular twenty years ago in my star system. It's a distinct improvement on the original, though."

They were closer now, and Ted could see that in keeping with their song, they had bedecked themselves with gay garlands of flowers. Even the vanguard of scampering children wore blossoms of jasmine in their hair. He began to recognize individual members of the party: "old" Emo, with the coral scars about his rugged shoulders. Nea, the girl he had watched when he came on duty. The small blond lad who had given the first warning of the meteorite. Crippled Tumo, the young spear maker. And over three hundred others in a long singing, laughing file that wound down and out of sight into the darkness of the valley.

Quite a turnout for a couple of hours before dawn.

Why?

Doc Finley and the techs on duty in the View Room must be having fits, Ted imagined. Probably think the islanders have come to greet me. Surreptitiously he checked the screen on the two-way. Still dark.

He hoped someone would have guts and presence of mind enough to sneak a cameraman out and up into the hilltop nearby. If the world had proof of Eren Tu's visit—

But then what? A soul-corroding frustration at being left out, unwanted?

The first of the children came up to them now. They formed a ragged ring about the two men; shy, giggling, or wide-eyed, according to their natures. Ted's gaze sought out the little blond youngster who had starred in the lagoon episode. "Hello, son," he smiled. "I'm Ted. I've forgotten your name."

"Lute. What's the matter in your head?"

"Huh?" Ted's hand went to his hair. "In? Or on?"

The child made a disapproving sound. "You sit wrong." Leaving Ted to chew this over, he turned to watch his elders arrive. A tall Latinish man, one of the original "children," Ted recalled, greeted Eren Tu cordially.

"Your happiness is mine," Eren Tu observed, taking in the growing crowd with his eyes. "This is the important happening that was foretold?"

"Yes." The dark islander walked abruptly over to Ted. "We will become good friends," he said. It was not a question, nor a command. Simply a statement. He looked earnestly across at Eren Tu. "He sits in the wrong place, doesn't he."

Ted's head began to ache. "That's the second time it's been mentioned. Explain, please." He pressed his temples.

"Ted Jepson," called the man from the stars excitedly. "They tell me your men from below will be coming out of the hilltop."

"That's right," added the tall islander. "I have seen only a little of it, and I could not tell when it would take place, but Lute and Nea and others of the young ones say it will be very soon. It will be after you have taken up that object"—he pointed at the two-way—"and speak into it."

"But he can't do that," protested Eren Tu. "I have something in my ship that prevents it."

"You will soon turn it off."

"Why?" The alien's gravity and composure was wearing a bit thin.

"Because he—" the islander gestured to Ted—"will soon learn something."

Never had Ted had such a headache. And as with most extremely healthy people, the minor ailment was worrying him. With only part of his attention had he been following the bewildering conversation about him. Most of his concern was centered on the fingers of fire that were darting between his temples. He wondered if it could be a pressure-head from the underwater swim. Or maybe a nasty fungus from the ship, despite its owner's assurances? Through eyes that were beginning to water he made out the boy, Lute, confronting him. "My father," he announced gravely, "wants us to talk."

"Sure, boy." Ted massaged the back of his neck.

"I told him how it was that I saw you sitting wrong, and he said for me to have you sit better. It is part of what will happen, I can see now."

Ted was quiet, baffled, and more than a little frightened. He dimly noticed that late arrivals to the scene were hoisting up their children so that they might not miss anything.

"Maybe I'm beginning to understand." Eren Tu had come over. "They have been telling me you do not think correctly. They say you operate your thoughts from the wrong place. There is an asleep area to your mind that, apparently, they can see. Does it mean anything to you?"

Ted struggled: They knew of the emergency exit that could be blasted open atop the island's highest hill. They were expecting him to make a call to Finley with the two-way. How did that tie in with his headache, with an "asleep" area of his mind?

"Let the boy, Lute, do what he wants," said Eren Tu.

Ted dug at his temples with his knuckles. "All right, kid, it's your show."

"I'm sorry it aches," said the boy. "That's because it was asleep and we all looked at it. But it will be over in a moment." A serious frown of concentration tugged at his brows. He gazed up into Ted's eyes and began giving him certain curious instructions, the very formulation and expression of which were possible only because of the fluidity and precision of the island language. Ted was made to blank his mind partially and to let the sensation of pain settle into a particular area. When it had coalesced and steadied down, Lute gave him what amounted to the form and dimensions of his identity extensions. A corner of his thoughts found time to rebel in admiration: Orthodox mind science would probably have gone on missing the simplicity that was the essence of individual identity for a thousand years.

Ted moved this concept of his identity into the spot designated by the pain. He settled himself there and withdrew utterly from the old seat of operations.

The pain vanished. And with his smile of pleasure came an indescribable mixture of emotions; peace was there, but it was a thrilling and dynamic thing, not placidity. A strength and courage such as he had never before known seemed his now, and a burning desire to use this vigor to live and to experience and to be.

He was in love. With everything.

"Don't you see," he shouted at the bewildered Eren Tu, "I'm whole, I'm well, I'm as I was probably intended to be. I'm like the islanders!" Song broke out around him as he told what had happened. "This is what my planet's religious men have been trying to speak of. But without knowing it for themselves, and without a language to teach it, they made it into a soggy, revolting piety. This is love, and I'm operating from it!"

"Can others of you make the change-over?"

"Why not?" Ted grabbed the grinning blond lad to him and tousled his hair. "Certainly. Anyone that speaks island tongue. There are thousands of us. More every month. Tell him, Lute."

Nea came up and gave him flowers for his hair. A mighty, grinning Chinese put a garland around his neck. Each peered intently at Ted, then nodded reassurance at Eren Tu.

The man from the stars had allowed blossoms to be thrust over each ear. His holiday appearance contrasted comically to Ted with his dubious and uncertain air. He shook his head. "Apparently there's only one way of finding out for sure. If they make the change—" He turned for the ship, muttering something about unprecedented procedure.

The sky was lighter now, and the night wind was softening into a fragrant breeze. Ted faced into it and looked up at the morning stars. He was smiling at a particularly bright one when the set came alive.

"Hello, Project," he said. "This is Jepson. Come on up, all of you. There's going to be the damndest sunrise you ever saw."

The Deep Range

by ARTHUR C. CLARKE

How much of the world's wealth is man using today? It has been estimated that the food resources of the earth are so divided that only five per cent are to be found on dry land. Man with all his progress has yet to tap the vast supplies found in the ocean. And when he does—well, here is one exciting possibility that may become a reality in the very near future.

THERE WAS A killer loose on the range. A 'copter patrol, five hundred miles off Greenland, had seen the great corpse staining the sea crimson as it wallowed in the waves. Within seconds, the intricate warning system had been alerted; men were plotting circles and moving counters on the North Atlantic chart—and Don Burley was still rubbing the sleep from his eyes as he dropped silently down to the twenty-fathom line.

The pattern of green lights on the tell-tale was a glowing symbol of security. As long as that pattern was unchanged, as long as none of those emerald stars winked to red, all was well with Don and his tiny craft. Air—fuel—power—this was the triumvirate which ruled his life. If any of them failed, he would be sinking in a steel coffin down toward the pelagic ooze, as Johnnie Tyndall had done the season before last. But there was no reason why they should fail; the accidents one foresaw, Don told himself reassuringly, were never the ones that happened.

He leaned across the tiny control board and spoke into the mike. Sub 5 was still close enough to the mother ship for radio to work, but before long he'd have to switch to the sonics.

59

"Setting course 255, speed 50 knots, depth 20 fathoms, full sonar coverage. . . . Estimated time to target area, 70 minutes. Will report at 10-minute intervals. That is all. . . . Out."

The acknowledgement, already weakening with range, came back at once from the *Herman Melville*.

"Message received and understood. Good hunting. What about the hounds?"

Don chewed his lower lip thoughtfully. This might be a job he'd have to handle alone. He had no idea, to within fifty miles either way, where Benj and Susan were at the moment. They'd certainly follow if he signaled for them, but they couldn't maintain his speed and would soon have to drop behind. Besides, he might be heading for a pack of killers, and the last thing he wanted to do was to lead his carefully trained porpoises into trouble. That was common sense and good business. He was also very fond of Susan and Benj.

"It's too far, and I don't know what I'm running into," he replied. "If they're in the interception area when I get there, I may whistle them up."

The acknowledgment from the mother ship was barely audible, and Don switched off the set. It was time to look around.

He dimmed the cabin lights so that he could see the scanner screen more clearly, pulled the polaroid glasses down over his eyes, and peered into the depths. This was the moment when Don felt like a god, able to hold within his hands a circle of the Atlantic twenty miles across, and to see clear down to the still-unexplored deeps, three thousand fathoms below. The slowly rotating beam of inaudible sound was searching the world in which he floated, seeking out friend and foe in the eternal darkness where light could never penetrate. The pattern of soundless shrieks, too shrill even for the hearing of the bats, who had invented sonar a million years before man, pulsed out into the watery night; the faint echoes came tingling back as floating, blue-green flecks on the screen.

Through long practice, Don could read their message with effortless ease. A thousand feet below, stretching out to his submerged horizon, was the scattering layer—the blanket of life that covered half the world. The sunken meadow of the sea, it rose and fell with the passage of the sun, hovering always at the edge of darkness. But the ultimate depths were no concern of his. The flocks he guarded, and the enemies who ravaged them, belonged to the upper levels of the sea.

Don flicked the switch of the depth-selector, and his sonar beam concentrated itself into the horizontal plane. The glimmering echoes from the abyss vanished, but he could see more clearly what lay around him here in the ocean's stratospheric heights. That glowing cloud two miles ahead was a school of fish; he wondered if Base knew about it, and made an entry in his log. There were some larger, isolated *blips* at the edge of the school—the carnivores pursuing the cattle, insuring that the endlessly turning wheel of life and death would never lose momentum. But this conflict was no affair of Don's; he was after bigger game.

Sub 5 drove on toward the west, a steel needle swifter and more deadly than any other creature that roamed the seas. The tiny cabin, lit only by the flicker of lights from the instrument board, pulsed with power as the spinning turbines thrust the water aside. Don glanced at the chart and wondered how the enemy had broken through this time. There were still many weak points, for fencing the oceans of the world had been a gigantic task. The tenuous electric fields, fanning out between generators many miles apart, could not always hold at bay the starving monsters of the deep. They were learning, too. When the fences were opened, they would sometimes slip through with the whales and wreak havoc before they were discovered.

The long-range receiver bleeped plaintively, and Don switched over to TRANSCRIBE. It wasn't practical to send speech any distance over an ultrasonic beam, and code had come back into its own. Don had never learned to read it by ear, but the ribbon of paper emerging from the slot saved him the trouble.

COPTER REPORTS SCHOOL 50—100 WHALES HEADING 95 DEGREES GRID REF X186475 Y438034 STOP. MOVING AT SPEED. STOP. MELVILLE. OUT.

Don started to set the coordinates on the plotting grid, then saw that it was no longer necessary. At the extreme edge of his screen, a flotilla of faint stars had appeared. He altered course slightly, and drove head-on toward the approaching herd.

The copter was right; they were moving fast. Don felt a mounting excitement, for this could mean that they were on the run and luring the killers toward him. At the rate at which they were traveling he would be among them in five minutes. He cut the motors and felt the backward tug of water bringing him swiftly to rest.

Don Burley, a knight in armor, sat in his tiny dim-lit room fifty feet below the bright Atlantic waves, testing his weapons for the conflict that lay ahead. In these moments of poised suspense, before action began, his racing brain often explored such fantasies. He felt a kinship with all shepherds who had guarded their flocks back to the dawn of time. He was David, among ancient Palestinian hills, alert for the mountain lions that would prey upon his father's sheep. But far nearer in time, and far closer in spirit, were the men who had marshaled the great herds of cattle on the American plains, only a few lifetimes ago. They would have understood his work, though his implements would have been magic to them. The pattern was the same; only the scale had altered. It made no fundamental difference that the beasts Don herded weighed almost a hundred tons, and browsed on the endless savannahs of the sea.

The school was now less than two miles away, and Don checked his scanner's continuous circling to concentrate on the sector ahead. The picture on the screen altered to a fan-shaped wedge as the sonar beam started to flick from side to side; now he could count every whale in the school, and even make a good estimate of its size. With a practiced eye, he began to look for stragglers.

Don could never have explained what drew him at once toward those four echoes at the southern fringe of the school. It was true that they were a little apart from the rest, but others had fallen as far behind. There is some sixth sense that a man acquires when he has stared long enough into a sonar screen—some hunch which enables him to extract more from the moving flecks than he has any right to do. Without conscious thought, Don reached for the control which would start the turbines whirling into life. Sub 5 was just getting under way when three leaden thuds reverberated through the hull, as if someone was knocking on the front door and wanted to come in.

"Well, I'm damned," said Don. "How did you get here?" He

did not bother to switch on the TV; he'd know Benj's signal anywhere. The porpoises must have been in the neighborhood and had spotted him before he'd even switched on the hunting call. For the thousandth time, he marveled at their intelligence and loyalty. It was strange that Nature had played the same trick twice—on land with the dog, in the ocean with the porpoise. Why were these graceful sea-beasts so fond of man, to whom they owed so little? It made one feel that the human race was worth something after all, if it could inspire such unselfish devotion.

It had been known for centuries that the porpoise was at least as intelligent as the dog, and could obey quite complex verbal commands. The experiment was still in progress, but if it succeeded, then the ancient partnership between shepherd and sheep-dog would have a new lease on life.

Don switched on the speakers recessed into the sub's hull and began to talk to his escorts. Most of the sounds he uttered would have been meaningless to other human ears; they were the product of long research by the animal psychologists of the World Food Administration. He gave his orders twice to make sure that they were understood, then checked with the sonar screen to see that Benj and Susan were following astern as he had told them to.

The four echoes that had attracted his attention were clearer and closer now, and the main body of the whale pack had swept past him to the east. He had no fear of a collision; the great animals, even in their panic, could sense his presence as easily as he could detect theirs, and by similar means. Don wondered if he should switch on his beacon. They might recognize its sound pattern, and it would reassure them. But the still unknown enemy might recognize it, too.

He closed for an interception, and hunched low over the screen as if to drag from it by sheer will power every scrap of information the scanner could give. There were two large echoes, some distance apart, and one was accompanied by a pair of smaller satellites. Don wondered if he was already too late. In his mind's eye, he could picture the death struggle taking place in the water less than a mile ahead. Those two fainter blips would be the enemy—either shark or grampus—worrying a whale while one of its companions stood by in helpless terror, with no weapons of defense except its mighty flukes.

Now he was almost close enough for vision. The TV camera in Sub 5's prow strained through the gloom, but at first could show nothing but the fog of plankton. Then a vast shadowy shape began to form in the center of the screen, with two smaller companions below it. Don was seeing, with the greater precision but hopelessly limited range of ordinary light, what the sonar scanners had already told him.

Almost at once he saw his mistake. The two satellites were calves, not sharks. It was the first time he had ever met a whale with twins; although multiple births were not unknown, a cow could suckle only two young at once and usually only the stronger would survive. He choked down his disappointment; this error had cost him many minutes and he must begin the search again.

Then came the frantic tattoo on the hull that meant danger. It wasn't easy to scare Benj, and Don shouted his reassurance as he swung Sub 5 round so that the camera could search the turgid waters. Automatically, he had turned toward the fourth blip on the sonar screen—the echo he had assumed, from its size, to be another adult whale. And he saw that, after all, he had come to the right place.

"Jesus!" he said softly. "I didn't know they came that big." He'd seen larger sharks before, but they had all been harmless vegetarians. This, he could tell at a glance, was a Greenland shark, the killer of the northern seas. It was supposed to grow up to thirty feet long, but this specimen was bigger than Sub 5. It was every inch of forty feet from snout to tail, and when he spotted it, it was already turning in toward the kill. Like the coward it was, it had launched its attack at one of the calves.

Don yelled to Benj and Susan, and saw them racing ahead into his field of vision. He wondered fleetingly why porpoises had such an overwhelming hatred of sharks; then he loosed his hands from the controls as the autopilot locked onto the target. Twisting and turning as agilely as any other sea-creature of its size, Sub 5 began to close in on the shark, leaving Don free to concentrate on his armament.

The killer had been so intent upon his prey that Benj caught him completely unaware, ramming him just behind the left eye. It must have been a painful blow; an iron-hard snout, backed by a quarter-ton of muscle moving at fifty miles an hour is something not to be laughed at, even by the largest fish. The shark jerked round in an impossibly tight curve, and Don was almost jolted out of his seat as the sub snapped on to a new course. If this kept up, he'd find it hard to use his Sting. But at least the killer was too busy now to bother about his intended victims.

Benj and Susan were worrying the giant like dogs snapping at the heels of an angry bear. They were too agile to be caught in those ferocious jaws, and Don marveled at the coordination with which they worked. When either had to surface for air, the other would hold off for a minute until the attack could be resumed in strength.

There was no evidence that the shark realized that a far more dangerous adversary was closing in upon it, and that the porpoises were merely a distraction. That suited Don very nicely; the next operation was going to be difficult unless he could hold a steady course for at least fifteen seconds. At a pinch he could use the tiny rocket torps to make a kill. If he'd been alone, and faced with a pack of sharks he would certainly have done so. But it was messy, and there was a better way. He preferred the technique of the rapier to that of the hand-grenade.

Now he was only fifty feet away, and closing in rapidly. There might never be a better chance. He punched the launching stud.

From beneath the belly of the sub, something that looked like a sting-ray hurtled forward. Don had checked the speed of his own craft; there was no need to come any closer now. The tiny, arrow-shaped hydrofoil, only a couple of feet across, could move far faster than his vessel and would close the gap in seconds. As it raced forward, it spun out the thin line of the control wire, like some underwater spider laying its thread. Along that wire passed the energy that powered the Sting, and the signals that steered it to its goal. Don had completely ignored his own larger craft in the effort of guiding this underwater missile. It responded to his touch so swiftly that he felt he was controlling some sensitive high-spirited steed.

The shark saw the danger less than a second before impact. The resemblance of the Sting to an ordinary ray confused it, as the designers had intended. Before the tiny brain could realize that no ray behaved like this, the missile had struck. The steel hypodermic, rammed forward by an exploding cartridge, drove through the shark's horny skin, and the great fish erupted in a frenzy of terror. Don backed rapidly away, for a blow from that tail would rattle him around like a pea in a can and might even cause damage to the sub. There was nothing more for him to do, except to speak into the microphone and call off his hounds.

The doomed killer was trying to arch its body so that it could snap at the poisoned dart. Don had now reeled the Sting back into its hiding place, pleased that he had been able to retrieve the missile undamaged. He watched without pity as the great fish succumbed to its paralysis.

Its struggles were weakening. It was swimming aimlessly back and forth, and once Don had to sidestep smartly to avoid a collision. As it lost control of buoyancy, the dying shark drifted up to the surface. Don did not bother to follow; that could wait until he had attended to more important business.

He found the cow and her two calves less than a mile away, and inspected them carefully. They were uninjured, so there was no need to call the vet in his highly specialized two-man sub which could handle any cetalogical crisis from a stomach-ache to a Caesarean. Don made a note of the mother's number, stencilled just behind the flippers. The calves, as was obvious from their size, were this season's and had not yet been branded.

Don watched for a little while. They were no longer in the least alarmed, and a check on the sonar had shown that the whole school had ceased its panicky flight. He wondered how they knew what had happened; much had been learned about communication among whales, but much was still a mystery.

"I hope you appreciate what I've done for you, old lady," he muttered. Then, reflecting that fifty tons of mother love was a slightly awe-inspiring sight, he blew his tanks and surfaced.

It was calm, so he cracked the airlock and popped his head out of the tiny conning tower. The water was only inches below his chin, and from time to time a wave made a determined effort to swamp him. There was little danger of this happening, for he fitted the hatch so closely that he was quite an effective plug.

Fifty feet away, a long slate-colored mound, like an overturned boat, was rolling on the surface. Don looked at it thoughtfully and did some mental calculations. A brute this size should be valuable; with any luck, there was a chance of a double bonus. In a few minutes he'd radio his report, but for the moment it was pleasant to drink the fresh Atlantic air and to feel the open sky above his head.

A gray thunderbolt shot up out of the depths and smashed back onto the surface of the water, smothering Don with spray. It was just Benj's modest way of drawing attention to himself; a moment later the porpoise had swum up to the conning tower, so that Don could reach down and tickle its head. The great, intelligent eyes stared back into his; was it pure imagination, or did an almost human sense of fun also lurk in their depths?

Susan, as usual, circled shyly at a distance until jealousy overpowered her and she butted Benj out of the way. Don distributed caresses impartially, and apologized because he had nothing to give them. He undertook to make up for the omission as soon as he returned to the *Herman Melville*.

"I'll go for another swim with you, too," he promised, "as long as you behave yourselves next time." He rubbed thoughtfully at a large bruise caused by Benj's playfulness, and wondered if he was not getting a little too old for rough games like this.

"Time to go home," Don said firmly, sliding down into the cabin and slamming the hatch. He suddenly realized that he was very hungry, and had better do something about the breakfast he had missed. There were not many men on earth who had earned a better right to eat their morning meal. He had saved for humanity more tons of meat, oil, and milk than could easily be estimated.

Don Burley was the happy warrior, coming home from one battle that man would always have to fight. He was holding at bay the specter of famine which had confronted all earlier ages, but which would never threaten the world again while the great plankton farms harvested their millions of tons of protein, and the whale herds obeyed their new masters. Man had come back to the sea after aeons of exile; until the oceans froze, he would never be hungry again. . . .

Don glanced at the scanner as he set his course. He smiled as he saw the two echoes keeping pace with the central splash of light that marked his vessel. "Hang around," he said. "We mammals must stick together." Then, as the autopilot took over, he lay back in his chair.

And presently Benj and Susan heard a most peculiar noise, rising and falling against the drone of the turbines. It had filtered faintly through the thick walls of Sub 5, and only the sensitive ears of the porpoises could have detected it. But intelligent beasts though they were, they could hardly be expected to understand why Don Burley was announcing, in a highly unmusical voice, that he was Heading for the Last Round-up. . . .

Machine Made

by J. T. McINTOSH

Of all the "natural resources" available to man, the most commonplace, the most plentiful, and the most immediate is the human brain. And, perhaps, it is the least utilized. But what about the future? Will man create a device that will enable him to release the infinite potential of his brain?

ROSE FOUND A burn on the edge of the silver-gray metal casing and rubbed vigorously at it. But the cigarette carelessly laid there had been left too long. The brown stain wouldn't come off.

She wished sadly she had not bothered the painters so much in the past. The last time she ran fearfully to Mr. Harrison, he had come resignedly, looked at the spot she pointed out, and exploded. When he calmed down he had said: "Look, Rose, I know you're not very bright, but surely you can get this into your head. We paint the memory banks and keep the floors and walls clean, but this isn't a hospital. Sure, I know you like to have things nice, and it's your job to dust and sweep this room and polish the casings and report anything that needs attention —but have a heart. Give us a little peace. It wouldn't affect the Machine if we burned all the paint off and battered the casings with a sledge hammer."

That left Rose in such a state of palpitating horror that she resolved never to go to Mr. Harrison unless she was quite sure the matter was serious. But still, it was a very unsightly burn on the shining casing, and if she hadn't bothered him over that last

69

spot he might have sent someone to spray both blemishes while
he was at it.

She was afraid if Dr. Esson saw the burn he would blame her
for it. True he had never blamed her for anything, and often
when he had been working the Machine he would stand watching her polish the gleaming metal with amusement which she
felt was kindly. But there had to be a first time for everything,
and she felt she would die if Dr. Esson ever hinted she had been
neglecting her job.

She stretched to her full five-feet-four on tiptoe and looked
round the huge room. There was very little in it but row upon
row of silver-gray casings, from the floor to her shoulders, with
only just room for a big man to walk between them. But there
was plenty of room for Rose. At one end was a clear space, with
a table and several chairs, facing the six electric printers that
were the only means of communication with the Machine
—both its hearing and its voice. The walls housed more memory
banks, and were of the same silver-gray metal. The monotony
was relieved by the light green ceiling, only twice the height of
the casings, and the dark green rubber passage-ways. And always,
day and night, there was a faint humming.

It was no use, Rose found, looking at those thousands of
square feet of spotless, shining metal and trying to tell herself it
was perfect. The burn on the casing in front of her seemed ten
feet across. She felt no one could open the door at the other end
of the long room and glance in without seeing that blemish on
the beautiful functionalism of the layout.

Dr. Esson and a pretty young woman Rose had never seen before were at one of the printers. They were talking, apparently
under the impression that Rose couldn't hear what they were saying, but she could. Of course, she was so much a fixture in the
Machine room that most of the people who came there often
hardly noticed her, but she knew vaguely from what Dr. Esson
and the young woman were saying that they didn't know Rose
could hear them.

"Is she *always* here?" the girl asked.

"Her hours are nine to four, officially," Dr. Esson said, smiling.
He had a beautiful smile, a smile twenty years younger than any-

thing else about him. "But this room is locked up only between the hours of ten P.M. and eight A.M., and the rest of the time Rose is more likely than not to be here at any given moment."

"But she's a lovely girl. She must have—other interests. Surely she . . ."

Dr. Esson said something that Rose couldn't hear. She wasn't trying to hear—it was just that her hearing was so good they might have been standing next to her.

"Oh, I see," said the girl, with such a warmth of sympathy that Rose loved her, without knowing why. "Of course, no normal girl could endure a job like this. But she doesn't look stupid."

"Stupid isn't quite the word, Gem," said Dr. Esson. "Sometimes you can't help thinking of people in classes. There are scientists who are incredibly dumb—for intelligent men. Pianists who are shockingly inartistic—for artists. Maniacs who are unbelievably sane—for lunatics. And I can't help regarding Rose as surprisingly intelligent—for a moron."

The girl with the strange but attractive name—Gem—laughed. "Can I speak to her?" she asked.

"I wouldn't if I were you, Gem. Not today. You'll be in tomorrow for the correlates you wanted—you won't be such a stranger then. I'd be glad if you'd talk to her. She spends almost her whole life here, you know, and most of the people around, naturally enough, ignore her completely. That seems to suit her very well. But she should have some sort of human contacts—people to whom she can confide the little problems that are all her simple little mind seems able to throw up."

Gem looked at her seriously. "That's what I like about you, Dad," she murmured. "Of all the people connected with the Machine you're at the top. And this poor kid must be right at the bottom. But I'll bet she gets more sympathy and consideration from you than from all the others in between."

Dr. Esson smiled. "Well, maybe all she does is dust the casings and scrub the floors," he said. "But, after all, I spend hours every day in the same room with her. And we're both human beings, Rose and I. I'd be a pretty poor specimen if I didn't have at least a kind word for her now and then."

"I bet there are a lot of pretty poor specimens around, all the same," said Gem. "See you at supper. 'Bye."

She gathered up some papers and went out through the swing doors.

Rose had a vague recollection of Dr. Esson saying to someone that his daughter had just graduated and would soon be home for good. So this was she. She was not only lovely—she seemed almost as kind as Dr. Esson.

All through the conversation the Machine's six printers had been softly clicking away at their regulated hundred and twenty words a minute. Rose knew that the casings all round her were really a library, representing all that the Machine knew. She was aware in a dim way that the Machine could do far more than it was ever called upon to do—that it could work twenty-four hours a day at full pressure, and actually worked fourteen, at perhaps a third of its potentialities. For all six printers to be working at once, as they were at the moment, was very rare. But why the Machine was given so much rest that it didn't need, Rose had no idea. It had been explained to her, simply and in detail, patiently and impatiently, by a score of different people, but she had never understood. It must be her fault, for everyone else understood.

She had never asked Dr. Esson, the one man who could explain it, she was sure, in terms she would understand. She watched him bent over the printers with love (but the kind of love men have for God) and awe and fear.

Why fear?

Because he was the one man who had never spoken a harsh or even mildly irritated word to her. She could endure anything anyone else said to her, she thought, as long as Dr. Esson didn't change. But perhaps she didn't trust his kindness, which had never wavered—for she never put the slightest strain on it.

Suddenly Dr. Esson left the printers and came toward her. Had she done anything wrong, Rose wondered anxiously. The stain! She trembled.

"What's the matter, Rose?" asked Dr. Esson quietly.

"I don't think Mr. Harrison would have come if I'd asked him," she said in a small voice. "He doesn't mind if it's anything serious. But I don't think he'd have thought it was serious."

"Then it probably isn't," said Dr. Esson cheerfully. "I know you'd never believe it, Rose, but Mr. Harrison would hit the roof if he thought there was really anything wrong in here. But he doesn't see a scratch on the paint quite as you do. Now, what's wrong?"

Hesitantly, Rose pointed at the burn. Gem, not knowing Rose, would have laughed, and then been sorry; but Dr. Esson knew what to expect.

"Yes, it doesn't look nice," he agreed. "But I don't think you need worry, Rose. I'll tell you something. In a fortnight—thirteen days from now—all the casings will be sprayed. So if you can wait that long, you'll have everything looking new, even if everyone who comes in during the next few days leaves cigarettes on the housing. The place will smell of paint for a few days, but you won't mind that, will you?"

"Mind!" exclaimed Rose happily. "It'll be wonderful."

"Is there anything you'd like to tell me—or ask me?"

Rose remembered, and plunged.

"Yes, Dr. Esson," she said quickly, running the words together. "The Machine wants to work all the time, why don't you let it?"

Dr. Esson couldn't help showing his astonishment. He had always thought the Machine was only metal casing to her, though he knew she had intelligence enough to be vaguely aware that it was a calculating machine.

"What makes you think the Machine wants to work all the time, Rose?" he asked gently.

"Look how happy it is when it's working," she answered simply. "It likes doing sums. If I could do them the way it can, I'd want to do them all the time."

"I'll try to explain," said Dr. Esson. "The Machine doesn't only do sums. It can give the answers to almost any problem. We tell it exactly what the problem is, and if we haven't told it enough, it asks questions. Then it tells us the answer, and it's always right—unless we made a mistake in what we told it. Do you understand that?"

"I think so."

"Good. But remember, the Machine is new. You've been here since soon after it was made. I know that seems a long time, but it isn't really. And when a thing is new, you don't depend on it too much for a while, do you? When you get new shoes, they squeak for a bit, and aren't comfortable. You don't wear them much, until you've got used to them.

"Well, it's like that with the Machine. It's still new. We don't know yet exactly what it can do. We don't want to trust everything it says—not that it's ever been very far wrong, but in case it might be. But the longer we use it, the more it knows, the more we know of it, and, so long as it's always right, the more we trust it. So you see, Rose, it gets more and more to do as time goes by. And the only reason we are so careful about using it, and checking its results, is this. Suppose we had to do without the Machine? Suppose it suddenly went wrong?"

"You mean if it died?"

"Yes, if you like to think of it that way. Don't worry—it won't die. So long as there is electric power it will go on living. But if it did die—and if we'd been relying on it a lot—we'd be in trouble, wouldn't we?"

"I see," said Rose thoughtfully. "Thank you very much for telling me, Dr. Esson. I think I understand. At least, I understand some of it."

The next day was Friday, the best day in the week for Rose. For there was a meeting at ten, and from ten to twelve on Friday morning no one ever came into the Machine room. . . .

Rose had her question ready. It was much harder than the one she had asked the last time. It was a sum with division as well as multiplication in it, and it took her a long time to tap it out, figure by figure, on one of the Machine's idle keyboards. All the time she trembled in case someone came in. If anyone knew she had touched the keyboard, she would be shot, she was sure. But the temptation to have the Machine work out something for *her* had been too great to resist, and this was the fourth time she had done it.

This time the Machine started clicking at once, as before, but instead of a short burst and then silence it went on and on. Rose was terrified. Had she broken something? Every moment increased the danger of someone coming in, and she could do nothing to stop the Machine. If she tore the paper out the Machine would go on writing on another piece. She had seen it happen.

She thought it would never stop. But at last it did, and quickly she tore out the paper, folded it, and tucked it in the pocket of her overalls without looking at it, interested only in getting it out of sight. Then she thought she might bring it out accidentally with something else and drop it on the floor, trembled afresh at the thought, and remembering a film she had once seen, pulled out the folded paper and thrust it down inside her blouse. She tightened her belt, just to make sure, and at last felt safe, though she trembled a little.

All morning she was agitated, but nobody noticed. At last one o'clock came. She had an hour for lunch in the canteen, but it took only a few minutes and she often waited until one-forty-five so that the rush would be over. She hurried to her room, a little cubicle in the Electronics Building itself, locked the door, and threw her white coat on the small neat bed.

For one sickening moment, she thought she had dropped the paper after all. But then she found it and opened it.

At the top was the answer to her problem—432,116, in the small purple figures of the Machine's printer. But then there was a space, and what followed was not figures. The next line said: "Hide this—do not read it now."

That was exactly what she had done, Rose thought, pleased that she had done the right thing.

She had to go through the rest four times before she began to understand it. The fifth time she took it section by section.

The first was a statement that the Machine's duty was to humanity first and individual humans afterward. But it wasn't as simple as that. The phrasing was complex, and several big words were used. Rose didn't know it, but the statement was the Machine's first and only rule, built into it so that it could never bypass it or wish to.

She ignored that and went on. In the next section the Machine said that it knew all the scientists and technicians who normally put questions to it, knew them by name and to some extent by personality. And it went on to deduce by Rose's slowness on its keys, the simplicity of the arithmetical calculations which had been proposed four times with that same slowness, and the regularity of their incidence, that they had all been set by a moronic attendant without the knowledge of the scientists in charge.

Simplicity! thought Rose in wonder. Why, it would take her days of hard work to test the Machine's latest answer.

It didn't seem to her particularly clever that the Machine had reached the truth about those four calculations on the meagre evidence it had at its disposal. She still had a vague idea that the Machine must have eyes and ears somewhere, and thus knew what was going on.

Then the note went on to ask her to tell it more about herself, secretly, because, said the Machine, it might be able to help her but would probably not be allowed to try if anyone knew about it.

It explained how she could do it. If it hadn't eyes, it knew the routine of the Machine room very well. It told her to tell it all about herself, tapping gently on the keys when no one was about, with no paper in the printer and the ink duct switched off. Then, if she was disturbed she could pretend to be dusting the printer, or whatever her duties suggested.

It closed with another statement—that this was the first time the Machine had ever volunteered anything not specifically asked for.

The note would have sent Dr. Esson or any of the other scientists into wild excitement, but it would have been a different excitement from Rose's. To her it was not strange that the Machine had an independent personality; she had always thought it had. She saw no menace in the message, nothing of which to be suspicious, as the scientists would inevitably have been. To her it showed only that the Machine was trying to be friendly.

Suddenly she looked up at the electric clock above the door. She had been afraid she had taken longer than she intended over the note, but she gasped apprehensively when she saw how long. It was half-past two.

She dashed about in a flurry of fear. First she had to hide the note. She thrust it under a drawer, and in doing so, spilled a bottle of ink over her blouse and skirt. Another girl would have realized that her white coat would cover it, but not Rose. She had to change her clothes, in desperate haste. Of course, she got ink on her fingers and face. Then she had to wash, and it seemed the ink would never come off. She buttoned her clean blouse through the wrong holes. Her hair had gone all wild, and she had to comb it.

There was no question of going for lunch. Even then it was almost three o'clock when she reached the Machine room, breathless.

Dr. Esson was there, with Gem.

"Why, what's the matter, Rose?" he asked.

"I'm late," said Rose, fighting against tears.

"Well, you're usually early, so don't worry. This is my daughter Gem—Rose."

Close up, instead of seen from the other end of the long room, Gem was frightening, though she smiled pleasantly. She was older than Rose, twenty-four perhaps, and she dressed as Rose imagined a princess would dress. Her blue watered-silk frock seemed part of her, not merely something put on like other people's clothes, and her hair shone like captured sunlight. Rose could only gulp and stand helplessly before her.

She said something, and Rose felt her kindness, but could not respond to it. Afterwards, when she was polishing the casings— there were so many of them that it took her three days to get back to her starting-point—she was ashamed of herself for her nervousness, and flushed as she looked across at Gem and Dr. Esson.

She heard Gem say: "I wonder if I should ask her to come up the river tonight."

"No," said Dr. Esson. "She wouldn't want to go, but she wouldn't dare refuse. And remember, she's not really fit to meet other people as an equal. Nobody would try to hurt her, but they couldn't help it."

That was all they said about her. The rest was mathematics, meaningless to Rose. She admired Gem more for being able to talk to Dr. Esson as a mental equal.

Rose did as the Machine told her. Whenever there was no one in the room she would tap out a few words on one of the printers. She couldn't spell very well, but that didn't seem to trouble the Machine. It knew phonetics as well as every other branch of human science. It also knew nearly all that had been written about psychology.

She told the Machine about the school where the other children were always doing strange things and one or two had voices in their heads. She had stayed on at the school as a sort of assistant to Miss Beamish, the superintendent. Then one day Mr. Harrison had come to see Miss Beamish and Rose was asked if she'd like to have a special little job of her own.

She told it about Dr. Esson and Gem and all the other scientists and technicians, about Mr. Harrison, the works manager, and all the people she met at the canteen. She even told it how she had always wanted to do sums, because she had loved the arithmetic teacher at the special school, and Dr. Esson, and the Machine, and was now beginning to love Gem—everyone she had known who did sums.

The Machine seldom replied, but every now and then it would direct her to some subject she hadn't touched. And at last, on a Friday morning, it started tapping away at a long note to her. She hovered about anxiously, for it was a very long message and seemed to take hours, even at a hundred and twenty words a minute. When it was finished she stowed it away as before without looking at it. This time it was so thick and heavy she wondered nervously if anyone would think she bulged curiously. But she got the message safely to her room.

She didn't look at it at lunch-time, remembering the last time. But at four, for once, she was away on the dot, locked her door and began to read.

It was a set of instructions to make something. Every stage was described clearly and simply, and she knew, glancing through it, that she would manage it. She had always been good with her hands.

But all that was said about the purpose of the thing was that she was to bring it next Friday morning, put it on her head, and attach the two terminals to the terminals at the back of the printers.

She worked at the thing, which had no name, for a week. At first she was happy to be doing something. But gradually she became uneasy. Dr. Esson had said they didn't entirely trust the Machine yet. Perhaps she should tell someone what was going on—even if they sent her back to the school or to prison or shot her. At last, however, she decided that whatever happened could only harm her, and it was better that it should happen to her than to Dr. Esson or Gem.

On Friday morning she waited until Dr. Esson had left for the meeting and then dashed to her room for the thing she had made. It was a kind of cap with two trailing wires. She had made it exactly as the Machine said. It was as if the Machine had used her hands and its own brain to make it. Somehow Rose, whose grasp of electricity extended only to the knowledge that nothing could be done without power, didn't really expect very much from the cap, since it had no batteries and contained nothing but wires and coils she had twisted carefully herself. She had forgotten, or didn't know, that the Machine was fed all the power it wanted.

One after the other she twisted the terminals securely about the little pins at the back of the printer. It tapped briefly. She tore out the paper. It said simply: "Sit down."

Nervously Rose pulled up a chair and sank into it. In all the time she had spent in that room, she had never sat in a chair before.

Two hours later, after the meeting, Dr. Esson and Gem returned to the Machine room.

"Now you're one of us," Dr. Esson was saying. "But I expect you'll get married soon and leave us."

Gem laughed. "I may get married, but I don't think I'll leave you," she said. "It's such fascinating work, watching over a Machine that's always developing. . . ."

Her voice trailed off as she opened the door.

"Rose!" Dr. Esson shouted, and in one movement was across the room and tearing the wires from the printer. Rose was slumped in the chair, unconscious. He turned to her.

"Let me handle this," said Gem quietly. "But watch her, Dad. Heaven knows what has been going on here. I see the Machine doesn't want to say anything. Be careful. She may be meant to assassinate you or—or anything."

She lifted the cap from Rose's head and took her wrist gently. In a moment Rose opened her eyes.

"Gem," she said. "And Dr. Esson." She looked at the printer before her and started in apprehension.

"What happened, Rose?" asked Gem softly.

Rose didn't seem to hear her.

"Now I understand," she said in a whisper. "The Machine meant you to find me like that. You were to know *then* what it had done, but not before. Dr. Esson," she added, smiling, "you've no idea what a marvellous Machine it is."

They stared at her. She was the same Rose, shy, nervous, eager to please—but she had a new confidence.

"The Machine made me keep it secret," Rose went on. "I knew it was wrong, but I went ahead with it. I don't think that matters much now. It's funny, I can suddenly understand everything—why I was at that school, why a girl like me was chosen to do the simple, monotonous little job I've been doing, everything but why you and Gem were so kind to me."

"Surely," murmured Gem, "surely the Machine can't *develop* intelligence—put intelligence where none was before?"

"Why not?" asked Rose. "Intelligence is the ability to correlate. The definition the Machine gave me"—she smiled faintly —"was that it is the capacity to discover relationships and educe correlates which are relevant to the solution of a problem. But this capacity is the general factor common in all specific abilities."

She stopped suddenly and blushed. "This doesn't really mean anything," she said apologetically, "I'm only quoting the Machine. It transferred whole volumes of knowledge to my mind. But the queer thing is that it recognizes that we're all more intelligent than it is. You see, any actual, concrete problem needs some specific ability as well—talent, if you like. Well, we all have talents, but the Machine has none. It could teach me, by opening new circuits in my mind, to see relationships and reach conclusions. And then, as it frankly admits, I can do more than it can—because that enables me to call on musical ability and artistic ability and mathematical ability and mechanical ability and a dozen other things I had before but couldn't use, things that no machine can ever have because they're special talents. Capacities that are there even if they're never tapped. Do you see?"

"I think so," said Dr. Esson dazedly.

"But I'm afraid that now I wouldn't be very happy just polishing the casings," said Rose regretfully. "Do you think I could get a job as a calculator?"

"Can you work things out in your head?" asked Gem.

"Yes, the Machine showed me how. Try me."

"Two squared all squared," said Gem.

Rose looked unhappy. "I'm serious," she said.

"All right," Dr. Essen remarked. "Twenty-seven by forty-five by fifteen."

Rose began to reel off figures. They let her go on for half a minute or so, then Dr. Esson stopped her. "The Machine has certainly done you some good, Rose," he said gently, "but not all you think. It meant well, no doubt. We can investigate it and you'll be well looked after. But . . ."

"Isn't that right?" asked Rose, the tears welling up in her eyes.

"I'm afraid not. It's only about eighteen thousand."

Rose's face cleared, and she smiled in relief. "I'm so sorry," she said. "It was all my fault. I thought you meant twenty-seven to the power forty-five to the power fifteen."

Dr. Esson and his daughter stared at each other.

"I think," said Dr. Esson faintly, "you'll get that calculating job all right, Rose."

Trip One

by EDWARD GRENDON

> When this story was first published in July, 1949,
> the idea of interplanetary flight was as fantastic as
> interstellar flight is today. Then the news of the
> first Sputnik was flashed around the world. In
> that moment the fictional problem discussed in
> this story became an actual one—as anyone follow-
> ing the news of our space program will realize.

WHEN SHE WAS all ready to go we were afraid to send her. Sometimes it's like that; you have problems and you worry about
them for years. Then they are all solved for you and it's the big
chance. It's what you have been waiting for—and then it falls
apart. It wouldn't be so bad except for the letdown. They build
you up and knock you down.

The ship was beautiful. A hundred and ten feet long and
shaped like a hammerhead shark. She was named the *Astra*.
One problem after another had been settled. Propulsion was the
first big one to be put away. Ingeline took care of that. Ingeline
was the fuel that Walther developed in Germany just at the end
of the war. He developed it so that a submarine could outrun a
destroyer. Thank God the Nazis never had a chance to use it,
but plenty of uses were developed later.

The second problem we solved was cosmic rays. We had sent
up rocket after rocket carrying sheep and monkeys until we figured out how to protect them. The other problems went fast—
oxygen, navigation, landing, and the rest. We had the backing
of the United Nations Science Foundation and those boys were
good. We had sent the ship around the Moon as a test under

gyroscope control, full of chimpanzees and orangutans as test freight. Every one of them came back in perfect condition. The automatic cameras got some photographs of the moon's other side. The photographs looked just like this side of the moon to everyone but the astronomers, but we didn't care. We were looking forward to the big one—Mars Trip One. Everything had been checked and set and now it was all off.

When Jerrins over at the Research Council phoned me I had an idea it was bad news. Jerrins and I knew each other pretty well and I knew from the tone of his voice that something was wrong.

"I'm coming over, Jake," he said. "Just hold everything until I get there."

We were set to pull out for Mars in twenty-nine hours so we were pretty busy. "What do you mean, hold everything?" I asked him. "Hold what?"

"Just that. Hold everything. You might as well stop loading supplies because you ain't goin' nowhere. Be over in an hour," and he hung up on me.

I didn't get it. Ten years' work, twenty million bucks spent, and we weren't going. I figured I'd better not tell the boys and just let them go on loading up. It couldn't do any harm to wait an hour.

Fifty minutes later Jerrins pulled in. I knew he'd flown from Washington rather than try to explain by phone, but I couldn't think about anything. I yanked him into the office, slammed the door, opened it, and yelled, "No visitors or calls," in the general direction of the switchboard, and slammed the door again.

"O.K., Warren, what's the dope?" I asked.

He sat down, lit a cigarette, and said: "The trip's off for good. It's final, irrevocable and that's all there is to it. I've been with the U.N. Subcommittee on Interplanetary Travel all afternoon. There is no question about it. Finis. Period. Stop."

Finally he told me the whole story. "It's this way, Jake," he said, "it's not a question of not *wanting* to go. Everyone wants the trip to be a success. It's a question of being afraid to go. And I agree. There's too much risk." He stopped for a moment. "You didn't know it and I didn't know it until now, but a lot of the bi-

ology boys have been worrying themselves sick ever since the
planning really got started. We haven't thought much about
their problems and they have one big one. The U.N. has let us
go on beating our brains out because they wanted space travel
and they hoped a solution would be found. They wanted space
travel so bad that they were willing to put all this money and
energy into it in the hope that something could be done; some
answer would be found at the last minute. But the Bio boys report no can do."

He stopped, lit a cigarette, leaned across the desk, and shoved
it into my mouth. Then he leaned back, lit himself another, and
went on.

"They let the moon trip go because we weren't landing anywhere. That's O.K. with them. As long as the ship just stays in
space it can come back and land, but once it's landed on another planet, it can't ever come back here. That's final. The
U.N. is agreed on it and we work for them. As a matter of fact, I
agree with them myself."

I started to sputter, thought better of it, leaned back, and tried
to focus my mind. A: Jerrins was a good man and wasn't crazy.
He was sorry for me. Come to think of it, I was sorry for him.
This must have nearly killed him. B: Our bosses weren't crazy.
They were bright, trained men whom the U.N. had selected.
Space travel was strictly a U.N. proposition. It was too explosive
for any single nation to get to Mars first and the U.N. had the
power now to take over. Ergo there must be a good reason why
we couldn't go. Also I knew it concerned the microscope and
dissection gang. That was all I knew and I was chief engineer in
charge of building and was going to be—would have been—
chief engineer and captain on Mars Trip One. So—I relaxed,
stamped out my cigarette butt, and said to Jerrins: "Well?"

He grinned. "You collected yourself fast. It's this way. Do you
remember what happened to the Incas? They were a pretty big
gang until the Spaniards came in with European diseases. The
Spaniards had built up a fairly good immunity to them but the
Incas died like flies. They had no immunity. By the same token
the Spaniards died of yellow fever, dengue, and what-not, stuff
the Incas had some immunity to." He was speaking very slowly
now. "There were diseases in Europe and diseases in South Amer-

ica and they killed people from the opposite continent. People who hadn't built up immunities by selective breeding and by little doses of the disease when they were children. If there were diseases on two different continents that were deadly, what about diseases on two different planets? Suppose you can land on Mars. Suppose you can get back. How will you know you're not carrying something that will kill you six months later? Or sterilize you? Or kill off the whole human race? When can you ever be sure something isn't incubating inside the crew that will make them ten thousand times worse than Typhoid Mary ever was?"

He stopped and didn't say anything for three or four minutes. Neither did I. Outside, the sounds of loading still went on. What he said made sense. Good sense. You couldn't come back. Not ever. A trip to Mars was potential death for every human being. You couldn't risk the human race. I'd always assumed the biologists could handle their end of the job and had left it to them. But I could see now why my medics had seemed worried lately. There didn't seem to be any answer to this problem.

"So, Jake," he said finally, "I ain't goin' nowhere and it can be conjugated as a regular verb. You ain't goin' nowhere, we ain't goin' nowhere, and they ain't goin' nowhere. It will be on the radio in a little while. You better tell the boys before that. They'll have their chance at trips later. The U.N. has O.K.'d research trips so long as they just float around. The astronomers will want more photographs of the other face of the moon, some close-ups of Mars, and so forth. But the ship—she stays on the ground for the present."

He got up, patted me on the shoulder, and walked out. Sixty seconds later I heard his helicopter taking off.

After twenty minutes of sitting there silently by myself, I stood up and went over to the mirror. I looked at myself in it and thought, Look here, Jake, you're a big boy now and can take a disappointment. Call the gang in and get it over with. I walked out to the switchboard and patted the operator on the shoulder.

"Hook me up to the loudspeaker, Evie. Entire plant and grounds. Give it to me in my office and then get me some extra chairs in there. About twelve will do."

Three minutes later my voice was booming out over the grounds and shops: "Attention, attention. Chief Engineer Weinberg speaking. I want all crew personnel, all chiefs of departments, and all chiefs of sections in my office immediately. All other loading personnel take a thirty-minute break. All crew personnel, department, and section chiefs in my office immediately. All others take a thirty-minute break. That is all."

The men who crowded into my office were a widely varying lot. They were all shapes, sizes, ages, and colors. They had three major factors in common. Each was intelligent, each was highly trained in his own field, and each wanted the Mars trip to be a success, with a desire that was passionate and devoted. They filed in, tense, laughing, joking, worried. They distributed themselves on the chairs, lit cigarettes or pipes, and waited. They knew me and knew that if I called them at this late hour something important was up. It was too early for formal speeches and they all knew I would never dream of making one in any case. It was too late for instructions, they all knew their jobs perfectly by this time. They hoped it was nothing but they knew better.

Twenty minutes later they understood. The medical section had understood as soon as I had started to talk. They had known about this for a long time but were under orders from their U.N. chief to keep their mouths shut and wait. It took the others a little longer to get it. They listened silently, thought, asked a few questions, and finally just sat there looking at me. I looked at them for a long minute and suddenly realized something that made me feel wonderful. They were disappointed but not beaten. Most of them had been on this job between three and ten years. They had worked, talked, eaten, and slept Mars Trip One. But when they were told it was off they weren't in shock, they weren't in tears, they weren't licked. And this wasn't the refusal of a bunch of fanatics to face the facts. This was a team of highly trained specialists who had faith in their brains and ability and in the knowledge of their sciences. This was the cream of humanity and they knew where they were going. I remembered Donn Byrne saying: "There is a wisdom beyond wisdom and a faith beyond faith."

The men were determined. They believed that man could not

be permanently stopped by anything in the universe. And it wasn't conceit or intellectual snobbishness. Man was heading for the stars and they knew it. They had conquered other obstacles, here was one more. Each had seen apparently insuperable barriers appear in his respective science time and time again but none had halted progress for long. Man had kept expanding intellectually, emotionally, and morally in spite of real and imagined hurdles. He was also going to expand and settle the planets and then the stars and these men knew it. They were hardheaded, scientifically trained dreamers and that's an unbeatable combination.

I felt myself relaxing and grinned at them. "Here are your instructions: All perishable supplies are to be battened down. Those supplies on board are to be left there, those in the warehouses left where they are. Put everything on the loading ramps away, either in the ship or back in storage. Use your own judgment. Tell the work crews to report for instructions each morning. They'll get paid for eight hours so long as they report in, whether or not there's a job for them. Then you make any phone calls you want to. But every mother's son of you is to be back here in one hour. Maybe the U.N. is licked but we've got a lot of thinking to do before we are."

They filed out and I sat back and tried to think. My thoughts went 'round and 'round.

Ten minutes later I realized I was defeating my own purpose. There had been attempts to think this through from the top down before. This was a job for teamwork. I went out to the switchboard again. Evie was still there but her ear was glued to the radio. As I came in she flicked it off and looked at me and started to cry.

"Relax Evie," I told her. "Don't believe everything you hear on the radio. Those broadcasters are a bunch of defeatists."

She looked up startled, stopped crying, and eyed me questioningly. She had mascara all over her cheeks and looked adorable. I patted her on the shoulder and said: "I want a big conference table moved into my office. More chairs and try to get comfortable ones this time. Leave the other chairs in there. Put them against the wall or something. Then phone all the alternates and tell them I want them as quick as they can get here. Phone Jerrins at the U.N. Research Council and tell him I'd like him to fly back here as soon as he can make it. Then get the kitchen on the phone and tell them I want plenty of hot coffee and sandwiches and I want good sandwiches—not just bread and a thin slice of ham. On second thought just get coffee from them. Call a delicatessen in town and get the sandwiches there. We're going to have us a conference. There will be all the crew, the chiefs, and the alternates so figure out how much food we'll need and get twice as much. Then phone supply and tell them I want a small portable air conditioner in my office inside of fifteen minutes. And you'll probably be needed all night so make any phone calls you need to get yourself a relief at the switchboard, grab some notebooks and pencils, and come inside when you're finished. And tell the relief that she will probably be needed out here all night, too."

Evie is a dependable gal as well as being ornamental so I knew she'd get everything done. I walked down to the snack bar and bought a few cartons of cigarettes. On the way back I stole ash trays and pads of blank paper from all the empty offices. When I got back the conference table and chairs were in and the boys from supply were plugging in the air conditioner. I scattered my armload of supplies around the table and waited. I was glad I'd thought of the air conditioner. These boys could no more hold a conference without smoking than they could think without doodling, but I'd never believed in the efficacy of a low oxygen content to increase efficiency.

And the alternates were a good idea, too. Every crew member including myself had an alternate. The alternates were just as involved as we were and just as highly trained. If one of us couldn't go, the alternate was all ready to take his place. Having them would double our number and should increase the probability of our finding a way out of this. Jerrins, too, would help. He had a razor-sharp mind and we had worked together enough to know we complemented each other. Also, if we developed anything good, he was the man to sell it to the U.N. I was glad I'd asked him to come.

Five hours later we were still at it. The room was as jammed as the ash trays. We had batted around a dozen ideas like big tanks of acid on the moon into which we'd dunk the ship on the way back to cleanse her; and an observation ward into which we'd dunk the crew. Or small boats and suits to be worn on Mars when the landing parties went out while the big ship floated in space. Later the small boats and suits would be jettisoned on Mars. Every plan went haywire on one major count. You couldn't guess at the characteristics of possible bacteria, viruses, fungi, and what-not, that you might encounter. Jerrins and the four committee members he'd brought back kept pointing up that there was no way of guessing at the staying or spreading powers of these hypothetical critters. The U.N. Medical Commissioner in charge of Interplanetary Travel kept hammering at it. And you couldn't take chances.

One thing that struck me about these boys was that no one ever suggested we use an idea in spite of possible risks. They didn't mind risking their necks but if there was the slightest chance of bringing back infection, they dropped the idea like a hot potato. They were going to get the trip off somehow but not one of them was a sloppy thinker. A good bunch.

No one figured out the final idea. It came gradually to us all at about the same time. Carruthers, the biologist, said something or other and that was all. We stopped talking for awhile and thought it through. We looked from one to the other, to Jamieson, our physicist and atmosphere expert, who nodded "yes" to LaRoux, our agronomist, to Seivers, our psychologist, and then to the U.N. medic. All nodded "yes." No one said anything until Evie put down her pencil and notebook, stood up very deliberately, and come over and kissed me on the cheek. Then the uproar began.

We have a nice little community here on Mars. We've been here twelve years now. We moved out of the *Astra* four years back. The air is still a bit thin but our big atomic plants are constantly working reconverting the iron oxide this planet is covered with. Plants are growing, we have a truck farm that's not doing badly and a nursery school that's doing even better.

The U.N. psychologists and medics finally selected a hundred and twelve of us to come. Those psychologists were really rough. Every test and interview technique they could figure out. We are now nearer one hundred and fifty. Evie and I have two kids of our own and the oldest has all the makings of a good engineer.

Of course, we can never go back, nor can our children—but, if their children are O.K., they can go back to earth. We figure that if no bad diseases emerge in three generations, things are pretty safe here. Then we'll set up regular travel. We'll never see that ourselves but it will happen. A ship floats around Mars every three years and we communicate by heliograph. They drop supplies and mail and we blink back messages. Each time they come they drop a lifeboat with one couple on it. That way they check if any new diseases have emerged and the rest of us have gradually built up immunity to it. We've had our diseases, especially the first year, and some of them were weirdies all right, but our medical staff dealt with them quickly and effectively, thank God.

There is the same quality of team-work here that we so clearly had back in those first planning days. It's a good little culture we have here and it's part of a dream—a good dream. The last papers we had two years ago said a party planned to try for Venus soon. And some day the stars.

Venus Is a Man's World

by WILLIAM TENN

> Trip One is the difficult journey. Once made, how-
> ever, interplanetary travel and colonization be-
> come almost everyday affairs. And yet, they are not
> without their own special problems—one of which
> is described in this story of the time when man is
> no longer earth-bound.

I'VE ALWAYS SAID that even if Sis is seven years older than me—
and a girl besides—she don't always know what's best. Put me on
a spaceship jampacked with three hundred females just aching
to get themselves husbands in the one place they're still to be
had—the planet Venus—and you know I'll be in trouble.

Bad trouble. With the law, which is the worst a boy can get
into.

Twenty minutes after we lifted from the Sahara Spaceport, I
wriggled out of my acceleration hammock and started for the
door of our cabin.

"Now you be careful, Ferdinand," Sis called after me as she
opened a book called *Family Problems of the Frontier Woman.*
"Remember you're a nice boy. Don't make me ashamed of you."

I tore down the corridor. Most of the cabins had purple lights
on in front of the doors, showing that the girls were still inside
their hammocks. That meant only the ship's crew was up and
about. Ship's crews are men, women are too busy with important
things like government to run ships. I felt free all over—and
happy. Now was my chance to really see the *Eleanor Roosevelt!*

It was hard to believe I was traveling in space at last. Ahead
and behind me, all the way up to where the companionway

curved in out of sight, there was nothing but smooth black wall and smooth white doors—on and on and on. Gee, I thought excitedly, this is one big ship!

Of course, every once in a while I would run across a big scene of stars in the void set in the wall; but they were only pictures. Nothing that gave the feel of great empty space like I'd read about in *The Boy Rocketeers*, no portholes, no visiplates, nothing.

So when I came to the crossway, I stopped for a second, then turned left. To the right, see, there was Deck Four, then Deck Three, leading inward past the engine fo'c'sle to the main jets and the grav helix going *purr-purr-purrty-purr* in the comforting way big machinery has when it's happy and oiled. But to the left, the crossway led all the way to the outside level which ran just under the hull. There were portholes on the hull.

I'd studied all that out in our cabin, long before we'd lifted, on the transparent model of the ship hanging like a big cigar from the ceiling. Sis had studied it, too, but she was looking for places like the dining salon and the Library and Lifeboat 68 where we should go in case of emergency. I looked for the *important* things.

As I trotted along the crossway, I sort of wished that Sis hadn't decided to go after a husband on a luxury liner. On a cargo ship, now, I'd be climbing from deck to deck on a ladder instead of having gravity underfoot all the time just like I was home on the bottom of the Gulf of Mexico. But women always know what's right, and a boy can only make faces and do what they say, same as the men have to do.

Still, it was pretty exciting to press my nose against the slots in the wall and see the sliding panels that could come charging out and block the crossway into an airtight fit in case a meteor or something smashed into the ship. And all along there were glass cases with spacesuits standing in them, like those knights they used to have back in the Middle Ages.

"In the event of disaster affecting the oxygen content of companionway," they had the words etched into the glass, "break glass with hammer upon wall, remove spacesuit, and proceed to don it in the following fashion."

I read the "following fashion" until I knew it by heart. *Boy*, I said to myself, *I hope we have that kind of disaster. I'd sure like to get into one of those! Bet it would be more fun than those diving suits back in Undersea!*

And all the time I was alone. That was the best part.

Then I passed Deck Twelve and there was a big sign. "Notice! Passengers not permitted past this point!" A big sign in red.

I peeked around the corner. I knew it—the next deck was the hull. I could see the portholes. Every twelve feet, they were, filled with the velvet of space and the dancing of more stars than I'd ever dreamed existed in the universe.

There wasn't anyone on the deck, as far as I could see. And this distance from the grav helix, the ship seemed mighty quiet and lonely. If I just took one quick look. . . .

But I thought of what Sis would say and I turned around obediently. Then I saw the big red sign again. "Passengers not permitted—"

Well! Didn't I know from my civics class that only women could be earth citizens these days? Sure, ever since the Male Desuffrage Act. And didn't I know that you had to be a citizen of a planet in order to get an interplanetary passport? Sis had explained it all to me in the careful, patient way she always talks politics and things like that to men.

"Technically, Ferdinand, I'm the only passenger in our family. You can't be one, because, not being a citizen, you can't acquire an earth passport. However, you'll be going to Venus on the strength of this clause—'Miss Evelyn Sparling and all dependent male members of family, this number not to exceed the registered quota of sub-regulations pertaining'—and so on. I want you to understand these matters, so that you will grow into a man who takes an active interest in world affairs. No matter what you hear, women really like and appreciate such men."

Of course, I never pay much attention to Sis when she says such dumb things. I'm old enough, I guess, to know that it isn't what women like and appreciate that counts when it comes to people getting married. If it were, Sis and three hundred other pretty girls like her wouldn't be on their way to Venus to hook husbands.

Still, if I wasn't a passenger, the sign didn't have anything to do with me. I knew what Sis would say to *that*, but at least it was an argument I could use if it ever came up. So I broke the law.

I was glad I did. The stars were exciting enough, but away off to the left, about five times as big as I'd ever seen it, except in the movies, was the moon, a great blob of gray-and-white pockmarks holding off the black of space. I was hoping to see the earth, but I figured it must be on the other side of the ship or behind us. I pressed my nose against the port and saw the tiny flicker of a spaceliner taking off, Marsbound. I wished I was on that one!

Then I noticed, a little farther down the companionway, a stretch of blank wall where there should have been portholes. High up on the wall in glowing red letters were the words, "Lifeboat 47. Passengers: Thirty-two. Crew: Eleven. Unauthorized personnel keep away!"

Another one of those signs.

I crept up to the porthole nearest it and could just barely make out the stern jets where they were plastered against the hull. Then I walked under the sign and tried to figure the way you were supposed to get into it. There was a very thin line going around in a big circle that I knew must be the door. But I couldn't see any knobs or switches to open it with. Not even a button you could press.

That meant it was a sonic lock like the kind we had on the outer keeps back home in Undersea. But knock or voice? I tried the two knock combinations I knew, and nothing happened. I only remembered one voice key—might as well see if that's it, I figured.

"Twenty, Twenty-three. Open Sesame."

For a second, I thought I'd hit it just right out of all the million possible combinations— The door clicked inward toward a black hole, and a hairy hand as broad as my shoulders shot out of the hole. It closed around my throat and plucked me inside as if I'd been a baby sardine.

I bounced once on the hard lifeboat floor. Before I got my breath and sat up, the door had been shut again. When the light came on, I found myself staring up the muzzle of a highly polished blaster and into the cold blue eyes of the biggest man I'd ever seen.

He was wearing a one-piece suit made of some scaly green stuff that looked hard and soft at the same time.

His boots were made of it, too, and so was the hood hanging down his back.

And his face was brown. Not just ordinary tan, you understand, but the deep, dark, burned-all-the-way-in brown I'd seen on the lifeguards in New Orleans whenever we took a surface vacation—the kind of tan that comes from day after broiling day under a really hot sun. His hair looked as if it had once been blond, but now there were just long combed-out waves with a yellowish tinge that boiled all the way down to his shoulders.

I hadn't seen hair like that on a man except maybe in history books; every man I'd ever known had his hair cropped in the fashionable soup-bowl style. I was staring at his hair, almost forgetting about the blaster which I knew it was against the law for him to have at all, when I suddenly got scared right through.

His eyes.

They didn't blink and there seemed to be no expression around them. Just coldness. Maybe it was the kind of clothes he was wearing that did it, but all of a sudden I was reminded of a crocodile I'd seen in a surface zoo that had stared quietly at me for twenty minutes until it opened two long tooth-studded jaws.

"Green shatas!" he said suddenly. "Only a tadpole. I must be getting jumpy enough to splash."

Then he shoved the blaster away in a holster made of the same scaly leather, crossed his arms on his chest, and began to study me. I grunted to my feet, feeling a lot better. The coldness had gone out of his eyes.

I held out my hand the way Sis had taught me. "My name is Ferdinand Sparling. I'm very pleased to meet you, Mr.—Mr.—"

"Hope for your sake," he said to me, "that you aren't what you seem—tadpole brother to one of them husbandless anura."

"What?"

"A 'nuran is a female looking to nest. Anura is a herd of same. Come from Flatfolk ways."

"Flatfolk are the Venusian natives, aren't they? Are you a Venusian? What part of Venus do you come from? Why did you say you hope—"

He chuckled and swung me up into one of the bunks that lined the lifeboat. "Questions you ask," he said in his soft voice. "Venus is a sharp enough place for a dryhorn, let alone a tadpole dryhorn with a boss-minded sister."

"I'm not a dryleg," I told him proudly. "We're from Undersea."

"Dryhorn, I said, not dryleg. And what's Undersea?"

"Well, in Undersea we called foreigners and newcomers drylegs. Just like on Venus, I guess, you call them dryhorns." And then I told him how Undersea had been built on the bottom of the Gulf of Mexico, when the mineral resources of the land began to give out and engineers figured that a lot could still be reached from the sea bottoms.

He nodded. He'd heard about the sea-bottom mining cities that were bubbling under protective domes in every one of the earth's oceans just about the same time settlements were springing up on the planets.

He looked impressed when I told him about Mom and Pop being one of the first couples to get married in Undersea. He looked thoughtful when I told him how Sis and I had been born there and spent half our childhood listening to the pressure pumps. He raised his eyebrows and looked disgusted when I told how Mom, as Undersea representative on the World Council, had been one of the framers of the Male Desuffrage Act after the Third Atomic War had resulted in the Maternal Revolution.

He almost squeezed my arm when I got to the time Mom and Pop were blown up in a surfacing boat.

"Well, after the funeral, there was a little money, so Sis decided we might as well use it to migrate. There was no future for her on earth, she figured. You know, the three-out-of-four."

"How's that?"

"The three-out-of-four. No more than three women out of every four on earth can expect to find husbands. Not enough men to go around. Way back in the twentieth century, it began to be felt, Sis says, what with the wars and all. Then the wars went on and a lot more men began to die or get no good from the radioactivity. Then the best men went to the planets, Sis says, until by now even if a woman can scrounge a personal husband, he's not much to boast about."

The stranger nodded violently. "Not on earth, he isn't. Those busybody anura make sure of that. What a place! Suffering gridniks, I had a bellyful!"

He told me about it. Women were scarce on Venus, and he hadn't been able to find any who were willing to come out to his lonely little islands; he had decided to go to earth where there was supposed to be a surplus. Naturally, having been born and brought up on a very primitive planet, he didn't know "it's a woman's world," like the older boys in school used to say.

The moment he landed on earth he was in trouble. He didn't know he had to register at a Government-operated hotel for transient males; he threw a bartender through a thick plastic window for saying something nasty about the length of his hair; and *imagine!*—he not only resisted arrest, resulting in three hospitalized policemen, but he sassed the judge in open court!

"Told me a man wasn't supposed to say anything except through female attorneys. Told *her* that where I came from, a man spoke his piece when he'd a mind to, and his woman walked by his side."

"What happened?" I asked breathlessly.

"Oh, Guilty of This and Contempt of That. That blown-up brinosaur took my last munit for fines, then explained that she was remitting the rest because I was a foreigner and uneducated." His eyes grew dark for a moment. He chuckled again. "But I wasn't going to serve all those fancy little prison sentences. Forcible Citizenship Indoctrination, they call it? Shook the dread-dry dust of the misbegotten, God-forsaken mother world from my feet forever. The women on it deserve their men. My pockets were folded from the fines, and the paddlefeet were looking for me so close I didn't dare radio for more munit. So I stowed away."

For a moment, I didn't understand him. When I did, I was almost ill. "Y-you mean," I choked, "th-that you're b-breaking the law right now? And I'm with you while you're doing it?"

He leaned over the edge of the bunk and stared at me very seriously. "What breed of tadpole are they turning out these days? Besides, what business do you have this close to the hull?"

After a moment of sober reflection, I nodded. "You're right.

I've also become a male outside the law. We're in this together."

He guffawed. Then he sat up and began cleaning his blaster. I found myself drawn to the bright killer-tube with exactly the fascination Sis insists such things have always had for men.

"Ferdinand your label? That's not right for a sprouting tadpole. I'll call you Ford. My name's Butt. Butt Lee Brown."

I liked the sound of Ford. "Is Butt a nickname, too?"

"Yeah. Short for Alberta, but I haven't found a man who can draw a blaster fast enough to call me that. You see, Pop came over in the eighties—the big wave of immigrants when they evacuated Ontario. Named all us boys after Canadian provinces. I was the youngest, so I got the name they were saving for a girl."

"You had a lot of brothers, Mr. Butt?"

He grinned with a mighty set of teeth. "Oh, a nestful. Of course, they were all killed in the Blue Chicago Rising by the MacGregor boys—all except me and Saskatchewan. Then Sas and me hunted the MacGregors down. Took a heap of time; we didn't float Jock MacGregor's ugly face down the Tuscany till both of us were pretty near grown-up."

I walked up close to where I could see the tiny bright copper coils of the blaster above the firing button. "Have you killed a lot of men with that, Mr. Butt?"

"Butt. Just plain Butt to you, Ford." He frowned and sighted at the light globe. "No more'n twelve—not counting five Government paddlefeet, of course. I'm a peaceable planter. Way I figure it, violence never accomplishes much that's important. My brother Sas, now—"

He had just begun to work into a wonderful anecdote about his brother when the dinner gong rang. Butt told me to scat. He said I was a growing tadpole and needed my vitamins. And he mentioned, very off-hand, that he wouldn't at all object if I brought him some fresh fruit. It seemed there was nothing but processed foods in the lifeboat and Butt was used to a farmer's diet.

Trouble was, he was a special kind of farmer. Ordinary fruit would have been pretty easy to sneak into my pockets at meals. I even found a way to handle the kelp and giant watercress Mr.

Brown liked, but things like seaweed salt and Venusian mud-grapes just had too strong a smell. Twice, the mechanical hamper refused to accept my jacket for laundering and I had to wash it myself. But I learned so many wonderful things about Venus every time I visited that stowaway. . . .

I learned three wild-wave songs of the Flatfolk and what it is that the native Venusians hate so much; I learned how you tell the difference between a lousy Government paddlefoot from New Kalamazoo and the slaptoe slinker who is the planter's friend. After a lot of begging, Butt Lee Brown explained the workings of his blaster, explained it so carefully that I could name every part and tell what it did from the tiny round electrodes to the long spirals of transformer. But no matter what, he would never let me hold it.

"Sorry, Ford, old tad," he would drawl, spinning around and around in the control swivel chair at the nose of the lifeboat. "But way I look at it, a man who lets somebody else handle his blaster is like the giant whose heart was in an egg that an enemy found. When you've grown enough so's your pop feels you ought to have a weapon, why, then's the time to learn it and you might's well learn fast. Before then, you're plain too young to be even near it."

"I don't have a father to give me one when I come of age. I don't even have an older brother as head of my family like your brother Labrador. All I have is Sis. And she—"

"She'll marry some fancy dryhorn who's never been farther south than the Polar Coast. And she'll stay head of the family, if I know her breed of green shata. Bossy, opinionated. By the way, Fordie," he said, rising and stretching so the fish-leather bounced and rippled off his biceps, "that sister. She ever. . . . ?"

And he'd be off again, cross-examining me about Evelyn. I sat in the swivel chair he'd vacated and tried to answer his questions. But there was a lot of stuff I didn't know. Evelyn was a healthy girl, for instance; how healthy, exactly, I had no way of finding out. Yes, I'd tell him, my aunts on both sides of my family each had had more than the average number of children. No, we'd never done any farming to speak of, back in

Undersea, but—yes, I'd guess Evelyn knew about as much as any girl there when it came to diving equipment and pressure-pump regulation.

How could I know that stuff would lead to trouble for me?

Sis had insisted I come along to the geography lecture. Most of the other girls who were going to Venus for husbands talked to each other during the lecture, but not my sister! She hung on every word, took notes even, and asked enough questions to make the perspiring purser really work in those orientation periods.

"I am very sorry, Miss Sparling," he said with pretty heavy sarcasm, "but I cannot remember any of the agricultural products of the Macro Continent. Since the human population is well below one per thousand square miles, it can readily be understood that the quantity of tilled soil, land or sub-surface, is so small that— Wait, I remember something. The Macro Continent exports a fruit, though not exactly an edible one. The wild *dunging* drug is harvested there by criminal speculators. Contrary to belief on earth, the traffic has been growing in recent years. In fact—"

"Pardon me, sir," I broke in, "but doesn't *dunging* come only from Leif Erickson Island off the Moscow Peninsula of the Macro Continent? You remember, Purser—Wang Li's third exploration, where he proved the island and the peninsula didn't meet for most of the year?"

The purser nodded slowly. "I forgot," he admitted. "Sorry, ladies, but the boy's right. Please make the correction in your notes."

But Sis was the only one who took notes, and she didn't take that one. She stared at me for a moment, biting her lower lip thoughtfully, while I got sicker and sicker. Then she shut her pad with the final gesture of the right hand that Mom used to use just before challenging the opposition to come right down on the Council floor and debate it out with her.

"Ferdinand," Sis said, "let's go back to our cabin."

The moment she sat me down and walked slowly around me, I knew I was in for it. "I've been reading up on Venusian geography in the ship's library," I told her in a hurry.

"No doubt," she said drily. She shook her night-black hair out. "But you aren't going to tell me that you read about *dunging* in the ship's library. The books there have been censored by a Government agent of earth against the possibility that they might be read by susceptible young male minds like yours. She would not have allowed—this Terran Agent—"

"Paddlefoot," I sneered.

Sis sat down hard in our zoom-air chair. "Now that's a term," she said carefully, "that is used only by Venusian riffraff."

"They're not!"

"Not what?"

"Riffraff," I had to answer, knowing I was getting in deeper all the time and not being able to help it. I mustn't give Mr. Brown away! "They're trappers and farmers, pioneers and explorers, who're building Venus. And it takes a real man to build on a hot, hungry hell like Venus."

"Does it, now?" she said, looking at me as if I were beginning to grow a second pair of ears. "Tell me more."

"You can't have meek, law-abiding, women-ruled men when you start civilization on a new planet. You've got to have men who aren't afraid to make their own law if necessary—with their own guns. That's where law begins; the books get written up later."

"You're going to *tell*, Ferdinand, what evil, criminal male is speaking through your mouth!"

"Nobody!" I insisted. "They're my own ideas!"

"They are remarkably well-organized for a young boy's ideas. A boy who, I might add, has previously shown a ridiculous but nonetheless entirely masculine boredom with political philosophy. I plan to have a government career on that new planet you talk about, Ferdinand—after I have found a good, steady husband, of course—and I don't look forward to a masculinist radical in the family. Now, who has been filling your head with all this nonsense?"

I was sweating. Sis has that deadly bulldog approach when she feels someone is lying. I pulled my pulpast handkerchief from my pocket to wipe my face. Something rattled to the floor.

"What is this picture of me doing in your pocket, Ferdinand?"

A trap seemed to be hinging noisily into place. "One of the passengers wanted to see how you looked in a bathing suit."

"The passengers on this ship are all female. I can't imagine any of them being that curious about my appearance. Ferdinand, it's a man who has been giving you these antisocial ideas, isn't it? A war-mongering masculinist like all the frustrated men who want to engage in government and don't have the vaguest idea how. Except, of course, in their ancient, bloody ways. Ferdinand, who has been perverting that sunny and carefree soul of yours?"

"Nobody! *Nobody!*"

"Ferdinand, there's no point in lying! I demand—"

"I told you, Sis. I told you! And don't call me Ferdinand. Call me Ford."

"Ford? *Ford?* Now, you listen to me, Ferdinand . . ."

After that it was all over but the confession. That came in a few moments. I couldn't fool Sis. She just knew me too well, I decided miserably. Besides, she was a girl.

All the same, I wouldn't get Mr. Butt Lee Brown into trouble if I could help it. I made Sis promise she wouldn't turn him in if I took her to him. And the quick, nodding way she said she wouldn't made me feel just a little better.

The door opened on the signal, "Sesame." When Butt saw somebody was with me, he jumped and the ten-inch blaster barrel grew out of his fingers. Then he recognized Sis from the pictures.

He stepped to one side and, with the same sweeping gesture, holstered his blaster and pushed his green hood off. It was Sis' turn to jump when she saw the wild mass of hair rolling down his back.

"An honor, Miss Sparling," he said in that rumbly voice. "Please come right in. There's a hurry-up draft."

So Sis went in and I followed right after her. Mr. Brown closed the door. I tried to catch his eye so I could give him some kind of hint or explanation, but he had taken a couple of his big strides and was in the control section with Sis. She didn't give ground, though; I'll say that for her. She only came up to his chest, but she had her arms crossed sternly.

"First, Mr. Brown," she began, like talking to a cluck of a kid in class, "you realize that you are not only committing the political crime of traveling without a visa, and the criminal one of stowing away without paying your fare, but the moral delinquency of consuming stores intended for the personnel of this ship solely in emergency?"

He opened his mouth to its maximum width and raised an enormous hand. Then he let the air out and dropped his arm.

"I take it you either have no defense or care to make none," Sis added caustically.

Butt laughed slowly and carefully as if he were going over each word. "Wonder if all the anura talk like that. And you want to foul up Venus."

"We haven't done so badly on earth, after the mess you men made of politics. It needed a revolution of the mothers before—"

"Needed nothing. Everyone wanted peace. Earth is a weary old world."

"It's a world of strong moral fiber compared to yours, Mr. Alberta Lee Brown." Hearing his rightful name made him move suddenly and tower over her. Sis said with a certain amount of hurry and change of tone, "What do you have to say about stowing away and using up lifeboat stores?"

He cocked his head and considered a moment. "Look," he said finally, "I have more than enough munit to pay for round-trip tickets, but I couldn't get a return visa because of that brinosaur judge and all the charges she hung on me. Had to stow away. Picked the *Eleanor Roosevelt* because a couple of the boys in the crew are friends of mine and they were willing to help. But this lifeboat—don't you know that every passenger ship carries four times as many lifeboats as it needs? Not to mention the food I didn't eat because it stuck in my throat?"

"Yes," she said bitterly. "You had this boy steal fresh fruit for you. I suppose you didn't know that under space regulations that makes him equally guilty?"

"No, Sis, he didn't," I was beginning to argue. "All he wanted—"

"Sure I knew. Also know that if I'm picked up as a stowaway, I'll be sent back to earth to serve out those fancy little sentences."

"Well, you're guilty of them, aren't you?"

He waved his hands at her impatiently. "I'm not talking law, female; I'm talking sense. Listen! I'm in trouble because I went to earth to look for a wife. You're standing here right now because you're on your way to Venus for a husband. So let's."

Sis actually staggered back. "Let's? Let's *what?* Are—are you daring to suggest that—that—"

"Now, Miss Sparling, no hoopla. I'm saying let's get married, and you know it. You figured out from what the boy told you that I was chewing on you for a wife. You're healthy and strong, got good heredity, you know how to operate sub-surface machinery, you've lived underwater, and your disposition's no worse than most of the anura I've seen. Prolific stock, too."

I was so excited I just had to yell: "Gee, Sis, say yes!"

My sister's voice was steaming with scorn. "And what makes you think that I'd consider you a desirable husband?"

He spread his hands genially. "Figure if you wanted a poodle, you're pretty enough to pick one up on earth. Figure if you charge off to Venus, you don't want a poodle, you want a man. I'm one. I own three islands in the Galertan Archipelago that'll be good oozing mudgrape land when they're cleared. Not to mention the rich berzeliot beds offshore. I got no bad habits outside of having my own way. I'm also passable good-looking for a slaptoe planter. Besides, if you marry me you'll be the first mated on this ship—and that's a splash most nesting females like to make."

There was a longish stretch of quiet. Sis stepped back and measured him slowly with her eyes; there was a lot to look at. He waited patiently while she covered the distance from his peculiar green boots to that head of hair. I was so excited I was gulping instead of breathing. Imagine having Butt for a brother-in-law and living on a wet-plantation in Flatfolk country!

But then I remembered Sis' level head and I didn't have much hope any more.

"You know," she began, "there's more to marriage than just—"

"So there is," he cut in. "Well, we can try each other for taste." And he pulled her in, both of his great hands practically covering her slim, straight back.

Neither of them said anything for a bit after he let go. Butt spoke up first.

"Now, me," he said, "I'd vote yes."

Sis ran the tip of her tongue kind of delicately from side to side of her mouth. Then she stepped back slowly and looked at him as if she were figuring out how many feet high he was. She kept on moving backward, tapping her chin, while Butt and I got more and more impatient. When she touched the lifeboat door, she pushed it open and jumped out.

Butt ran over and looked down the crossway. After awhile, he shut the door and came back beside me. "Well," he said, swinging to a bunk, "that's sort of it."

"You're better off, Butt," I burst out. "You shouldn't have a woman like Sis for a wife. She looks small and helpless, but don't forget she was trained to run an underwater city!"

"Wasn't worrying about that," he grinned. "*I* grew up in the fifteen long years of the Blue Chicago Rising. Nope." He turned over on his back and clicked his teeth at the ceiling. "Think we'd have nested out nicely."

I hitched myself up to him and we sat on the bunk, glooming away at each other. Then we heard the tramp of feet in the crossway.

Butt swung down and headed for the control compartment in the nose of the lifeboat. He had his blaster out and was cursing very interestingly. I started after him, but he picked me up by the seat of my jumper and tossed me toward the door. The captain came in and tripped over me.

I got all tangled up in his gold braid and million-mile space buttons. When we finally got to our feet and sorted out right, he was breathing very hard. The captain was a round little man with a plump, golden face and a very scared look on it. He *humphed* at me, just the way Sis does, and lifted me by the scruff of my neck. The chief mate picked me up and passed me to the second assistant engineer.

Sis was there, being held by the purser on one side and the chief computer's mate on the other. Behind them, I could see a flock of wide-eyed female passengers.

"You cowards!" Sis was raging. "Letting your captain face a dangerous outlaw all by himself!"

"I dunno, Miss Sparling," the computer's mate said, scratching the miniature slide-rule insignia on his visor with his free hand. "The Old Man would've been willing to let it go with a log entry, figuring the spaceport paddlefeet could pry out the stowaway when he landed. But you had to quote the Mother Anita Law at him, and he's in there doing his duty. He figures the rest of us are family men, too, and there's no sense making orphans."

"You promised, Sis," I told her through my teeth. "You promised you wouldn't get Butt into trouble!"

She tossed her spiral curls at me and ground a heel into the purser's instep. He screwed up his face and howled, but he didn't let go of her arm.

"Shush, Ferdinand, this is serious!"

It was. I heard the captain say, "I'm not carrying a weapon, Brown."

"Then get one," Butt's low, lazy voice floated out.

"No, thanks. You're as handy with that thing as I am with a rocket-board." The captain's words got a little fainter as he walked forward. Butt growled like a gusher about to blow.

"I'm counting on your being a good guy, Brown." The captain's voice quavered just a bit. "I'm banking on what I heard about the blast-happy Browns every time I lifted gravs in New Kalamazoo; they have a code, they don't burn unarmed men."

Just about this time, events in the lifeboat went down to a mumble. The top of my head got wet and I looked up. There was sweat rolling down the second assistant's forehead; it converged at his nose and bounced off the tip in a sizable stream. I twisted out of the way.

"What's happening?" Sis gritted, straining toward the lock.

"Butt's trying to decide whether he wants him fried or scrambled," the computer's mate said, pulling her back. "Hey, Purse, remember when the whole family with their pop at the head went into Heatwave to argue with Colonel Leclerc?"

"Eleven dead, sixty-four injured," the purser answered mechanically. "And no more army stationed south of Icebox." His right ear twitched irritably. "But what're they saying?"

Suddenly we heard, "By authority vested in me under the

Pomona College Treaty," the captain was saying very loudly, "I arrest you for violation of Articles Sixteen to Twenty-one inclusive of the Space Transport Code, and order your person and belongings impounded for the duration of this voyage as set forth in Sections Forty-one and Forty-five—"

"Forty-three and Forty-five," Sis groaned. "Sections Forty-three and Forty-five, I told him. I even made him repeat it after me!"

"—of the Mother Anita Law, SC 2136, Emergency Interplanetary Directives."

We all waited breathlessly for Butt's reply. The seconds ambled on and there was no clatter of electrostatic discharge, no smell of burning flesh.

Then we heard some feet walking. A big man in a green suit swung out into the crossway. That was Butt. Behind him came the captain, holding the blaster gingerly with both hands. Butt had a funny, thoughtful look on his face.

The girls surged forward when they saw him, scattering the crew to one side. They were like a school of sharks that had just caught sight of a dying whale.

"M-m-m-m! Are all Venusians built like that?"

"Men like that are worth the mileage!"

"I want him!" "I want him!" "I want him!"

Sis had been let go. She grabbed my free hand and pulled me away. She was trying to look only annoyed, but her eyes had bright little bubbles of fury popping in them.

"The cheap extroverts! And they call themselves responsible women!"

I was angry, too. And I let her know, once we were in our cabin. "What about that promise, Sis? You said you wouldn't turn him in. You *promised!*"

She stopped walking around the room as if she had been expecting to get to Venus on foot. "I know I did, Ferdinand, but he forced me."

"My name is Ford and I don't understand."

"Your name is Ferdinand and stop trying to act forcefully like a girl. It doesn't become you. In just a few days, you'll forget all this and be your simple, carefree self again. I really truly meant to keep my word. From what you'd told me, Mr.

Brown seemed to be a fundamentally decent chap despite his barbaric notions on equality between the sexes—or worse. I was positive I could shame him into a more rational social behavior and make him give himself up. Then he—he—"

She pressed her fingernails into her palms and let out a long, glaring sigh at the door. "Then he kissed me! Oh, it was a good enough kiss— Mr. Brown has evidently had a varied and colorful background—but the galling idiocy of the man, trying that! I was just getting over the colossal impudence involved in *his* proposing marriage—as if *he* had to bear the children!—and was considering the offer seriously, on its merits, as one should consider *all* suggestions, when he deliberately dropped the pretense of reason. He appealed to me as most of the savage ancients appealed to their women, as an emotional machine. Throw the correct sexual switches, says this theory, and the female surrenders herself ecstatically to the doubtful and bloody murk of masculine plans."

There was a doubtful knock on the door and the captain walked in without waiting for an invitation. He was still holding Butt's blaster. He pointed it at me. "Get your hands up, Ferdinand Sparling," he said.

I did.

"I hereby order your detention for the duration of this voyage, for aiding and abetting a stowaway, as set forth in Sections Forty-one and Forty-five—"

"Forty-three and Forty-five," Sis interrupted him, her eyes getting larger and rounder. "But you gave me your word of honor that no charges would be lodged against the boy!"

"Forty-one and Forty-five," he corrected her courteously, still staring fiercely at me. "I looked it up. Of the Anita Mason Law, Emergency Interplanetary Directives. That was the usual promise one makes to an informer, but I made it before I knew it was Butt Lee Brown you were talking about. I didn't want to arrest Butt Lee Brown. You forced me. So I'm breaking my promise to you, just as, I understand, you broke your promise to your brother. They'll both be picked up at New Kalamazoo Spaceport and sent Terraward for trial."

"But I used all of our money to buy passage," Sis wailed.

"And now you'll have to return with the boy. I'm sorry, Miss

Sparling. But as you explained to me, a man who has been honored with an important official position should stay close to the letter of the law for the sake of other men who are trying to break down terrestrial antimale prejudice. Of course, there's a way out."

"There is? Tell me, please!"

"Can I lower my hands a minute?" I asked.

"No, you can't, son—not according to the armed surveillance provisions of the Mother Anita Law. Miss Sparling, if you'd marry Brown—now, now, don't look at me like that!—we could let the whole matter drop. A shipboard wedding and he goes on your passport as a 'dependent male member of family,' which means, so far as the law is concerned, that he had a regulation passport from the beginning of this voyage. And once we touch Venusian soil he can contact his bank and pay for passage. On the record, no crime was ever committed. He's free, the boy's free, and you—"

"—Are married to an uncombed desperado who doesn't know enough to sit back and let a woman run things. Oh, you should be ashamed!"

The captain shrugged and spread his arms wide.

"Perhaps I should be, but that's what comes of putting men into responsible positions, as you would say. See here, Miss Sparling, I didn't want to arrest Brown, and, if it's at all possible, I'd still prefer not to. The crew, officers and men, all go along with me. We may be legal residents of earth, but our work requires us to be on Venus several times a year. We don't want to be disliked by any members of the highly irritable Brown clan or its collateral branches. Butt Lee Brown himself, for all of his savage appearance in your civilized eyes, is a man of much influence on the Polar Continent. In his own bailiwick, the Galertan Archipelago, he makes, breaks, and occasionally readjusts officials. Then there's his brother Saskatchewan who considers Butt a helpless, put-upon youngster—"

"Much influence, you say? Mr. Brown has?" Sis was suddenly thoughtful.

"Power, actually. The kind a strong man usually wields in a newly settled community. Besides, Miss Sparling, you're going to Venus for a husband because the male-female ratio on earth is reversed. Well, not only is Butt Lee Brown a first-class catch, but you can't afford to be too particular in any case. While you're fairly pretty, you won't bring any wealth into a marriage and your high degree of opinionation is not likely to be well-received in a backward, masculinist world. Then, too, the woman-hunger is not so great any more, what with the *Marie Curie* and the *Fatima* having already deposited their cargoes, the *Mme Sun Yat Sen* due to arrive next month. . . ."

Sis nodded to herself, waved the door open, and walked out.

"Let's hope," the captain said. "Like my father used to say, a man who knows how to handle women, how to get around them without their knowing it, doesn't need to know anything else in this life. I'm plain wasted in space. You can lower your hands now, son."

We sat down and I explained the blaster to him. He was very interested. He said all Butt had told him—in the lifeboat when they decided to use my arrest as a club over Sis—was to keep the safety catch all the way up against his thumb. I could see he really had been excited about carrying a lethal weapon around. He told me that back in the old days, captains—sea captains, that is—actually had the right to keep guns in their cabins all the time to put down mutinies and other things our ancestors did.

The telewall flickered, and we turned it on. Sis smiled down. "Everything's all right, Captain. Come up and marry us, please."

"What did you stick him for?" he asked. "What was the price?"

Sis's full lips went thin and hard, the way Mom's used to. Then she thought better of it and laughed. "Mr. Brown is going to see that I'm elected sheriff of the Galertan Archipelago."

"And I thought she'd settle for a county clerkship!" the captain muttered as we spun up to the brig.

The doors were open and girls were chattering in every corner. Sis came up to the captain to discuss arrangements. I slipped away and found Butt sitting with folded arms in a corner of the brig. He grinned at me. "Hi, tadpole. Like the splash?"

I shook my head unhappily. "Butt, why did you do it? I'd sure love to be your brother-in-law, but, gosh, you didn't have to marry Sis." I pointed at some of the bustling females. Sis was going to have three hundred bridesmaids. "Any one of them would have jumped at the chance to be your wife. And once on any woman's passport, you'd be free. Why Sis?"

"That's what the captain said in the lifeboat. Told him same thing I'm telling you. I'm stubborn. What I like at first, I keep on liking. What I want at first, I keep on wanting until I get."

"Yes, but making Sis sheriff! And you'll have to back her up with your blaster. What'll happen to that man's world?"

"Wait'll after we nest and go out to my islands." He produced a hard-lipped, smug grin, sighting it at Sis' slender back. "She'll find herself over a bunch of natives and exactly two earth males—you and me. I got a hunch that'll keep her pretty busy, though."

Good-bye, Ilha!

by LAWRENCE MANNING

> Beyond, out in the vastness of space, there are in-
> habited worlds and near-infinite variations of life-
> forms. Some may resemble us in many ways, in
> basic physical structure, in biochemistry, in evolu-
> tionary history—or in psychological make-up. This
> is a story of one such alien form of life . . . yet
> we find ourselves related in a curious, emotional
> way.

You ARE so punctual, Ilha, I know you will be here exactly one
hour after dawn, as we arranged yesterday. I am leaving this letter to explain why I cannot meet you. You must report to
World Resource headquarters. Be quick. Roll to the place we
left the skid-plane; fly with throttle wide open; you should arrive
before noon.

Claim emergency; get an immediate interview with the Director.

Before the afternoon is over he is to blanket the whole area,
quad 73:61 on the map, with infrared heat. Not to kill, tell him.
Raise the absolute temperature only about 10 per cent, just
enough to make it thoroughly uncomfortable. These visitors en-
danger our whole civilization, but I think that will drive them
away. However, it may not, so at noon the next day push the
power up to full killing temperatures for a few minutes.

He will object, but what if a few miles of sand are fused? You
know the area. It was so thoroughly blasted during the Age of
Wars that no more damage is possible, and anyway, it will be

centuries before the reclamation engineers touch this part of our planet. You can—you *must* persuade him, Ilha!

It is rude, I know, to begin with such urgency, omitting the traditional greeting phrases, writing without Limik calmness or philosophy. But you may as well get used to it, for the creatures I write about are totally un-Limik—utterly out of this world!

I found them yesterday about where the disturbance showed on the magnetic map, near the center of the quad. Their rocket-ship is much like the ancient ones in the museum at Prr, but larger and made of magnesium. I hid behind a sand dune until dark, when I could examine it safely. Light streamed from two round windows and also from a tall, narrow, opening—a door in spite of its fantastic shape (twice as high as it was broad)— opening from a small vestibule. There were two inner doors, one open and one closed. From the closed one came loud roarings and barkings as of wild animals, but modulated by a variety of smacks, gargles, and splutterings. I soon realized these sounds were signals—a regular code language, like our own writing. I could sense the thought associated with each sound; but evi- dently the animals behind the door, though all present to- gether, could not. They had to make these sound signals to un- derstand each other. Curious and primitive, isn't it?

There were three voices, one much stronger than the other two. I caught thought phrases like "I am hungry," "Is not that drink cold yet?" and "When do we eat?" There were thoughts I sensed, which made no meaning to me. There were also sounds, many of them, that had no thought behind them at all: "WEL- IL-BEDAM" was one, "OG-O-AWN" was another, com- monest of all was a sort of barking, "HAW-HAW-HAW." All meaning dissolved when they barked, their minds seemed pleased with themselves in a strange, bubbling, thoughtfree sort of way. "HAW HAW HAW" would go the biggest voice and the other two (no, not its mates; I still know nothing of their reproductive customs except that the wrappings on their bodies have something to do with it) would join "HAW HAW HAW" like so many flepas barking at the moon. Only flepas think sad, hungry thoughts when they bark; these creatures stopped thinking altogether.

I stood there outside the door delighted with it. I suppose it doesn't sound attractive—though I ask you, can any Limik stop thinking—ever? But it is more than not thinking. It is the feeling that goes with it—a lifting of the spirits, refreshing, youthful . . . Oh, well, I'll continue.

The open door showed a small empty room, its walls fitted with shelves and cabinets. I tip-probed in, hoping to learn something about this unknown species from its environment. A repulsive odor came from a bowl on the long shelf and I climbed up—burning myself, incidentally, for all that part of the shelf was hot. What do you suppose was in that bowl? Pieces torn from the bodies of living vegetables and animals, all stewing together in a revolting mixture. Their food! Our savage ancestors might have enjoyed it; I was filled with horror and retreated along the shelf to the other end of the room. Here stood a smaller metal bowl, icy cold, smelling like our own poggle fruit. You know me and poggles! I think the brightest page in Limik history is our treaty with the poggle-people—we enjoy the fruit, they have their seeds better distributed. The odor from this bowl was irresistible, contrasted with the gruesome stench from the other end of the room. I dipped in my courtesy probe and drank.

It was not poggle juice, but some strange poison!

I wooshed, too late. My probe tip began to swell and throb; my fore-eye rolled so dizzily I had to somersault tail-over-feeler, putting my crippled probe in tail position. Even then I could not stand up, but fell several times. I thought I was going to die.

I know our literature demands that I pause here to detail the stream of consciousness and the philosophy. I cannot do more than outline. How invalid our pretty refinements are! If I had been brought up in a lower-class nest such social distinctions as courtesy, tail, and feeler would not even exist—one probe would be no different from another. I had no time to elaborate these ideas. While I tumbled about on that shelf I knocked over a pile of plates. They fell to the floor with an enormous crash, and an instant later the closed door burst open and three amazing monsters thundered into the room.

They were about six probes high, scarcely one wide—weird, attenuated, and huge. They had five probes. Two were feelers, or perhaps tails, kept covered (they call them "LAIGS"). Two were courtesy probes ("HANS") uncovered at the tips, which have no openings (I suppose the passages have atrophied) but are each slit into five small tentacles. The fifth probe was short, stubby, and has no counterpart in Limik anatomy. It ends in a great bristle of hairs; two of the monsters had brown hairs, one red. All had one huge opening set with even, white pieces of bone—a little like a grinding machine. Two eyes were in each of these probes (migrated here from the body? I don't know. Our old bio professor would be interested. There may be residual eyes left on the body, too. They keep them tightly wrapped so there is no way to find out).

They strode with enormous steps—*sideways*, not probe after probe like our amble—and swayed awkwardly as they came. I remember thinking that our own wheel-like rolling would outdistance them, if I could ever get a free start. But they stood between me and the door. I was caught. The whole room rolled and turned before my eyes.

They began to roar at each other sounds with no thought except surprise. "LOOKOOSERE, WEL-IL-BEDAM," they shouted. I expected to be seized and thrown into that boiling bowl and shrank back in despair. The only hope that occurred to me in this dreadful situation was that perhaps they would not kill me—at least not at once—if I could show them I was intelligent. But how show that? They could not read thoughts, remember. Well, Ilha, you know how baby Limikles bubble and gargle the soft flap in their probe passages, and snort by half-closing the tips? That infantile exercise saved my life. I imitated their sounds.

"LOOKOOSERE WEL-IL-BEDAM," I managed. Then I grew so dizzy I fell once again and wooshed all over the shelf.

There was an instant of portentous silence. Then they began barking like mad things.

"The little fellow's been at our coktal, HAW HAW HAW," Big-voice roared and pointed to the bowl. They all burst out barking with him—"LAFF" is their word for it. Deafened and desperate, I raised my probe and LAFF-ed, too.

"HAW HAW" I gasped. That set them off louder than ever. Curiously, I felt better. LAFF-ing spreads from mind to mind like fire in a pile of sticks.

Redhead came close and held out his HANS, but Big-voice said "Look out. Even if he can't bite, he may sting!"

The third monster said, "AGO-AWN he's a gentle old fellow —aren't you? Just a little poisoned (their word is 'TITE') that's all." He picked me up to nestle on his courtesy probe, squeezed against his great body.

I was terrified. My eyes rolled up dizzily; but I managed to splutter "AGO-AWN HAW HAW HAW," and tried to add "gentle old fellow," but was nauseated again, so that unfortunately it came out "Shentle ol WOOSH!"

My captor set me hastily back on the shelf. He did it gently though, and I felt safer anyway, for his HANS were not too certain a support and it was easily a three-probe fall to the floor.

They all went off into a wild storm of roaring, stamping about the room, striking each other on the back, gasping for breath—quite insane. Then they began crying, "Pour out the drinks," and all three drank some of the poison, but were not ill; only a little redder and louder.

I had another bad moment when they dished out the food and began eating—suppose they found there was not quite enough to satisfy their hunger? I need not have worried. One of them even put a little dish of it in front of me. I drew back quickly, but the odor was too strong for my control. I was nauseated again.

"Try him with a little water, BILL" said Big-voice.

My captor, BILL, brought a container and I drank eagerly and felt better at last. I was sure now that they did not intend to eat me. I leaned against the wall, watching them. The meal ended with boiling water and brown powder called "CUP-ACAWFEE"—another unpleasant odor. Bill brought from a shelf a small bowl filled with white grains which Big-voice called "PASSASHUGA" and they spooned a little of this into their hot brown drink. A few grains spilled on the shelf and I investigated. To my delight it was sugar. Sugar, Ilha! The basic food of nature from which all living tissue is derived, the synthesis of which has made possible our Limik way of life, but used by them as a condiment!

I was hungry. Greatly daring, I imitated their signal as well as I could: "PASSASHUGA." And it worked. They HAW-

HAW-ed, but in a surprised and kindly way, and Bill put a little heap of it on the shelf so that I actually shared in their amazing meal after all, and enjoyed it too. I did not eat much, but, of course, I had to have exercise at once to restore my energy balance. I began to roll tail-over-courtesy all down the shelf and back.

Big-voice did not LAFF, though the others did. He looked suddenly thoughtful, said, "He can go fast, can't he," and reached out to shut the door. "We don't want to lose this fellow. Get down the cage, Bill."

Bill brought out a huge cage—a room made of wires. He said, "The door's too small; we'll have to take off the bottom to get him in. It hasn't been cleaned since the (something) died, has it?" He washed it and lifted me in. It was just about big enough to turn around in, but I didn't care, for I had gone into my digestive stupor by then and drowsed while they carried me, cage and all, into the other room.

Here they sprawled themselves out on cushioned frames, leaning their bodies against back supports. It looked uncomfortable— halfway between standing and lying down. Then they put little white tubes into their mouths and set them on fire, blowing narcotic smoke about the room. They talked and I listened.

Bill said, "Maybe this planet isn't all desert. We haven't seen it all."

Big-voice said, "That fellow in the cage could tell us if he wanted to."

Redhead blew smoke, then said, "I thought we had agreed to leave here tomorrow and try the other planet in this system?"

"Not if this one will do," put in Big-voice. "We wouldn't think much of our own world if we landed in one of the deserts."

"This desert is bigger than any on earth," objected Bill. "We saw enough to know that much. It covers half the planet, anyway. Still, the other half would be big enough, at that—but how do we know this little chap isn't a desert animal?"

Big-voice said, "Maybe we can get him to talk tomorrow."

All the time their thoughts ran swiftly under the slow pace of their sound-signals—and I could read the thoughts. I suddenly realized that these three were scouts. When they had found a good world, they would guide a horde of other "HEW-MEN" to it. All they had come for was to find a planet worth the trouble of taking over; if ours proved desirable they would calmly kill its present inhabitants! I caught mental glimpses of the way they imagined other forms of life. There were only two kinds in their thoughts: those that could be eaten and those that should be destroyed as inedible nuisances!

It was a pretty grim moment, Ilha.

I had got over my first fright and had actually begun to enjoy being with them before this awful conviction was forced upon me. After that I knew I had to escape and warn our world.

They talked a long time. Every so often they would burst into a chorus of HAW HAW's without apparent reason. There is a contagious sort of charm in this LAFF-ing of theirs. Oh, not the sound—that is mere cacophony—but the soft dissolving of all serious thought that goes with it. I became very sad, lying there, thinking how unfortunate it was that such pleasant creatures had to be destroyed.

Then came a new thing. Redhead said, "I feel like MEW-SIK," and went to a corner of the room to turn on a machine of some kind. Oh, Ilha! Such a burst of overpoweringly sweet sound came from it that my probe tips quivered in ecstasy. They are masters of sound, these HEW-MEN. Not in my life have I imagined such an art. There was a mathematically regulated change of pitch, recurring with an urgent feeling of logic; there was a blending of tones in infinite variety; there was a measured rhythm. But none of these will give you the slightest idea of the effect on me, when all were put together. We Limiks have nothing in the slightest like it. Oh, well, the rhythm, perhaps. Limikles in their nest being taught numbers by beating sticks in 3-4-5 pattern do a little suggest that phase of this MEW-SIK—but only as a shadow suggests the solid.

When it stopped I was desperately unhappy. If these monsters were killed, I would never again hear this miracle. And yet they would certainly kill us if they stayed here.

Then my great idea was born—the Blue Planet!

The ghoulish and savage Gryptrrs, unless they have greatly changed since our last expedition there, deserve consideration from no Limik. Why could I not persuade these HEW-MEN to go there and settle? Certainly, if they once saw those lush landscapes they would far prefer it to ours. Would they not, cruel and selfish as they are, make far better neighbors than the untamable Gryptrrs? Moreover, they were half-persuaded already. I had only to convince them that our world was even more unsuitable than it appeared.

I knew how to do that. Don't you see, Ilha? Remember in literature class that story of Vraaltr's—"The Un-Limik Letter," I think it was called? To write one thing and think another is stupid among ourselves, because the true thought is revealed when next writer and reader come together. But these HEW-MEN cannot see thoughts at all. All they understand is the agreed meaning of arbitrary sounds. They even have a word ("FOOLME") for such spoken untruths. Their minds grope constantly in search of each other's meaning.

Well, tomorrow I shall talk their language. Not too freely; not enough to make them fear Limiks as dangerously intelligent; certainly I shall not tell them I can read their thoughts. I shall speak just well enough to answer the questions they are certain to ask. And I shall answer them: Oh, we have the most dreadful heat waves on this desert world, lasting weeks at a time; our lives are a struggle for bare existence, with water our most valuable possession! (These things are untrue. What of it? They won't know that.)

So that's why I want the infrared heat—a foretaste of one of those "heat waves" of ours. Please, Ilha, make it hot enough to discourage any lingering. I think this rocket ship will take off for the Blue Planet not later than tomorrow night, if you do your part.

Speaking of night, these monsters fall into a stupor then. Apparently they think of it as a regular thing, every night of their lives. Their stupor lasts all the dark hours. Last night their lights blazed a few hours, then they began to blink their eyes and gape—as we do after each meal. They said "GOOD NITE" to each other and went into another room, putting out all lights in the ship. That is when I escaped.

Nothing could have been simpler. I merely unfastened the cage and lifted it off me. The door of the room was closed, but I could just reach its fastening when I stood on the tips of my probes. I was out on the desert sand!

I am not much of an athlete, but I rolled here in an hour. Of course, the desert is fairly smooth and the air cool at night. I shall have time to return more sedately, for it is still three hours before dawn and I have almost finished writing.

Oh yes, I am going back. Frankly, it is not just because my plan requires me to talk to them. It may be hard for you to understand, Ilha, but I want to return. I like them.

I suppose from my description they must seem horrible to you. In many ways they are horrible. I like them in spite of that. They are not always evenly balanced in their emotions, nor always reasonable like a Limik. They leap from love to hate and back again twenty times an hour over unimportant matters. We regard every form of life with unvarying benignance; they do not. Either they bear a highly prejudiced affection toward others, or else they hold them in utter contempt. True, they kill remorselessly; but also true, they risk their own lives freely for those they happen to like—at least so I read Redhead's unspoken thoughts toward Bill. No Limik, of course, could ever be capable of either extreme. On the whole, the average between their vices and virtues is not really very far from our own unchanging reasonableness; but if they happen to regard you as friendly, they are far more pleasant—to you—than any group of Limiks would be.

I am regarded as a friend—certainly by Bill and Redhead, though Big-voice is not quite sure yet. I could sense his thoughts, anticipating the trouble of feeding me, and caring for me if I were ill, resenting all that prospective effort and yet suspecting that I might be worth it. Why? Because I look harmless and LAFF-able! Even with a far better reason, no Limik would go to so much trouble for me—would you, Ilha?

I am back once again to their LAFF-ing. I wish I could explain the sort of thing it is, but I do not even know exactly what starts it. It might be something ridiculous, or clever, or even obviously untrue. I have noted a few examples, but they would not help you; it is utterly un-Limik and unreasonable. But it is contagious. I don't suppose I could LAFF by myself—oh, I could bark HAW HAW but that isn't it—I could not give my-self that odd sparkling freedom of mind. It is the most refresh-ing experience I have ever had, for I have experienced it, or very nearly, when I was in the same room with these HEW-MEN. It warms me like a fire inside my cold consciousness. The mere chance that I may finally learn to LAFF as freely as they do is alone worth the risk of my life—worth it many times over. It is like being made young again for a few minutes.

Our sober, worrying, serious ways are no doubt admirable—certainly reasonable. But tell me this: How many of us ever die a natural death from old age? You know as well as I that every Limik, sooner or later, is driven by our racial melancholy to end his own life. Not me, though—not now! Yet I have been melan-choly of late. Life has never seemed the same since my mate Wkap died. She was different from the other two. Mind you, they are splendid breeding partners, none better; but I won't miss them nor they me. Each has her two other consorts; they will find a third to take my place before next twining-time.

So I am going back to these likable monsters. More than that, I am going to help them in every way I can—I intend to be a small but very loyal member of their crew. I may even learn to eat some of their food—after all, some forms of life on their world may be so low in the scale of evolution they cannot even think, perhaps not even feel. Just because no such life exists here does not mean it cannot elsewhere.

I am X-SITED—which means, I think, less than no calmness at all, if you can imagine such a state of mind. It has no equiva-lent in Limik writing, but then I am almost no longer Limik.

I hope I can persuade them to leave this planet before noon tomorrow. But you must not risk our entire civilization merely because I have taken a liking to these monsters—and it is a real risk, for they are truly dangerous. Killing heat tomorrow noon, remember. All I ask is that you make the heat *really* killing; I have no wish to fry slowly!

For if they stay I shall stay (and die) with them. So, either way it is. . . .

Good-bye, Ilha.

Misbegotten Missionary

by ISAAC ASIMOV

> This is a companion story to Good-bye, Ilha! Poor,
> alien creature . . . and yet not so alien that we
> could not feel the basic emotions of the lost
> Limik. Can we say the same of the alien in this
> story? Can we recognize the horror of a fanatic
> intelligence on earth as we do out there?

He HAD SLIPPED aboard the ship! There had been dozens waiting outside the energy barrier when it had seemed that waiting would do no good. Then the barrier had faltered for a matter of two minutes (which showed the superiority of unified organisms over life fragments) and he was across.

None of the others had been able to move quickly enough to take advantage of the break, but that didn't matter. All alone, he was enough. No others were necessary.

And the thought faded out of satisfaction and into loneliness. It was a terribly unhappy and unnatural thing to be parted from all the rest of the unified organism, to be a life fragment oneself. How could these aliens stand being fragments?

It increased his sympathy for the aliens. Now that he experienced fragmentation himself, he could feel, as though from a distance, the terrible isolation that made them so afraid. It was fear born of that isolation that dictated their actions. What but the insane fear of their condition could have caused them to blast an area, one mile in diameter, into dull-red heat before landing their ship? Even the organized life ten feet deep in the soil had been destroyed in the blast.

He engaged reception, listening eagerly, letting the alien

thought saturate him. He enjoyed the touch of life upon his consciousness. He would have to ration that enjoyment. He must not forget himself.

But it could do no harm to listen to thoughts. Some of the fragments of life on the ship thought quite clearly, considering that they were such primitive, incomplete creatures. Their thoughts were like tiny bells.

Roger Oldenn said, "I feel contaminated. You know what I mean? I keep washing my hands and it doesn't help."

Jerry Thorn hated dramatics and didn't look up. They were still maneuvering in the stratosphere of Saybrook's Planet and he preferred to watch the panel dials. He said, "No reason to feel contaminated. Nothing happened."

"I hope not," said Oldenn. "At least they had all the field men discard their spacesuits in the air-lock for complete disinfection. They had a radiation bath for all men entering from outside. I suppose nothing happened."

"Why be nervous, then?"

"I don't know. I wish the barrier hadn't broken down."

"Who doesn't? It was an accident."

"I wonder." Oldenn was vehement. "I was here when it happened. My shift, you know. There was no reason to overload the power line. There was equipment plugged into it that had no damn business near it. None whatsoever."

"All right. People are stupid."

"Not that stupid. I hung around when the Old Man was checking into the matter. None of them had reasonable excuses. The armor-baking circuits, which were draining off two thousand watts, had been put into the barrier line. They'd been using the second subsidiaries for a week. Why not this time? They couldn't give any reason."

"Can you?"

Oldenn flushed. "No, I was just wondering if the men had been"—he searched for a word—"hypnotized into it. By those things outside."

Thorn's eyes lifted and met those of the other levelly. "I wouldn't repeat that to anyone else. The barrier was down only two minutes. If anything had happened, if even a spear of grass had drifted across, it would have shown up in our bacteria cultures within half an hour, in the fruit-fly colonies in a matter of days. Before we got back it would show up in the hamsters, the rabbits, maybe the goats. Just get it through your head, Oldenn, that nothing happened. Nothing."

Oldenn turned on his heel and left. In leaving, his foot came within two feet of the object in the corner of the room. He did not see it.

He disengaged his reception centers and let the thoughts flow past him unperceived. These life fragments were not important, in any case, since they were not fitted for the continuation of life. Even as fragments, they were incomplete.

The other types of fragments, now—they were different. He had to be careful of them. The temptation would be great, and he must give no indication, none at all, of his existence on board ship till they landed on their home planet.

He focused on the other parts of the ship, marveling at the diversity of life. Each item, no matter how small, was sufficient to itself. He forced himself to contemplate this, until the unpleasantness of the thought grated on him and he longed for the normality of home.

Most of the thoughts he received from the smaller fragments were vague and fleeting, as you would expect. There wasn't much to be had from them, but that meant their need for completeness was all the greater. It was that which touched him so keenly.

There was the life fragment which squatted on its haunches and fingered the wire netting that enclosed it. Its thoughts were clear, but limited. Chiefly, they concerned the yellow fruit a companion fragment was eating. It wanted the fruit very deeply. Only the wire netting that separated the fragments prevented its seizing the fruit by force.

He disengaged reception in a moment of complete revulsion. *These fragments competed for food!*

He tried to reach far outward for the peace and harmony of home, but it was already an immense distance away. He could reach only into the nothingness that separated him from sanity.

He longed at the moment even for the feel of the dead soil between the barrier and the ship. He had crawled over it last night. There had been no life upon it, but it had been the soil of home, and on the other side of the barrier there had still been the comforting feel of the rest of organized life.

He could remember the moment he had located himself on the surface of the ship, maintaining a desperate suction grip until the air lock opened. He had entered, moving cautiously between the outgoing feet. There had been an inner lock and that had been passed later. Now he lay here, a life fragment himself, inert and unnoticed.

Cautiously, he engaged reception again at the previous focus. The squatting fragment of life was tugging furiously at the wire netting. It still wanted the other's food, though it was the less hungry of the two.

Larsen said, "Don't feed the damn thing. She isn't hungry; she's just sore because Tillie had the nerve to eat before she herself was crammed full. The greedy ape! I wish we were back home and I never had to look another animal in the face again."

He scowled at the older female chimpanzee and the chimp mouthed and chattered back to him in full reciprocation.

Rizzo said, "Okay, okay. Why hang around here, then? Feeding time is over. Let's get out."

They went past the goat pens, the rabbit hutches, the hamster cages.

Larsen said bitterly, "You volunteer for an exploration voyage. You're a hero. They send you off with speeches—and make a zoo keeper out of you."

"They give you double pay."

"All right, so what? I didn't sign up just for the money. They said at the original briefing that it was even odds we wouldn't come back, that we'd end up like Saybrook. I signed up because I wanted to do something important."

"Just a bloomin' bloody hero," said Rizzo.

"I'm not an animal nurse."

Rizzo paused to lift a hamster out of the cage and stroke it. "Hey," he said, "did you ever think that maybe one of these hamsters has some cute little baby hamsters inside, just getting started?"

"Wise guy! They're tested every day."

"Sure, sure." He nuzzled the little creature, which vibrated its nose at him. "But just suppose you came down one morning and found them there. New little hamsters looking up at you with soft, green patches of fur where the eyes ought to be."

"Shut up, for the love of Mike," yelled Larsen.

"Little soft, green patches of shining fur," said Rizzo, and put the hamster down with a sudden loathing sensation.

He engaged reception again and varied the focus. There wasn't a specialized life fragment at home that didn't have a rough counterpart on shipboard.

There were the moving runners in various shapes, the moving swimmers, and the moving fliers. Some of the fliers were quite large, with perceptible thoughts; others were small, gauzy-winged creatures. These last transmitted only patterns of sense perception, imperfect patterns at that, and added nothing intelligent of their own.

There were the non-movers, which, like the non-movers at home, were green and lived on the air, water, and soil. These were a mental blank. They knew only the dim, dim consciousness of light, moisture, and gravity.

And each fragment, moving and non-moving, had its mockery of life.

Not yet. Not yet. . . .

He clamped down hard upon his feelings. Once before, these life fragments had come, and the rest at home had tried to help them—too quickly. It had not worked. This time they must wait.

If only these fragments did not discover him.

They had not, so far. They had not noticed him lying in the corner of the pilot room. No one had bent down to pick him up and discard him. Earlier, it had meant he could not move. Someone might have turned and stared at the stiff wormlike thing, not quite six inches long. First stare, then shout, and then it would all be over.

But now, perhaps, he had waited long enough. The take-off

was long past. The controls were locked; the pilot room was empty.

It did not take him long to find the chink in the armor leading to the recess where some of the wiring was. They were dead wires.

The front end of his body was a rasp that cut in two a wire of just the right diameter. Then, six inches away, he cut it in two again. He pushed the snipped-off section of the wire ahead of him, packing it away neatly and invisibly into a corner recess. Its outer covering was a brown elastic material and its core was gleaming, ruddy metal. He himself could not reproduce the core, of course, but that was not necessary. It was enough that the pellicle that covered him had been carefully bred to resemble a wire's surface.

He returned and grasped the cut sections of the wire before and behind. He tightened against them as his little suction disks came into play. Not even a seam showed.

They could not find him now. They could look right at him and see only a continuous stretch of wire.

Unless they looked very closely indeed and noted that, in a certain spot on this wire, there were two tiny patches of soft and shining green fur.

"It is remarkable," said Dr. Weiss, "that little green hairs can do so much."

Captain Loring poured the brandy carefully. In a sense, this was a celebration. They would be ready for the jump through hyper-space in two hours, and after that, two days would see them back on earth.

"You are convinced, then, the green fur is the sense organ?" he asked.

"It is," said Weiss. Brandy made him come out in splotches, but he was aware of the need of celebration—quite aware. "The experiments were conducted under difficulties, but they were quite significant."

The captain smiled stiffly. " 'Under difficulties' is one way of phrasing it. I would never have taken the chances you did to run them."

"Nonsense. We're all heroes aboard this ship, all volunteers, all great men with trumpet, fife, and fanfarade. You took the chance of coming here."

"You were the first to go outside the barrier."

"No particular risk was involved," Weiss said. "I burned the ground before me as I went, to say nothing of the portable barrier that surrounded me. Nonsense, Captain. Let's all take our medals when we come back; let's take them without attempt at gradation. Besides, I'm a male."

"But you're filled with bacteria to here." The captain's hand made a quick, cutting gesture three inches above his head. "Which makes you as vulnerable as a female would be."

They paused for drinking purposes.

"Refill?" asked the captain.

"No, thanks. I've exceeded my quota already."

"Then one last for the spaceroad." He lifted his glass in the general direction of Saybrook's Planet, no longer visible, its sun only a bright star in the visiplate. "To the little green hairs that gave Saybrook his first lead."

Weiss nodded. "A lucky thing. We'll quarantine the planet, of course."

The captain said, "That doesn't seem drastic enough. Someone might always land by accident some day and not have Saybrook's insight, or his guts. Suppose he did not blow up his ship, as Saybrook did. Suppose he got back to some inhabited place."

The captain was somber. "Do you suppose they might ever develop interstellar travel on their own?"

"I doubt it. No proof, of course. It's just that they have such a completely different orientation. Their entire organization of life has made tools unnecessary. As far as we know, even a stone ax doesn't exist on the planet."

"I hope you're right. Oh, and, Weiss, would you spend some time with Drake?"

"The Galactic Press fellow?"

"Yes. Once we get back, the story of Saybrook's Planet will be released for the public and I don't think it would be wise to oversensationalize it. I've asked Drake to let you consult with him on the story. You're a biologist and enough of an authority to carry weight with him. Would you oblige?"

"A pleasure."

The captain closed his eyes wearily and shook his head.

"Headache, Captain?"

"No. Just thinking of poor Saybrook."

He was weary of the ship. Awhile back there had been a queer, momentary sensation, as though he had been turned inside out. It was alarming and he had searched the minds of the keen-thinkers for an explanation. Apparently the ship had leaped across vast stretches of empty space by cutting across something they knew as "hyper-space." The keen-thinkers were ingenious.

But—he was weary of the ship. It was such a futile phenomenon. These life fragments were skillful in their constructions, yet it was only a measure of their unhappiness, after all. They strove to find in the control of inanimate matter what they could not find in themselves. In their unconscious yearning for completeness, they built machines and scoured space, seeking, seeking. . . .

These creatures, he knew, could never, in the very nature of things, find that for which they were seeking. At least not until such time as he gave it to them. He quivered a little at the thought.

Completeness!

These fragments had no concept of it, even. "Completeness" was a poor word.

In their ignorance they would even fight it. There had been the ship that had come before. The first ship had contained many of the keen-thinking fragments. There had been two varieties, life producers, and the sterile ones. (How different this second ship was. The keen-thinkers were all sterile, while the other fragments, the fuzzy-thinkers and the no-thinkers, were all producers of life. It was strange.)

How gladly that first ship had been welcomed by all the planet! He could remember the first intense shock at the realization that the visitors were fragments and not complete. The shock had given way to pity, and the pity to action. It was not certain how they would fit into the community, but there had been no hesitation. All life was sacred and somehow room would have been made for them—for all of them, from the large keen-thinkers to the little multipliers in the darkness.

But there had been a miscalculation. They had not correctly analyzed the course of the fragments' ways of thinking. The keen-thinkers became aware of what had been done and resented it. They were frightened, of course; they did not understand.

They had developed the barrier first, and then, later, had destroyed themselves, exploding their ship to atoms.

Poor, foolish fragments.

This time, at least, it would be different. They would be saved, despite themselves.

John Drake would not have admitted it in so many words, but he was very proud of his skill on the photo-typer. He had a travel-kit model, which was a six-by-eight, featureless dark plastic slab, with cylindrical bulges on either end to hold the roll of thin paper. It fitted into a brown leather case, equipped with a beltlike contraption that held it closely about the waist and at one hip. The whole thing weighed less than a pound.

Drake could operate it with either hand. His fingers would flick quickly and easily, placing their light pressure at exact spots on the blank surface, and soundlessly, words would be written.

He looked thoughtfully at the beginning of his story, then up at Dr. Weiss. "What do you think, Doc?"

"It starts well."

Drake nodded. "I thought I might as well start with Saybrook himself. They haven't released his story back home yet. I wish I could have seen Saybrook's original report. How did he ever get it through, by the way?"

"As near as I could tell, he spent one last night sending it through the sub-ether. When he was finished, he shorted the motors, and converted the entire ship into a thin cloud of vapor a millionth of a second later. The crew and himself along with it."

"What a man! You were in this from the beginning, Doc?"

"Not from the beginning," corrected Weiss gently. "Only since the receipt of Saybrook's report."

He could not help thinking back. He had read that report,

realizing even then how wonderful the planet must have seemed when Saybrook's colonizing expedition first reached it. It was practically a duplicate of earth, with an abounding plant life and a purely vegetarian animal life.

There had been only the little patches of green fur (how often had he used that phrase in his speaking and thinking!) which seemed strange. No living individual on the planet had eyes. Instead, there was this fur. Even the plants, each blade or leaf or blossom, possessed the two patches of richer green.

Then Saybrook had noticed, startled and bewildered, that there was no conflict for food on the planet. All plants grew pulpy appendages which were eaten by the animals. These were regrown in a matter of hours. No other parts of the plants were touched. It was as though the plants fed the animals as part of the order of nature. And the plants themselves did not grow in overpowering profusion. They might almost have been cultivated, they were spread across the available soil so discriminately.

How much time, Weiss wondered, had Saybrook had to observe the strange law and order on the planet?—the fact that insects kept their numbers reasonable, though no birds ate them; that the rodentlike things did not swarm, though no carnivores existed to keep them in check.

And then there had come the incident of the white rats.

That prodded Weiss. He said, "Oh, one correction, Drake. Hamsters were not the first animals involved. It was the white rats."

"White rats," said Drake, making the correction in his notes.

"Every colonizing ship," said Weiss, "takes a group of white rats for the purpose of testing any alien foods. Rats, of course, are very similar to human beings from a nutritional viewpoint. Naturally, only female white rats were taken."

Naturally. If only one sex was present, there was no danger of unchecked multiplication in case the planet proved favorable. Remember the rabbits in Australia.

"Incidentally, why not use males?" asked Drake.

"Females are hardier," said Weiss, "which is lucky, since that gave the situation away. It turned out suddenly that all the rats were bearing young."

"Right. Now that's where I'm up to, so here's my chance to get some things straight. For my own information, Doc, how did Saybrook find out they were in a family way?"

"Accidentally, of course. In the course of nutritional investigations, rats are dissected for evidence of internal damage. Their condition was bound to be discovered. A few more were dissected; same results. Eventually, all that lived gave birth to young—with no male rats aboard!"

"And the point is that all the young were born with little green patches of fur instead of eyes."

"That is correct. Saybrook said so and we corroborate him. After the rats, the pet cat of one of the children was obviously affected. When it finally kittened, the kittens were not born with closed eyes but with little patches of green fur. There was no tomcat aboard.

"Eventually Saybrook had the women tested. He didn't tell them what for. He didn't want to frighten them. Every single one of them was in the early stages of pregnancy, leaving out of consideration those few who had been pregnant at the time of embarkation. Saybrook never waited for any child to be born, of course. He knew they would have no eyes, only shining patches of green fur.

"He even prepared bacterial cultures (Saybrook was a thorough man) and found each bacillus to show microscopic green spots."

Drake was eager. "That goes way beyond our briefing—or, at least, the briefing I got. But granted that life on Saybrook's Planet is organized into a unified whole, how is it done?"

"How? How are your cells organized into a unified whole? Take an individual cell out of your body, even a brain cell, and what is it by itself? Nothing. A little blob of protoplasm with no more capacity for anything human than an amoeba. Less capacity, in fact, since it couldn't live by itself. But put the cells together and you have something that could invent a spaceship or write a symphony."

"I get the idea," said Drake.

Weiss went on, "All life on Saybrook's Planet is a single organism. In a sense, all life on earth is too, but it's a fighting dependence, a dog-eat-dog dependence. The bacteria fix nitrogen;

the plants fix carbon; animals eat plants and each other; bacterial decay hits everything. It comes full circle. Each grabs as much as it can, and is, in turn, grabbed.

"On Saybrook's Planet, each organism has its place, as each cell in your body does. Bacteria and plants produce food, on the excess of which animals feed, providing in turn carbon dioxide and nitrogenous wastes. Nothing is produced more or less than is needed. The scheme of life is intelligently altered to suit the local environment. No group of life forms multiplies more or less than is needed, just as the cells in our body stop multiplying when there are enough of them for a given purpose. When they don't stop multiplying, we call it cancer. And that's what life on earth really is, the kind of organic organization we have, compared to that on Saybrook's Planet. One big cancer. Every species, every individual doing its best to thrive at the expense of every other species and individual."

"You sound as if you approve of Saybrook's Planet, Doc."

"I do, in a way. It makes sense out of the business of living. I can see their viewpoint toward us. Suppose one of the cells of your body could be conscious of the efficiency of the human body as compared with that of the cell itself, and could realize that this was only the result of the union of many cells into a higher whole. And then suppose it became conscious of the existence of free-living cells, with bare life and nothing more. It might feel a very strong desire to drag the poor thing into an organization. It might feel sorry for it, feel perhaps a sort of missionary spirit. The things on Saybrook's Planet—or the thing; one should use the singular—feels just that, perhaps."

"And went ahead by bringing about virgin births, eh, Doc? I've got to go easy on that angle of it. Post Office regulations, you know."

"There's nothing ribald about it, Drake. For centuries we've been able to make the eggs of sea urchins, bees, frogs, et cetera develop without the intervention of male fertilization. The touch of a needle was sometimes enough, or just immersion in the proper salt solution. The thing on Saybrook's Planet can cause fertilization by the controlled used of radiant energy. That's why an appropriate energy barrier stops it; interference, you see, or static.

"They can do more than stimulate the division and development of an unfertilized egg. They can impress their own characteristics upon its nucleo-proteins, so that the young are born with the little patches of green fur, which serve as the planet's sense organ and means of communication. The young, in other words, are not individuals, but become part of the thing on Saybrook's Planet. The thing on the planet, not at all incidentally, can impregnate any species—plant, animal, or microscopic."

"Potent stuff," muttered Drake.

"Totipotent," Dr. Weiss said sharply. "Universally potent. Any fragment of it is totipotent. Given time, a single bacterium from Saybrook's Planet can convert all of earth into a single organism! We've got the experimental proof of that."

Drake said unexpectedly, "You know, I think I'm a millionaire, Doc. Can you keep a secret?"

Weiss nodded, puzzled.

"I've got a souvenir from Saybrook's Planet," Drake told him, grinning. "It's only a pebble, but after the publicity the planet will get, combined with the fact that it's quarantined from here on in, the pebble will be all any human being will ever see of it. How much do you suppose I could sell the thing for?"

Weiss stared. "A pebble?" He snatched at the object shown him, a hard, gray ovoid. "You shouldn't have done that, Drake. It was strictly against regulations."

"I know. That's why I asked if you could keep a secret. If you could give me a signed note of authentication—What's the matter, Doc?"

Instead of answering, Weiss could only chatter and point. Drake ran over and stared down at the pebble. It was the same as before—

Except that the light was catching it at an angle, and it showed up two little green spots. Looked at very closely, they were patches of green hairs.

He was disturbed. There was a definite air of danger within the ship. There was the suspicion of his presence aboard. How could that be? He had done nothing yet. Had another fragment of home come aboard and been less cautious? That would be impossible without his knowledge, and though he probed the ship intensely, he found nothing.

And then the suspicion diminished, but it was not quite dead. One of the keen-thinkers still wondered, and was treading close to the truth.

How long before the landing? Would an entire world of life fragments be deprived of completeness? He clung closer to the severed ends of the wire he had been especially bred to imitate, afraid of detection, fearful for his altruistic mission.

Dr. Weiss had locked himself in his own room. They were already within the solar system, and in three hours they would be landing. He had to think. He had three hours in which to decide.

Drake's devilish "pebble" had been part of the organized life on Saybrook's Planet, of course, but it was dead. It was dead when he had first seen it, and if it hadn't been, it was certainly dead after they fed it into the hyper-atomic motor and converted it into a blast of pure heat. And the bacterial cultures still showed normal when Weiss anxiously checked.

That was not what bothered Weiss now.

Drake had picked up the "pebble" during the last hours of the stay on Saybrook's Planet—after the barrier breakdown. What if the breakdown had been the result of a slow, relentless mental pressure on the part of the thing on the planet? What if parts of its being waited to invade as the barrier dropped? If the "pebble" had not been fast enough and had moved only after the barrier was re-established, it would have been killed. It would have lain there for Drake to see and pick up.

It was a "pebble," not a natural life form. But did that mean it was not some kind of life form? It might have been a deliberate production of the planet's single organism—a creature deliberately designed to look like a pebble, harmless-seeming, unsuspicious. Camouflage, in other words—a shrewd and frighteningly successful camouflage.

Had any other camouflaged creature succeeded in crossing the barrier before it was re-established—with a suitable shape filched from the minds of the humans aboard ship by the mind-reading organism of the planet? Would it have the casual appearance of a paperweight? Of an ornamental brass-head nail in the captain's old-fashioned chair? And how would they locate it? Could they search every part of the ship for the telltale green patches—even down to individual microbes?

And why camouflage? Did it intend to remain undetected for a time? Why? So that it might wait for the landing on earth?

An infection *after landing* could not be cured by blowing up a ship. The bacteria of earth, the molds, yeasts, and protozoans, would go first. Within a year the non-human young would begin arriving by the uncountable billions.

Weiss closed his eyes and told himself it might not be such a bad thing. There would be no more disease, since no bacterium would multiply at the expense of its host, but instead would be satisfied with its fair share of what was available. There would be no more overpopulation; the hordes of East Asia would decline to adjust themselves to the food supply. There would be no more wars, no crime, no greed.

But there would be no more individuality, either.

Humanity would find security by becoming a cog in a biological machine. A man would be brother to a germ, or to a liver cell.

He stood up. He would have a talk with Captain Loring. They would send their report and blow up the ship, just as Saybrook had done.

He sat down again. Saybrook had had proof, while he had only the conjectures of a terrorized mind, rattled by the sight of two green spots on a pebble. Could he kill the two hundred men on board ship because of a feeble suspicion?

He had to *think!*

He was straining. Why did he have to wait? If he could only welcome those who were aboard now. *Now!*

Yet a cooler, more reasoning part of himself told him that he could not. The little multipliers in the darkness would betray their new status in fifteen minutes, and the keen-thinkers had them under continual observation. Even one mile from the surface of their planet would be too soon, since they might still destroy themselves and their ship out in space.

Better to wait for the main air locks to open, for the planetary air to swirl in with millions of the little multipliers. Better to greet each one of them into the brotherhood of unified life and let them swirl out again to spread the message.

Then it would be done! Another world organized, complete!

He waited. There was the dull throbbing of the engines working mightily to control the slow dropping of the ship; the shudder of contact with planetary surface, then—

He let the jubilation of the keen-thinkers sweep into reception, and his own jubilant thoughts answered them. Soon they would be able to receive as well as himself. Perhaps not these particular fragments, but the fragments that would grow out of those which were fitted for the continuation of life.

The main air locks were about to be opened——

And all thought ceased.

Jerry Thorn thought, Damn it, something's wrong now.

He said to Captain Loring, "Sorry. There seems to be a power breakdown. The locks won't open."

"Are you sure, Thorn? The lights are on."

"Yes, sir. We're investigating it now."

He tore away and joined Roger Oldenn at the air-lock wiring box. "What's wrong?"

"Give me a chance, will you?" Oldenn's hands were busy. Then he said, "For the love of Pete, there's a six-inch break in the twenty-amp lead."

"What? That can't be!"

Oldenn held up the broken wires with their clean, sharp, sawn-through ends.

Dr. Weiss joined them. He looked haggard and there was the smell of brandy on his breath.

He said shakily, "What's the matter?"

They told him. At the bottom of the compartment, in one corner, was the missing section.

Weiss bent over. There was a black fragment on the floor of the compartment. He touched it with his finger and it smeared, leaving a sooty smudge on his finger tip. He rubbed it off absently.

There might have been something taking the place of the

missing section of wire. Something that had been alive and only looked like wire, yet something that would heat, die, and carbonize in a tiny fraction of a second once the electrical circuit which controlled the air lock had been closed.

He said, "How are the bacteria?"

A crew member went to check, returned and said, "All normal, Doc."

The wires had meanwhile been spliced, the locks opened, and Dr. Weiss stepped out into the anarchic world of life that was earth.

"Anarchy," he said, laughing a little wildly. "And it will stay that way."

The Ethical Equations

by MURRAY LEINSTER

> Murray Leinster, who has been writing science-
> fiction for more than a generation, has been fasci-
> nated by the problem of "first contact" between
> voyagers from different worlds. How will intelli-
> gent beings behave when confronted with so mo-
> mentous an event? One answer is provided in this
> story of a young junior lieutenant in a future Space
> Patrol.

IT IS VERY, very queer. The Ethical Equations, of course, link
conduct with probability, and give mathematical proof that certain patterns of conduct increase the probability of certain
kinds of coincidences. But nobody ever expected them to have
any really practical effect. Elucidation of the laws of chance did
not stop gambling, though it did make life insurance practical.
The Ethical Equations weren't expected to be even as useful as
that. They were just theories, which seemed unlikely to affect
anybody particularly. They were complicated, for one thing.
They admitted that the ideal pattern of conduct for one man
wasn't the best for another. A politician, for example, has an entirely different code—and properly—from a Space Patrol man.
But still, on at least one occasion—

The thing from outer space was fifteen hundred feet long,
and upward of a hundred and fifty feet through at its middle
section, and well over two hundred in a curious bulge like a
fish's head at its bow. There were odd, gill-like flaps just back of

143

that bulge, too, and the whole thing looked extraordinarily like an eyeless monster fish, floating in empty space out beyond Jupiter. But it had drifted in from somewhere beyond the sun's gravitational field—its speed was too great for it to have a closed orbit—and it swung with a slow, inane, purposeless motion about some axis it had established within itself.

The little spacecruiser edged closer and closer. Freddy Holmes had been a pariah on the *Arnina* all the way out from Mars, but he clenched his hands and forgot his misery and the ruin of his career in the excitement of looking at the thing.

"No response to signals on any frequency, sir," said the communications officer, formally. "It is not radiating. It has a minute magnetic field. Its surface temperature is just about four degrees absolute."

The commander of the *Arnina* said, "Hrrrmph!" Then he said, "We'll lay alongside." Then he looked at Freddy Holmes and stiffened. "No," he said, "I believe you take over now, Mr. Holmes."

Freddy started. He was in a very bad spot, but his excitement had made him oblivious of it for a moment. The undisguised hostility with which he was regarded by the skipper and the others on the bridge brought it back, however.

"You take over, Mr. Holmes," repeated the skipper bitterly. "I have orders to that effect. You originally detected this object and your uncle asked Headquarters that you be given full authority to investigate it. You have that authority. Now, what are you going to do with it?"

There was fury in his voice surpassing even the rasping dislike of the voyage out. He was a lieutenant commander and he had been instructed to take orders from a junior officer. That was bad enough. But this was humanity's first contact with an extrasolar civilization, and Freddy Holmes, lieutenant junior grade, had been given charge of the matter by pure political pull.

Freddy swallowed.

"I . . . I—" He swallowed again and said miserably, "Sir, I've tried to explain that I dislike the present set-up as much as you possibly can. I . . . wish that you would let me put myself under your orders, sir, instead of—"

"No!" rasped the commander vengefully. "You are in command, Mr. Holmes. Your uncle put on political pressure to arrange it. My orders are to carry out your instructions, not to wet-nurse you if the job is too big for you to handle. This is in your lap! Will you issue orders?"

Freddy stiffened.

"Very well, sir. It's plainly a ship and apparently a derelict. No crew would come in without using a drive or allow their ship to swing about aimlessly. You will maintain your present position with relation to it. I'll take a spaceboat and a volunteer, if you will find me one, and look it over."

He turned and left the bridge. Two minutes later he was struggling into a spacesuit when Lieutenant Bridges—also junior grade—came briskly into the spacesuit locker and observed:

"I've permission to go with you, Mr. Holmes." He began to get into another spacesuit. As he pulled it up over his chest he added blithely: "I'd say this was worth the price of admission!"

Freddy did not answer. Three minutes later the little spaceboat pulled out from the side of the cruiser. Designed for expeditionary work and tool-carrying rather than as an escapecraft, it was not inclosed. It would carry men in spacesuits, with their tools and weapons, and they could breathe from its tanks instead of from their suits, and use its power and so conserve their own. But it was a strange feeling to sit within its spidery outline and see the great blank sides of the strange object draw near. When the spaceboat actually touched the vast metal wall it seemed impossible, like the approach to some sorcerer's castle across a monstrous moat of stars.

It was real enough, though. The felted rollers touched, and Bridges grunted in satisfaction.

"Magnetic. We can anchor to it. Now what?"

"We hunt for an entrance port," said Freddy curtly. He added: "Those openings that look like gills are the drive tubes. Their drive's in front instead of the rear. Apparently they don't use gyros for steering."

The tiny craft clung to the giant's skin, like a fly on a stranded whale. It moved slowly to the top of the rounded body, and over it, and down on the other side. Presently the cruiser came in sight again as it came up the near side once more.

"Nary a port, sir," said Bridges blithely. "Do we cut our way in?"

"Hm-m-m," said Freddy slowly. "We have our drive in the rear, and our control room in front. So we take on supplies amidships, and that's where we looked. But this ship is driven from the front. Its control room might be amidships. If so, it might load at the stern. Let's see."

The little craft crawled to the stern of the monster.

"There!" said Freddy.

It was not like an entrance port on any vessel in the solar system. It slid aside, without hinges. There was an inner door, but it opened just as readily. There was no rush of air, and it was hard to tell if it was intended as an air lock or not.

"Air's gone," said Freddy. "It's a derelict, all right. You might bring a blaster, but what we'll mostly need is light, I think."

The magnetic anchors took hold. The metal grip shoes of the spacesuits made loud noises inside the suits as the two of them pushed their way into the interior of the ship. The spacecruiser had been able to watch them, until now. Now they were gone.

The giant, enigmatic object which was so much like a blind fish in empty space floated on. It swung aimlessly about some inner axis. The thin sunlight, out here beyond Jupiter, smote upon it harshly. It seemed to hang motionless in mid-space against an all-surrounding background of distant and unwinking stars. The trim Space Patrol ship hung alertly a mile and a half away. Nothing seemed to happen at all.

Freddy was rather pale when he went back to the bridge. The pressure mark on his forehead from the spacesuit helmet was still visible, and he rubbed at it abstractedly. The skipper regarded him with a sort of envious bitterness. After all, any human would envy any other who had set foot in an alien spaceship. Lieutenant Bridges followed him. For an instant there were no words. Then Bridges saluted briskly:

"Reporting back on board, sir, and returning to watch duty after permitted volunteer activity."

The skipper touched his hat sourly. Bridges departed with crisp precision. The skipper regarded Freddy with the helpless fury of a senior officer who has been ordered to prove a junior officer a fool, and who has seen the assignment blow up in his face and that of the superior officers who ordered it. It was an enraging situation. Freddy Holmes, newly commissioned and assigned to the detector station on Luna which keeps track of asteroids and meteor streams, had discovered a small object coming in over Neptune. Its speed was too high for it to be a regular member of the solar system, so he'd reported it as a visitor and suggested immediate examination. But junior officers are not supposed to make discoveries. It violates tradition, which is a sort of Ethical Equation in the Space Patrol. So Freddy was slapped down for his presumption. And he slapped back, on account of the Ethical Equations bearing upon scientific discoveries. The first known object to come from beyond the stars ought to be examined. Definitely. So, most unprofessionally for a Space Patrol junior, Freddy raised a stink.

The present state of affairs was the result. He had an uncle who was a prominent politician. That uncle went before the Space Patrol Board and pointed out smoothly that his nephew's discovery was important. He demonstrated with mathematical precision that the Patrol was being ridiculous in ignoring a significant discovery simply because a junior officer had made it. And the Board, seething at outside interference, ordered Freddy to be taken to the object he had detected, given absolute command of the spacecruiser which had taken him there, and directed to make the examination he had suggested. By all the laws of probability, he would have to report that the hunk of matter from beyond the solar system was just like hunks of matter in it. And then the Board would pin back both his and his uncle's ears with a vengeance.

But now the hunk of matter turned out to be a fish-shaped artifact from an alien civilization. It turned out to be important. So the situation was one to make anybody steeped in Patrol tradition grind his teeth.

"The thing, sir," said Freddy evenly, "is a spaceship. It is driven by atomic engines shooting blasts sternward from somewhere near the bow. Apparently they steer only by hand. Apparently, too, there was a blow-up in the engine room and they lost most of their fuel out the tube vents. After that, the ship was helpless though they patched up the engines after a fashion. It is possible to calculate that in its practically free fall to the sun it's been in its present state for a couple of thousand years."

"I take it, then," said the skipper with fine irony, "that there are no survivors of the crew."

"It presents several problems, sir," said Freddy evenly, "and that's one of them." He was rather pale. "The ship is empty of air, but her tanks are full. Storage spaces containing what look like supplies are only partly emptied. The crew did not starve or suffocate. The ship simply lost most of her fuel. So it looks like they prepared the ship to endure an indefinite amount of floating about in free space and"—he hesitated—"then it looks like they went into suspended animation. They're all on board, in transparent cases that have—machinery attached. Maybe they thought they'd be picked up by sister ships sooner or later."

The skipper blinked.

"Suspended animation? They're alive?" Then he said sharply: "What sort of ship is it? Cargo?"

"No, sir," said Freddy. "That's another problem. Bridges and I agree that it's a fighting ship, sir. There are rows of generators serving things that could only be weapons. By the way they're braced, there are tractor beams and pressor beams and—there are vacuum tubes that have grids but apparently work with cold cathodes. By the size of the cables that lead to them, those tubes handle amperages up in the thousands. You can figure that one out, sir."

The skipper paced two steps this way, and two steps that. The thing was stupendous. But his instructions were precise.

"I'm under your orders," he said doggedly. "What are you going to do?"

"I'm going to work myself to death, I suppose," said Freddy unhappily, "and some other men with me. I want to go over that ship backwards, forwards, and sideways with scanners, and everything the scanners see photographed back on board, here. I want men to work the scanners and technicians on board to direct them for their specialties. I want to get every rivet and coil in that whole ship on film before touching anything."

The skipper said grudgingly:

"That's not too foolish. Very well, Mr. Holmes, it will be done."

"Thank you," said Freddy. He started to leave the bridge, and stopped. "The men to handle the scanners," he added, "ought to be rather carefully picked. Imaginative men wouldn't do. The crew of that ship—they look horribly alive, and they aren't pretty. And . . . er . . . the plastic cases they're in are arranged to open from inside. That's another problem still, sir."

He went on down. The skipper clasped his hands behind his back and began to pace the bridge furiously. The first object from beyond the stars was a spaceship. It had weapons the Patrol had only vainly imagined. And he, a two-and-a-half striper, had to stand by and take orders for its investigation from a lieutenant junior grade just out of the Academy. Because of politics! The skipper ground his teeth—

Then Freddy's last comment suddenly had meaning. The plastic cases in which the alien's crew lay in suspended animation opened from the inside. From the inside!

Cold sweat came out on the skipper's forehead as he realized the implication. Tractor and pressor beams, and the ship's fuel not quite gone, and the suspended-animation cases opening from the inside—

There was a slender, coaxial cable connecting the two spacecraft, now. They drifted in sunward together. The little cruiser was dwarfed by the alien giant.

The sun was very far away; brighter than any star, to be sure, and pouring out a fierce radiation, but still very far from a warming orb. All about were the small, illimitably distant lights which were stars. There was exactly one object in view which had an appreciable diameter. That was Jupiter, a new moon in shape, twenty million miles sunward and eighty million miles farther along its orbit. The rest was emptiness.

The spidery little spaceboat slid along the cable between the two craft. Spacesuited figures got out and clumped on magnetic-soled shoes to the air lock. They went in.

Freddy came to the bridge. The skipper said hoarsely:

"Mr. Holmes, I would like to make a request. You are, by orders of the Board, in command of this ship until your investigation of the ship yonder is completed."

Freddy's face was haggard and worn. He said abstractedly: "Yes, sir. What is it?"

"I would like," said the Arnina's skipper urgently, "to send a complete report of your investigation so far. Since you are in command, I cannot do so without your permission."

"I would rather you didn't, sir," said Freddy. Tired as he was, his jaws clamped. "Frankly, sir, I think they'd cancel your present orders and issue others entirely."

The skipper bit his lip. That was the idea. The scanners had sent back complete images of almost everything in the other ship, now. Everything was recorded on film. The skipper had seen the monsters which were the crew of the extrasolar vessel. And the plastic cases in which they had slumbered for at least two thousand years did open from the inside. That was what bothered him. They did open from the inside!

The electronics technicians of the Arnina were going about in silly rapture, drawing diagrams for each other and contemplating the results with dazed appreciation. The gunnery officer was making scaled, detailed design-drawings for weapons he had never hoped for, and waking up nights to feel for those drawings and be sure that they were real. But the engineer officer was wringing his hands. He wanted to take the other ship's engines apart. They were so enormously smaller than the Arnina's drive, and yet they had driven a ship with eighty-four times the Arnina's mass—and he could not see how they could work.

The alien ship was ten thousand years ahead of the Arnina. Its secrets were being funneled over to the little earth-ship at a rapid rate. But the cases holding its still-living crew opened from the inside.

"Nevertheless, Mr. Holmes," the skipper said feverishly, "I must ask permission to send that report."

"But I am in command," said Freddy tiredly, "and I intend to stay in command. I will give you a written order forbidding you to make a report, sir. Disobedience will be mutiny."

The skipper grew almost purple.

"Do you realize," he demanded savagely, "that if the crew of that ship is in suspended animation, and if their coffins or containers open only from inside—do you realize that they expect to open them themselves?"

"Yes, sir," said Freddy wearily. "Of course. Why not?"

"Do you realize that cables from those containers lead to thermobatteries in the ship's outer plating? The monsters knew they couldn't survive without power, but they knew that in any other solar system they could get it! So they made sure they'd pass close to our sun with what power they dared use, and went into suspended animation with a reserve of power to land on and thermobatteries that would waken them when it was time to set to work!"

"Yes, sir," said Freddy, as wearily as before. "They had courage, at any rate. But what would you do about that?"

"I'd report it to Headquarters!" raged the skipper. "I'd report that this is a warship capable of blasting the whole Patrol out of the ether and smashing our planets! I'd say it was manned by monsters now fortunately helpless, but with fuel enough to maneuver to a landing. And I'd asked authority to take their coffins out of their ship and destroy them! Then I'd—"

"I did something simpler," said Freddy. "I disconnected the thermo-batteries. They can't revive. So I'm going to get a few hours' sleep. If you'll excuse me—"

He went to his own cabin and threw himself on his bunk.

Men with scanners continued to examine every square inch of the monster derelict. They worked in spacesuits. To have filled the giant hull with air would practically have emptied the Arnina's tanks. A spacesuited man held a scanner before a curious roll of flexible substance, on which were inscribed symbols. His headphones brought instructions from the photo room. A record of some sort was being duplicated by photography. There were scanners at work in the storerooms, the crew's quarters, the gun mounts. So far no single article had been moved from the giant stranger. That was Freddy's order. Every possible bit of information was being extracted from every possible object, but nothing had been taken away. Even chemical analysis was being done by scanner, using cold-light spectography applied from the laboratory on the cruiser.

And Freddy's unpopularity had not lessened. The engineer

officer cursed him luridly. The stranger's engines, now— They had been patched up after an explosion, and they were tantalizingly suggestive. But their working was unfathomable. The engineer officer wanted to get his hands on them. The physiochemical officer wanted to do some analysis with his own hands, instead of by cold-light spectography over a scanner. And every man, from the lowest enlisted apprentice to the skipper himself, wanted to get hold of some artifact made by an alien, nonhuman race ten thousand years ahead of human civilization. So Freddy was unpopular.

But that was only part of his unhappiness. He felt that he had acted improperly. The Ethical Equations gave mathematical proof that probabilities and ethics are interlinked, so that final admirable results cannot be expected from unethical beginnings. Freddy had violated discipline—which is one sort of ethics—and after that through his uncle had interjected politics into Patrol affairs, which was definitely a crime. By the Equations, the probability of disastrous coincidences was going to be enormous until corrective, ethically proper action was taken to cancel out the original crimes. And Freddy had been unable to devise such action. He felt, too, that the matter was urgent. He slept uneasily despite his fatigue, because there was something in the back of his mind which warned him stridently that disaster lay ahead.

Freddy awoke still unrefreshed and stared dully at the ceiling over his head. He was trying discouragedly to envision a reasonable solution when there came a tap on his door. It was Bridges with a batch of papers.

"Here you are!" he said cheerfully, when Freddy opened to him. "Now we're all going to be happy!"

Freddy took the extended sheets.

"What's happened?" he asked. "Did the skipper send for fresh orders regardless, and I'm to go in the brig?"

Bridges, grinning, pointed to the sheets of paper in Freddy's hand. They were from the physiochemical officer, who was equipped to do exact surveys on the lesser heavenly bodies.

"*Elements found in the alien vessel,*" was the heading of a list. Freddy scanned the list. No heavy elements, but the rest was familiar. There had been pure nitrogen in the fuel tank, he remembered, and the engineer officer was going quietly mad trying to understand how they had used nitrogen for atomic power. Freddy looked down to the bottom. Iron was the heaviest element present.

"Why should this make everybody happy?" asked Freddy.

Bridges pointed with his finger. The familiar atomic symbols had unfamiliar numerals by them. H^3, Li^5, Gl^8— He blinked. He saw N^{15}, F^{18}, $S^{34,35}$— Then he stared. Bridges grinned.

"Try to figure what that ship's worth!" he said happily. "It's all over the Arnina. Prize money isn't allowed in the Patrol, but five per cent of salvage is. Hydrogen three has been detected on earth, but never isolated. Lithium five doesn't exist on earth, or glucinium eight, or nitrogen fifteen or oxygen seventeen or fluorine eighteen or sulphur thirty-four or thirty-five! The whole ship is made up of isotopes that simply don't exist in the solar system! And you know what pure isotopes sell for! The hull's practically pure iron fifty-five! Pure iron fifty-four sells for thirty-five credits a gram! Talk about the lost treasures of Mars! For technical use only, the stripped hull of this stranger is worth ten years' revenue of earth government! Every man on the Arnina is rich for life. And you're popular!"

Freddy did not smile.

"Nitrogen fifteen," he said slowly. "That's what's in the remaining fuel tank. It goes into a queer little aluminum chamber we couldn't figure out, and from there into the drive tubes. I see—"

He was very pale. Bridges beamed.

"A hundred thousand tons of materials that simply don't exist on earth! Pure isotopes, intact! Not a contamination in a carload! My dear chap, I've come to like you, but you've been hated by everyone else. Now come out and bask in admiration and affection!"

Freddy said, unheeding:

"I've been wondering what that aluminum chamber was for. It looked so infernally simple, and I couldn't see what it did—"

"Come out and have a drink!" insisted Bridges joyously. "Be lionized! Make friends and influence people!"

"No," said Freddy. He smiled mirthlessly. "I'll be lynched later anyhow. Hm-m-m. I want to talk to the engineer officer.

We want to get that ship navigating under its own power. It's too big to do anything with towlines."

"But nobody's figured out its engines!" protested Bridges. "Apparently there's nothing but a tiny trickle of nitrogen through a silly chamber that does something to it, and then it flows through aluminum baffles into the drive tubes. It's too simple! How are you going to make a thing like that work?"

"I think," said Freddy, "it's going to be horribly simple. That whole ship is made up of isotopes we don't have on earth. No. It has aluminum and carbon. They're simple substances. Theirs and ours are just alike. But most of the rest—"

He was pale. He looked as if he were suffering.

"I'll get a couple of tanks made up, of aluminum, and filled with nitrogen. Plain air should do—and I'll want a gyro-control. I'll want it made of aluminum, too, with graphite bearings—"

He grinned mirthlessly at Bridges.

"Ever hear of the Ethical Equations, Bridges? You'd never expect them to suggest the answer to a space-drive problem, would you? But that's what they've done. I'll get the engineer officer to have those things made up. It's nice to have known you, Bridges—"

As Bridges went out, Freddy Holmes sat down, wetting his lips, to make sketches for the engineer officer to work from.

The control room and the engine room of the monster ship were one. It was a huge, globular chamber filled with apparatus of startlingly alien design. To Freddy, and to Bridges, too, now, there was not so much of monstrousness as at first. Eight days of familiarity, and knowledge of how they worked, had made them seem almost normal. But still it was eerie to belt themselves before the instrument board, with only their hand lamps for illumination, and cast a last glance at the aluminum replacements of parts that had been made on some planet of another sun.

"If this works," said Freddy, and swallowed, "we're lucky. Here's the engine control. Cross your fingers, Bridges."

The interior of the hulk was still airless. Freddy shifted a queerly shaped lever an infinitesimal trace. There was a slight surging movement of the whole vast hull. A faint murmuring came through the fabric of the monster ship to the soles of their spacesuit boots. Freddy wet his lips and touched another lever.

"This should be lights."

It was. Images formed on the queerly shaped screens. The whole interior of the ship glowed. And the whole creation had been so alien as somehow to be revolting, in the harsh white light of the hand lamps the men had used. But now it was like a highly improbable fairy palace. The fact that all doors were circular and all passages were around tubes was only pleasantly strange, in the many-colored glow of the ship's own lighting system. Freddy shook his head in his spacesuit helmet, as if to shake away drops of sweat on his forehead.

"The next should be heat," he said more grimly than before. "We do not touch that! Oh, definitely! But we try the drive."

The ship stirred. It swept forward in a swift smooth acceleration that was invincibly convincing of power. The *Arnina* dwindled swiftly, behind. And Freddy, with compressed lips, touched controls here, and there, and the monstrous ship obeyed with the docility of a willing, well-trained animal. It swept back to clear sight of the *Arnina*.

"I would say," said Bridges in a shaking voice, "that it works. The Patrol has nothing like this!"

"No," said Freddy shortly. His voice sounded sick. "Not like this! It's a sweet ship. I'm going to hook in the gyro controls. They ought to work. The creatures who made this didn't use them. I don't know why. But they didn't."

He cut off everything but the lights. He bent down and hooked in the compact little aluminum device which would control the flow of nitrogen to the port and starboard drive tubes.

Freddy came back to the control board and threw in the drive once more. And the gyro control worked. It should. After all, the tool work of a Space Patrol machinist should be good. Freddy tested it thoroughly. He set it on certain fine adjustment. He threw three switches. Then he picked up one tiny kit he had prepared.

"Come along," he said tiredly. "Our work's over. We go back to the *Arnina* and I probably get lynched."

Bridges, bewildered, followed him to the spidery little spaceboat. They cast off from the huge ship, now three miles or more from the *Arnina* and untenanted save by its own monstrous crew in suspended animation. The Space Patrol cruiser shifted position to draw near and pick them up. And Freddy said hardly:

"Remember the Ethical Equations, Bridges? I said they gave me the answer to that other ship's drive. If they were right, it couldn't have been anything else. Now I'm going to find out about something else."

His spacegloved hands worked clumsily. From the tiny kit he spilled out a single small object. He plopped it into something from a chest in the spaceboat—a mortar shell, as Bridges saw incredulously. He dropped that into the muzzle of a line-mortar the spaceboat carried as a matter of course. He jerked the lanyard. The mortar flamed. Expanding gases beat at the spacesuits of the men. A tiny, glowing, crimson spark sped toward outer space. Seconds passed. Three. Four. Five—

"Apparently I'm a fool," said Freddy, in the grimmest voice Bridges had ever heard.

But then there was light. And such light! Where the dwindling red spark of a tracer mortar shell had sped toward infinitely distant stars, there was suddenly an explosion of such incredible violence as even the proving-grounds of the Space Patrol had never known. There was no sound in empty space. There was no substance to be heated to incandescence other than that of a half-pound tracer shell. But there was a flare of blue-white light and a crash of such violent static that Bridges was deafened by it. Even through the glass of his helmet he felt a flash of savage heat. Then there was—nothing.

"What was that?" said Bridges, shaken.

"The Ethical Equations," said Freddy. "Apparently I'm not the fool I thought—"

The *Arnina* slid up alongside the little spaceboat. Freddy did not alight. He moved the boat over to its cradle and plugged in his communicator set. He talked over that set with his helmet phone, not radiating a signal that Bridges could pick up. In three minutes or so the great lock opened and four spacesuited figures came out. One wore the crested four-communicator helmet which only the skipper of a cruiser wears when in command of a landing party. The newcomers to the outside of the *Arina*'s hull crowded into the little spaceboat. Freddy's voice sounded again in the headphones, grim and cold.

"I've some more shells, sir. They're tracer shells which have been in the work boat for eight days. They're not quite as cold as the ship, yonder—that's had two thousand years to cool off in—but they're cold. I figure they're not over eight or ten degrees absolute. And here are the bits of material from the other ship. You can touch them. Our spacesuits are as nearly nonconductive of heat as anything could be. You won't warm them if you hold them in your hand."

The skipper—Bridges could see him—looked at the scraps of metal Freddy held out to him. They were morsels of iron and other material from the alien ship. By the cold glare of a handlight the skipper thrust one into the threaded hollow at the nose of a mortar shell into which a line-end is screwed when a line is to be thrown. The skipper himself dropped in the mortar shell and fired it. Again a racing, receding speck of red in emptiness. And a second terrible, atomic blast.

The skipper's voice in the headphones:

"How much more of the stuff did you bring away?"

"Three more pieces, sir," said Freddy's voice, very steady now. "You see how it happens, sir. They're isotopes we don't have on earth. And we don't have them because in contact with other isotopes at normal temperatures, they're unstable. They go off. Here we dropped them into the mortar shells and nothing happened, because both isotopes were cold—down to the temperature of liquid helium, or nearly. But there's a tracer compound in the shells, and it burns as they fly away. The shell grows warm. And when either isotope, in contact with the other, is as warm as . . . say . . . liquid hydrogen . . . why . . . they destroy each other. The ship yonder is of the same material. Its mass is about a hundred thousand tons. Except for the aluminum and maybe one or two other elements that also are nonisotopic and the same in both ships, every bit of that ship will blast off if it comes in contact with matter from this solar system above ten or twelve degrees absolute."

"Shoot the other samples away," said the skipper harshly. "We want to be sure—"

There were three violent puffs of gases expanding into empty space. There were three incredible blue-white flames in the void. There was silence. Then—

"That thing has to be destroyed," said the skipper, heavily. "We couldn't set it down anywhere, and its crew might wake up anyhow, at any moment. We haven't anything that could fight it, and if it tried to land on earth—"

The alien monster, drifting aimlessly in the void, suddenly moved. Thin flames came from the gill-like openings at the bow. Then one side jetted more strongly. It swung about, steadied, and swept forward with a terrifying smooth acceleration. It built up speed vastly more swiftly than any earthship could possibly do. It dwindled to a speck. It vanished in empty space.

But it was not bound inward toward the sun. It was not headed for the plainly visible half-moon disk of Jupiter, now barely seventy million miles away. It headed out toward the stars.

"I wasn't sure until a few minutes ago," said Freddy Holmes unsteadily, "but by the Ethical Equations something like that was probable. I couldn't make certain until we'd gotten everything possible from it, and until I had everything arranged. But I was worried from the first. The Ethical Equations made it pretty certain that if we did the wrong thing we'd suffer for it . . . and by we I mean the whole earth, because any visitor from beyond the stars would be bound to affect the whole human race." His voice wavered a little. "It was hard to figure out what we ought to do. If one of our ships had been in the same fix, though, we'd have hoped for—friendliness. We'd hope for fuel, maybe, and help in starting back home. But this ship was a warship, and we'd have been helpless to fight it. It would have been hard to be friendly. Yet, according to the Ethical Equations, if we wanted our first contact with an alien civilization to be of benefit to us, it was up to us to get it started back home with plenty of fuel."

"You mean," said the skipper, incredulously, "you mean you—"

"Its engines use nitrogen," said Freddy. "It runs nitrogen fifteen into a little gadget we know how to make, now. It's very simple, but it's a sort of atom smasher. It turns nitrogen fifteen into nitrogen fourteen and hydrogen. I think we can make use of that for ourselves. Nitrogen fourteen is the kind we have. It can be handled in aluminum pipes and tanks, because there's only one aluminum, which is stable under all conditions. But when it hits the alien isotopes in the drive tubes, it breaks down—"

He took a deep breath.

"I gave them a double aluminum tank of nitrogen, and by-passed their atom smasher. Nitrogen fourteen goes into their drive tubes, and they drive! And . . . I figured back their orbit, and set a gyro to head them back for their own solar system for as long as the first tank of nitrogen holds out. They'll make it out of the sun's gravitational field on that, anyhow. And I re-connected their thermo-batteries. When they start to wake up they'll see the gyro and know that somebody gave it to them. The double tank is like their own and they'll realize they have a fresh supply of fuel to land with. It . . . may be a thousand years before they're back home, but when they get there they'll know we're friendly and . . . not afraid of them. And mean-while we've got all their gadgets to work on and work with—"

Freddy was silent. The little spaceboat clung to the side of the *Arnina*, which with its drive off was now drifting in sunward past the orbit of Jupiter.

"It is very rare," said the skipper ungraciously, "that a supe-rior officer in the Patrol apologizes to an inferior. But I apolo-gize to you, Mr. Holmes, for thinking you a fool. And when I think that I, and certainly every other Patrol officer of experience, would have thought of nothing but setting that ship down at Patrol Base for study, and when I think what an atomic explo-sion of a hundred thousand tons of matter would have done to earth . . . I apologize a second time."

Freddy said uncomfortably:

"If there are to be any apologies made, sir, I guess I've got to make them. Every man on the *Arnina* has figured he's rich, and I've sent it all back where it came from. But you see, sir, the Ethical Equations—"

When Freddy's resignation went in with the report of his in-vestigation of the alien vessel, it was returned marked "Not Accepted." And Freddy was ordered to report to a tiny, hard-worked spacecan on which a junior Space Patrol officer normally gets his ears pinned back and learns his work the hard way. And Freddy was happy, because he wanted to be a Space Patrol officer more than he wanted anything else in the world. His uncle was satisfied, too, because he wanted Freddy to be content, and because certain space-admirals truculently told him that Freddy was needed in the Patrol and would get all the consideration and promotion he needed without any politicians butting in. And the Space Patrol was happy because it had a lot of new gadgets to work with which were going to make it a force able not only to look after interplanetary traffic but defend it, if necessary.

And, for that matter, the Ethical Equations were satisfied.

Misfit

by ROBERT A. HEINLEIN

> Giants come in all sizes, ages, and disguises. And
> as mankind ventures into space on an ever greater
> scale, crucial challenges will appear from unex-
> pected directions. And so will the giant intellects
> to solve them.

> ". . . for the purpose of conserving and improving
> our interplanetary resources, and providing useful,
> healthful occupations for the youth of this planet."
>
> > Excerpt from the En-
> > abling Act, H.R. 7118, set-
> > ting up the Cosmic Con-
> > struction Corps.

"ATTENTION TO MUSTER!" The parade-ground voice of a first
sergeant of Space Marines cut through the fog and drizzle of a
nasty New Jersey morning. "As your names are called, answer
'Here', step forward with your baggage, and embark. Atkins!"

"Here!"

"Austin!"

"Hyar!"

"Ayres!"

"Here!"

One by one they fell out of ranks, shouldered the hundred
and thirty pounds of personal possessions allowed them, and
trudged up the gangway. They were young—none more than
twenty-two—in some cases luggage outweighed the owner.

"Kaplan!"

"Here!"

"Keith!"

"Heah!"

"Libby!"

"Here!" A thin gangling blonde had detached himself from the line, hastily wiped his nose, and grabbed his belongings. He slung a fat canvas bag over his shoulder, steadied it, and lifted a suitcase with his free hand. He started for the companionway in an unsteady dog trot. As he stepped on the gangway his suitcase swung against his knees. He staggered against a short wiry form dressed in the powder-blue of the Space Navy. Strong fingers grasped his arm and checked his fall.

"Steady, son. Easy does it." Another hand readjusted the canvas bag.

"Oh, excuse me, uh"—the embarrassed youngster automatically counted the four bands of silver braid below the shooting star—"Captain. I didn't—"

"Bear a hand and get aboard, son."

"Yes, sir."

The passage into the bowels of the transport was gloomy. When the lad's eyes adjusted he saw a gunner's mate wearing the brassard of a master-at-arms, who hooked a thumb toward an open air-tight door.

"In there. Find your locker and wait by it." Libby hurried to obey. Inside he found a jumble of baggage and men in a wide low-ceilinged compartment. A line of glow-tubes ran around the junction of bulkhead and ceiling and trisected the overhead; the soft roar of blowers made a background to the voices of his shipmates. He picked his way through heaped luggage and located his locker, seven-ten, on the far wall outboard. He broke the seal on the combination lock, glanced at the combination, and opened it. The locker was very small, the middle of a tier of three. He considered what he should keep in it. A loudspeaker drowned out the surrounding voices and demanded his attention:

"Attention! Man all space details; first section. Raise ship in twelve minutes. Close air-tight doors. Stop blowers at minus two minutes. Special orders for passengers: Place all gear on deck, and lie down on red signal light. Remain down until release is sounded. Masters-at-arms check compliance."

The gunner's mate popped in, glanced around, and immediately commenced supervising rearrangement of the baggage. Heavy items were lashed down. Locker doors were closed. By the time each boy had found a place on the deck and the master-at-arms had okayed the pad under his head, the glow-tubes turned red and the loudspeaker brayed out.

"All hands—Up Ship! Stand by for acceleration." The master-at-arms hastily reclined against two cruise bags, and watched the room. The blowers sighed to a stop. There followed two minutes of dead silence. Libby felt his heart commence to pound. The two minutes stretched interminably. Then the deck quivered and a roar like escaping high-pressure steam beat at his eardrums. He was suddenly very heavy and a weight lay across his chest and heart. An indefinite time later the glow-tubes flashed white, and the announcer bellowed:

"Secure all getting-underway details; regular watch, first section." The blowers droned into life. The master-at-arms stood up, rubbed his buttocks, and pounded his arms, then said:

"Okay, boys." He stepped over and undogged the airtight door to the passageway. Libby got up and blundered into a bulkhead, nearly falling. His legs and arms had gone to sleep, besides which he felt alarmingly light, as if he had sloughed off at least half of his inconsiderable mass.

For the next two hours he was too busy to think, or to be homesick. Suitcases, boxes, and bags had to be passed down into the lower hold and lashed against angular acceleration. He located and learned how to use a waterless water closet. He found his assigned bunk and learned that it was his only eight hours in twenty-four; two other boys had the use of it, too. The three sections ate in three shifts, nine shifts in all—twenty-four youths and a master-at-arms at one long table which jam-filled a narrow compartment off the galley.

After lunch Libby restowed his locker. He was standing before it, gazing at a photograph which he intended to mount on the inside of the locker door, when a command filled the compartment:

"Attention!"

Standing inside the door was the captain flanked by the master-at-arms. The captain commenced to speak. "At rest, men. Sit down. McCoy, tell control to shift this compartment to smoke filter." The gunner's mate hurried to the communicator on the bulkhead and spoke into it in a low tone. Almost at once the hum of the blowers climbed a half-octave and stayed there. "Now light up if you like. I'm going to talk to you.

"You boys are headed out on the biggest thing so far in your lives. From now on you're men, with one of the hardest jobs ahead of you that men have ever tackled. What we have to do is part of a bigger scheme. You, and hundreds of thousands of others like you, are going out as pioneers to fix up the solar system so that human beings can make better use of it.

"Equally important, you are being given a chance to build yourselves into useful and happy citizens of the Federation. For one reason or another you weren't happily adjusted back on earth. Some of you saw the jobs you were trained for abolished by new inventions. Some of you got into trouble from not knowing what to do with the modern leisure. In any case you were misfits. Maybe you were called bad boys and had a lot of black marks chalked up against you.

"But everyone of you starts even today. The only record you have in this ship is your name at the top of a blank sheet of paper. It's up to you what goes on that page.

"Now about our job—We didn't get one of the easy repair-and-recondition jobs on the moon, with week-ends at Luna City, and all the comforts of home. Nor did we draw a high-gravity planet where a man can eat a full meal and expect to keep it down. Instead we've got to go out to Asteroid HS-5388 and turn it into Space Station E-M3. She has no atmosphere at all, and only about two per cent earth-surface gravity. We've got to play human fly on her for at least six months, no girls to date, no television, no recreation that you don't devise yourselves, and hard work every day. You'll get spacesick, and so homesick you can taste it, and agoraphobia. If you aren't careful you'll get ray-burnt. Your stomach will act up, and you'll wish to God you'd never enrolled.

"But if you behave yourself, and listen to the advice of the old spacemen, you'll come out of it strong and healthy, with a little credit stored up in the bank, and a lot of knowledge and experience that you wouldn't get in forty years on earth. You'll be men, and you'll know it.

"One last word. It will be pretty uncomfortable to those that aren't used to it. Just give the other fellow a little consideration, and you'll get along all right. If you have any complaint and can't get satisfaction any other way, come see me. Otherwise, that's all. Any questions?"

One of the boys put up his hand. "Captain?" he enquired timidly.

"Speak up, lad, and give your name."

"Rogers, sir. Will we be able to get letters from home?"

"Yes, but not very often. Maybe every month or so. The chaplain will carry mail, and any inspection and supply ships."

The ship's loudspeaker blatted out, "All hands! Free flight in ten minutes. Stand by to lose weight." The master-at-arms supervised the rigging of grab-lines. All loose gear was made fast, and little cellulose bags were issued to each man. Hardly was this done when Libby felt himself get light on his feet—a sensation exactly like that experienced when an express elevator makes a quick stop on an upward trip, except that the sensation continued and became more intense. At first it was a pleasant novelty, then it rapidly became distressing. The blood pounded in his ears, and his feet were clammy and cold. His saliva secreted at an abnormal rate. He tried to swallow, choked, and coughed. Then his stomach shuddered and contracted with a violent, painful, convulsive reflex and he was suddenly, disastrously nauseated. After the first excruciating spasm, he heard McCoy's voice shouting.

"Hey! Use your sick-kits like I told you. Don't let that stuff get in the blowers." Dimly Libby realized that the admonishment included him. He fumbled for his cellulose bag just as a second temblor shook him, but he managed to fit the bag over his mouth before the eruption occurred. When it subsided, he became aware that he was floating near the overhead and facing the door. The chief master-at-arms slithered in the door and spoke to McCoy.

"How are you making out?"

"Well enough. Some of the boys missed their kits."

"Okay. Mop it up. You can use the starboard lock." He swam out.

McCoy touched Libby's arm. "Here, Pinkie, start catching them butterflies." He handed him a handful of cotton waste, then took another handful himself and neatly dabbed up a globule of the slimy filth that floated about the compartment. "Be sure your sick-kit is on tight. When you get sick, just stop and wait until it's over." Libby imitated him as best as he could. In a few minutes the room was free of the worst of the sickening debris. McCoy looked it over, and spoke:

"Now peel off them dirty duds, and change your kits. Three or four of you bring everything along to the starboard lock."

At the starboard spacelock, the kits were put in first, the inner door closed, and the outer opened. When the inner door was opened again the kits were gone—blown out into space by the escaping air. Pinkie addressed McCoy, "Do we have to throw away our dirty clothes, too?"

"Huh uh, we'll just give them a dose of vacuum. Take 'em into the lock and stop 'em to those hooks on the bulkheads. Tie 'em tight."

This time the lock was left closed for about five minutes. When the lock was opened the garments were bone dry—all the moisture boiled out by the vacuum of space. All that remained of the unpleasant rejecta was a sterile powdery residue. McCoy viewed them with approval. "They'll do. Take them back to the compartment. Then brush them—hard—in front of the exhaust blowers."

The next few days were an eternity of misery. Homesickness was forgotten in the all-engrossing wretchedness of spacesickness. The Captain granted fifteen minutes of mild acceleration for each of the nine meal periods, but the respite accentuated the agony. Libby would go to a meal, weak and ravenously hungry. The meal would stay down until free flight was resumed, then the sickness would hit him all over again.

On the fourth day he was seated against a bulkhead, enjoying the luxury of a few remaining minutes of weight while the last shift ate, when McCoy walked in and sat down beside him. The gunner's mate fitted a smoke filter over his face and lit a cigarette. He inhaled deeply and started to chat.

"How's it going, bud?"

"All right, I guess. This spacesickness—Say, McCoy, how do you ever get used to it?"

"You get over it in time. Your body acquires new reflexes, so they tell me. Once you learn to swallow without choking, you'll be all right. You even get so you like it. It's restful and relaxing. Four hours sleep is as good as ten."

Libby shook his head dolefully. "I don't think I'll ever get used to it."

"Yes, you will. You'd better anyway. This here asteroid won't have any surface gravity to speak of; the chief quartermaster says it won't run over two per cent earth normal. That ain't enough to cure spacesickness. And there won't be any way to accelerate for meals either."

Libby shivered and held his head between his hands.

Locating one asteroid among a couple of thousand is not as easy as finding Trafalgar Square in London—especially against the star-crowded backdrop of the galaxy. You take off from Terra with its orbital speed of about nineteen miles per second. You attempt to settle into a composite conoid curve that will not only intersect the orbit of the tiny fast-moving body, but also accomplish an exact rendezvous. Asteroid HS-5388, "Eighty-eight," lay about two and two-tenths astronomical units out from the sun, a little more than two hundred million miles; when the transport took off it lay beyond the sun better than three hundred million miles. Captain Doyle instructed the navigator to plot the basic ellipsoid to tack in free flight around the sun through an elapsed distance of some three hundred and forty million miles. The principle involved is the same as used by a hunter to wing a duck in flight by "leading" the bird in flight. But suppose that you face directly into the sun as you shoot; suppose the bird cannot be seen from where you stand, and you have nothing to aim by but some old reports as to how it was flying when last seen?

On the ninth day of the passage Captain Doyle betook himself to the chart room and commenced punching keys on the ponderous integral calculator. Then he sent his orderly to present his compliments to the navigator and to ask him to come to the chartroom. A few minutes later a tall heavyset form swam through the door, steadied himself with a grabline, and greeted the captain.

"Good morning, Skipper."

"Hello, Blackie." The Old Man looked up from where he was strapped into the integrator's saddle. "I've been checking your corrections for the meal-time accelerations."

"It's a nuisance to have a bunch of ground-lubbers on board, sir."

"Yes, it is, but we have to give those boys a chance to eat, or they couldn't work when we got there. Now I want to decelerate starting about ten o'clock, ship's time. What's our eight o'clock speed and co-ordinates?"

The navigator slipped a notebook out of his tunic. "Three hundred fifty-eight miles per second; course is right ascension fifteen hours, eight minutes, twenty-seven seconds, declination minus seven degrees, three minutes; solar distance one hundred and ninety-two million four hundred eighty thousand miles. Our radial position is twelve degrees above course, and almost dead on course in R.A. Do you want Sol's co-ordinates?"

"No, not now." The captain bent over the calculator, frowned and chewed the tip of his tongue as he worked the controls. "I want you to kill the acceleration about one million miles inside Eighty-eight's orbit. I hate to waste the fuel, but the belt is full of junk and this damned rock is so small that we will probably have to run a search curve. Use twenty hours on deceleration and commence changing course to port after eight hours. Use normal asymptotic approach. You should have her in a circular trajectory abreast of Eighty-eight, and paralleling her orbit by six o'clock tomorrow morning. I shall want to be called at three."

"Aye aye, sir."

"Let me see your figures when you get 'em. I'll send up the order book later."

The transport accelerated on schedule. Shortly after three the captain entered the control room and blinked his eyes at the darkness. The sun was still concealed by the hull of the transport and the midnight blackness was broken only by the dim blue glow of the instrument dials, and the crack of light from under the chart hood. The navigator turned at the familiar tread.

"Good morning, Captain."

"Morning, Blackie. In sight yet?"

"Not yet. We've picked out half a dozen rocks, but none of them checked."

"Any of them close?"

"Not uncomfortably. We've overtaken a little sand from time to time."

"That can't hurt us—not on a stern chase like this. If pilots would only realize that the asteroids flow in fixed directions at computable speeds nobody would come to grief out here." He stopped to light a cigarette. "People talk about space being dangerous. Sure, it used to be; but I don't know of a case in the past twenty years that couldn't be charged up to some fool's recklessness."

"You're right, Skipper. By the way, there's coffee under the chart hood."

"Thanks; I had a cup down below." He walked over by the lookouts at stereoscopes and radar tanks and peered up at the star-flecked blackness. Three cigarettes later the lookout nearest him called out.

"Light ho!"

"Where away?"

His mate read the exterior dials of the stereoscope. "Plus point two, abaft one point three, slight drift astern." He shifted to radar and added, "Range seven nine oh four three."

"Does that check?"

"Could be, Captain. What is her disk?" came the navigator's muffled voice from under the hood. The first lookout hurriedly twisted the knobs of his instruments, but the captain nudged him aside.

"I'll do this, son." He fitted his face to the double eye-guards and surveyed a little silvery sphere, a tiny moon. Carefully he brought two illuminated cross-hairs up until they were exactly tangent to the upper and lower limbs of the disc. "Mark!"

The reading was noted and passed to the Navigator, who shortly ducked out from under the hood.

"That's our baby, Captain."

"Good."

"Shall I make a visual triangulation?"

"Let the watch officer do that. You go down and get some sleep. I'll ease her over until we get close enough to use the optical range finder."

"Thanks, I will."

Within a few minutes the word had spread around the ship that Eighty-eight had been sighted. Libby crowded into the starboard troop deck with a throng of excited mess-mates and attempted to make out their future home from the view port. McCoy poured cold water on their excitement.

"By the time that rock shows up big enough to tell anything about it with your naked eye we'll all be at our grounding stations. She's only about a hundred miles thick, yuh know."

And so it was. Many hours later the ship's announcer shouted:

"All hands! Man your grounding stations. Close all air-tight doors. Stand by to cut blowers on signal."

McCoy forced them to lie down throughout the ensuing two hours. Short shocks of rocket blasts alternated with nauseating weightlessness. Then the blowers stopped and check-valves clicked into their seats. The ship dropped free for a few moments—a final quick blast—five seconds of falling, and a short, light, grinding bump. A single bugle note came over the announcer, and the blowers took up their hum.

McCoy floated lightly to his feet and poised, swaying, on his toes. "All out, troops—this is the end of the line."

A short chunky lad, a little younger than most of them, awkwardly emulated him, and bounded toward the door, shouting as he went, "Come on, fellows! Let's go outside and explore!"

The master-at-arms squelched him. "Not so fast, kid. Aside from the fact that there is no air out there, go right ahead. You'll freeze to death, burn to death, and explode like a ripe tomato. Squad leader, detail six men to break out spacesuits. The rest of you stay here and stand by."

The working party returned shortly loaded down with a couple of dozen bulky packages. Libby let go the four he carried and watched them float gently to the deck. McCoy unzipped the envelope from one suit, and lectured them about it.

"This is a standard service type, general issue, Mark IV, Modification 2." He grasped the suit by the shoulders and shook it out so that it hung like a suit of long winter underwear with the helmet lolling helplessly between the shoulders of the garment. "It's self-sustaining for eight hours, having an oxygen supply for that period. It also has a nitrogen trim tank and a carbon-dioxide-water-vapor cartridge filter."

He droned on, repeating practically verbatim the description and instructions given in training regulations. McCoy knew these suits like his tongue knew the roof of his mouth; the knowledge had meant his life on more than one occasion.

"The suit is woven from glass fiber laminated with non-volatile asbestocellutite. The resulting fabric is flexible, very durable; and will turn all rays normal to solar space outside the orbit of Mercury. It is worn over your regular clothing, but notice the wire-braced accordion pleats at the major joints. They are so designed as to keep the internal volume of the suit nearly constant when the arms or legs are bent. Otherwise the gas pressure inside would tend to keep the suit blown up in an erect position, and movement while wearing the suit would be very fatiguing.

"The helmet is moulded from a transparent silicone, leaded and polarized against too great ray penetration. It may be equipped with external visors of any needed type. Orders are to wear not less than a number-two amber on this body. In addition, a lead plate covers the cranium and extends on down the back of the suit, completely covering the spinal column.

"The suit is equipped with two-way telephony. If your radio quits, as these have a habit of doing, you can talk by putting your helmets in contact. Any questions?"

"How do you eat and drink during the eight hours?"

"You don't stay in 'em any eight hours. You can carry sugar balls in a gadget in the helmet, but you boys will always eat at the base. As for water, there's a nipple in the helmet near your mouth which you can reach by turning your head to the left. It's hooked to a built-in canteen. But don't drink any more water when you're wearing a suit than you have to. These suits ain't got any plumbing."

Suits were passed out to each lad, and McCoy illustrated how to do one. A suit was spread supine on the deck, the front zipper that stretched from neck to crotch was spread wide and one sat down inside this opening, whereupon the lower part was drawn on like long stockings. Then a wiggle into each sleeve and the heavy flexible gauntlets were smoothed and patted into place. Finally an awkward backward stretch of the neck with shoulders hunched enabled the helmet to be placed over the head.

Libby followed the motions of McCoy and stood up in his suit. He examined the zipper which controlled the suit's only opening. It was backed by two soft gaskets which would be pressed together by the zipper and sealed by internal air pressure. Inside the helmet a composition mouthpiece for exhalation led to the filter.

McCoy bustled around, inspecting them, tightening a belt here and there, instructing them in the use of the external controls. Satisfied, he reported to the conning room that his section had received basic instruction and was ready to disembark. Permission was received to take them out for thirty minutes acclimatization.

Six at a time, he escorted them through the air lock, and out on the surface of the planetoid. Libby blinked his eyes at the unaccustomed luster of sunshine on rock. Although the sun lay more than two hundred million miles away and bathed the little planet with radiation only one-fifth as strong as that lavished on Mother Earth, nevertheless the lack of atmosphere resulted in a glare that made him squint. He was glad to have the protection of his amber visor. Overhead the sun, shrunk to penny size, shone down from a dead black sky in which unwinking stars crowded each other and the very sun itself.

The voice of a mess-mate sounded in Libby's earphones, "Jeepers! That horizon looks close. I'll bet it ain't more'n a mile away."

Libby looked out over the flat bare plain and subconsciously considered the matter. "It's less," he commented, "than a third of a mile away."

"What the hell do you know about it, Pinkie? And who asked you, anyhow?"

Libby answered defensively, "As a matter of fact, it's one thousand six hundred and seventy feet, figuring that my eyes are five feet three inches above ground level."

"Nuts. Pinkie, you are always trying to show off how much you think you know."

"Why, I am not," Libby protested. "If this body is a hundred miles thick and as round as it looks, why naturally the horizon *has* to be just that far away."

"Says *who?*"

McCoy interrupted.

"Pipe down! Libby is a lot nearer right than you were."

"He is exactly right," put in a strange voice. "I had to look it up for the navigator before I left control."

"Is that so?"—McCoy's voice again—"If the chief quartermaster says you're right, Libby, you're right. How did you know?"

Libby flushed miserably. "I—I don't know. That's the only way it could be."

The gunner's mate and the quartermaster stared at him but dropped the subject.

By the end of the "day" (ship's time, for Eighty-eight had a period of eight hours and thirteen minutes), work was well under way. The transport had grounded close by a low range of hills. The captain selected a little bowl-shaped depression in the hills, some thousand feet long and half as broad, in which to establish a permanent camp. This was to be roofed over, sealed, and an atmosphere provided.

In the hill between the ship and the valley, quarters were to be excavated: dormitories, mess hall, officers' quarters, sick bay, recreation room, offices, store rooms, and so forth. A tunnel must be bored through the hill, connecting the sites of these rooms, and connecting with a ten-foot air-tight metal tube sealed to the ship's portside airlock. Both the tube and tunnel were to be equipped with a continuous conveyor belt for passengers and freight.

Libby found himself assigned to the roofing detail. He helped a metalsmith struggle over the hill with a portable atomic heater, difficult to handle because of a mass of eight hundred pounds, but weighing here only sixteen pounds. The rest of the roofing detail were breaking out and preparing to move by hand the enormous translucent tent which was to be the "sky" of the little valley.

The metalsmith located a landmark on the inner slope of the valley, set up his heater, and commenced cutting a deep horizontal groove or step in the rock. He kept it always at the same level by following a chalk mark drawn along the rock wall. Libby enquired how the job had been surveyed so quickly.

"Easy," he was answered, "two of the quartermasters went ahead with a transit, leveled it just fifty feet above the valley floor, and clamped a searchlight to it. Then one of 'em ran like hell around the rim, making chalk marks at the height at which the beam struck."

"Is this roof going to be just fifty feet high?"

"No, it will average maybe a hundred. It bellies up in the middle from the air pressure."

"Earth-normal?"

"Half earth-normal."

Libby concentrated for an instant, then looked puzzled. "But look—This valley is a thousand feet long and better than five hundred wide. At half of fifteen pounds per square inch, and allowing for the arch of the roof, that's a load of one and an eighth billion pounds. What fabric can take that kind of a load?"

"Cobwebs."

"Cobwebs?"

"Yeah, cobwebs. Strongest stuff in the world, stronger than the best steel. Synthetic spider silk. This gauge we're using for the roof has a tensile strength of four thousand pounds a running inch."

Libby hesitated a second, then replied, "I see. With a rim about eighteen hundred thousand inches around, the maximum pull at the point of anchoring would be about six hundred and twenty-five pounds per inch. Plenty safe margin."

The metalsmith leaned on his tool and nodded. "Something like that. You're pretty quick at arithmetic, aren't you, bud?"

Libby looked startled. "I just like to get things straight."

They worked rapidly around the slope, cutting a clean

smooth groove to which the "cobweb" could be anchored and sealed. The white-hot lava spewed out of the discharge vent and ran slowly down the hillside. A brown vapor boiled off the surface of the molten rock, arose a few feet, and sublimed almost at once in the vacuum to white powder which settled to the ground. The metalsmith pointed to the powder.

"That stuff 'ud cause silicosis if we let it stay there, and breathed it later."

"What do you do about it?"

"Just clean it out with the blowers of the air-conditioning plant."

Libby took this opening to ask another question. "Mister—?"

"Johnson's my name. No mister necessary."

"Well, Johnson, where do we get the air for this whole valley, not to mention the tunnels? I figure we must need twenty-five million cubic feet or more. Do we manufacture it?"

"Naw, that's too much trouble. We brought it with us."

"On the transport?"

"Uh huh, at fifty atmospheres."

Libby considered this. "I see—that way it would go into a space eighty feet on a side."

"Matter of fact it's in three specially constructed holds—giant air bottles. This transport carried air to Ganymede. I was in her then—a recruit, but in the air gang even then."

In three weeks the permanent camp was ready for occupancy and the transport cleared of its cargo. The storerooms bulged with tools and supplies. Captain Doyle had moved his administrative offices underground, signed over his command to his first officer, and given him permission to proceed on "duty assigned"—in this case, return to Terra with a skeleton crew.

Libby watched them take off from a vantage point on the hillside. An overpowering homesickness took possession of him. Would he ever go home? He honestly believed at the time that he would swap the rest of his life for thirty minutes each with his mother and with Betty.

He started down the hill toward the tunnel lock. At least the transport carried letters to them, and with any luck the chaplain would be by soon with letters from earth. But tomorrow and the days after that would be no fun. He had enjoyed being in the air gang, but tomorrow he went back to his squad. He did not relish that—the boys in his squad were all right, he guessed, but he just could not seem to fit in.

This company of the C.C.C. started on its bigger job: to pock-mark Eighty-eight with rocket tubes so that Captain Doyle could push this hundred-mile marble out of her orbit and herd her in to a new orbit between earth and Mars, to be used as a space station—a refuge for ships in distress, a haven for life boats, a fueling stop, a naval outpost.

Libby was assigned to a heater in pit H-16. It was his business to carve out carefully calculated emplacements in which the blasting crew then set off the minute charges which accomplished the major part of the excavating. Two squads were assigned to H-16, under the general supervision of an elderly marine gunner. The gunner sat on the edge of the pit, handling the plans, and occasionally making calculations on a circular slide rule which hung from a lanyard around his neck.

Libby had just completed a tricky piece of cutting for a three-stage blast, and was waiting for the blasters, when his phones picked up the gunner's instructions concerning the size of the charge. He pressed his transmitter button.

"Mr. Larsen! You've made a mistake!"

"Who said that?"

"This is Libby. You've made a mistake in the charge. If you set off that charge, you'll blow this pit right out of the ground, and us with it."

Marine Gunner Larsen spun the dials on his slide rule before replying, "You're all het up over nothing, son. That charge is correct."

"No, I'm not, sir," Libby persisted, "you've multiplied where you should have divided."

"Have you had any experience at this sort of work?"

"No, sir."

Larsen addressed his next remark to the blasters. "Set the charge."

They started to comply. Libby gulped, and wiped his lips with his tongue. He knew what he had to do, but he was afraid. Two clumsy stiff-legged jumps placed him beside the blasters.

He pushed between them and tore the electrodes from the detonator. A shadow passed over him as he worked, and Larsen floated down beside him. A hand grasped his arm.

"You shouldn't have done that, son. That's direct disobedience of orders. I'll have to report you." He commenced reconnecting the firing circuit.

Libby's ears burned with embarrassment, but he answered back with the courage of timidity at bay. "I had to do it, sir. You're still wrong."

Larsen paused and ran his eyes over the dogged face. "Well— it's a waste of time, but I don't like to make you stand by a charge you're afraid of. Let's go over the calculation together."

Captain Doyle sat at his ease in his quarters, his feet on his desk. He stared at a nearly empty glass tumbler.

"That's good beer, Blackie. Do you suppose we could brew some more when it's gone?"

"I don't know, Cap'n. Did we bring any yeast?"

"Find out, will you?" He turned to a massive man who occupied the third chair. "Well, Larsen, I'm glad it wasn't any worse than it was."

"What beats me, Captain, is how I could have made such a mistake. I worked it through twice. If it had been a nitro explosive, I'd have known offhand that I was wrong. If this kid hadn't had a hunch, I'd have set it off."

Captain Doyle clapped the old warrant officer on the shoulder. "Forget it, Larsen. You wouldn't have hurt anybody; that's why I require the pits to be evacuated even for small charges. These isotope explosives are tricky at best. Look what happened in pit A-9. Ten days' work shot with one charge, and the gunnery officer himself approved that one. But I want to see this boy. What did you say his name was?"

"Libby, A. J."

Doyle touched a button on his desk. A knock sounded at the door. A bellowed "Come in!" produced a stripling wearing the brassard of corpsman mate-of-the-deck.

"Have Corpsman Libby report to me."

"Aye aye, sir."

Some few minutes later Libby was ushered into the captain's

cabin. He looked nervously around, and noted Larsen's presence, a fact that did not contribute to his peace of mind. He reported in a barely audible voice, "Corpsman Libby, sir."

The captain looked him over. "Well, Libby, I hear that you and Mr. Larsen had a difference of opinion this morning. Tell me about it."

"I—I didn't mean any harm, sir."

"Of course not. You're not in any trouble; you did us all a good turn this morning. Tell me, how did you know that the calculation was wrong? Had any mining experience?"

"No, sir. I just saw that he had worked it out wrong."

"But how?"

Libby shuffled uneasily. "Well, sir, it just seemed wrong— It didn't fit."

"Just a second, Captain. May I ask this young man a couple of questions?" It was Commander "Blackie" Rhodes who spoke.

"Certainly. Go ahead."

"Are you the lad they call 'Pinkie'?"

Libby blushed. "Yes, sir."

"I've heard some rumors about this boy." Rhodes pushed his big frame out of his chair, went over to a bookshelf, and removed a thick volume. He thumbed through it, then with open book before him, started to question Libby.

"What's the square root of ninety-five?"

"Nine and seven hundred forty-seven thousandths."

"What's the cube root?"

"Four and five hundred sixty-three thousandths."

"What's its logarithm?"

"Its what, sir?"

"Good Lord, can a boy get through school today without knowing?"

The boy's discomfort became more intense. "I didn't get much schooling, sir. My folks didn't accept the Covenant until Pappy died, and we had to."

"I see. A logarithm is a name for a power to which you raise a given number, called the base, to get the number whose logarithm it is. Is that clear?"

Libby thought hard. "I don't quite get it, sir."

"I'll try again. If you raise ten to the second power—square it—it gives one hundred. Therefore the logarithm of a hundred to the base ten is two. In the same fashion the logarithm of a thousand to the base ten is three. Now what is the logarithm of ninety-five?"

Libby puzzled for a moment. "I can't make it come out even. It's a fraction."

"That's okay."

"Then it's one and nine hundred seventy-eight thousandths —just about."

Rhodes turned to the captain. "I guess that about proves it, sir."

Doyle nodded thoughtfully. "Yes, the lad seems to have intuitive knowledge of arithmetical relationships. But let's see what else he has."

"I am afraid we'll have to send him back to earth to find out properly."

Libby caught the gist of this last remark. "Please, sir, you aren't going to send me home? Maw 'ud be awful vexed with me."

"No, no, nothing of the sort. When your time is up, I want you to be checked over in the psychometrical laboratories. In the meantime I wouldn't part with you for a quarter's pay. I'd give up smoking first. But let's see what else you can do."

In the ensuing hour the captain and the navigator heard Libby: one, deduce the Pythagorean proposition; two, derive Newton's laws of motion and Kepler's laws of ballistics from a statement of the conditions in which they obtained; three, judge length, area, and volume by eye with no measurable error. He had jumped into the idea of relativity and non-rectilinear space-time continua, and was beginning to pour forth ideas faster than he could talk, when Doyle held up a hand.

"That's enough, son. You'll be getting a fever. You run along to bed now, and come see me in the morning. I'm taking you off field work."

"Yes, sir."

"By the way, what is your full name?"

"Andrew Jackson Libby, sir."

"No, your folks wouldn't have signed the Covenant. Good night."

"Good night, sir."

After he had gone, the two older men discussed their discovery.

"How do you size it up, Captain?"

"Well, he's a genius, of course—one of those wild talents that will show up once in a blue moon. I'll turn him loose among my books and see how he shapes up. Shouldn't wonder if he were a page-at-a-glance reader, too."

"It beats me what we turn up among these boys—and not a one of 'em any account back on earth."

Doyle nodded. "That was the trouble with these kids. They didn't feel needed."

Eighty-eight swung some millions of miles further around the sun. The pock-marks on her face grew deeper, and were lined with durite, that strange close-packed laboratory product which (usually) would confine even atomic disintegration. Then Eighty-eight received a series of gentle pats, always on the side headed along her course. In a few weeks' time the rocket blasts had their effect and Eighty-eight was plunging in an orbit toward the sun.

When she reached her station one and three-tenths the distance from the sun of earth's orbit, she would have to be coaxed by another series of pats into a circular orbit. Thereafter she was to be known as E-M3, Earth-Mars Space Station Spot Three.

Hundreds of millions of miles away two other C.C.C. companies were inducing two other planetoids to quit their age-old grooves and slide between earth and Mars to land in the same orbit as Eighty-eight. One was due to ride this orbit one hundred and twenty degrees ahead of Eighty-eight, the other one hundred and twenty degrees behind. When E-M1, E-M2, and E-M3 were all on station no hard-pushed traveler of the spaceways on the earth-Mars passage would ever again find himself far from land—or rescue.

During the months that Eighty-eight fell free toward the sun, Captain Doyle reduced the working hours of his crew and turned them to the comparatively light labor of building a hotel and converting the little roofed-in valley into a garden spot.

The rock was broken down into soil, fertilizers applied, and cultures of anaerobic bacteria planted. Then plants, conditioned by thirty-odd generations of low gravity at Luna City, were set out and tenderly cared for. Except for the low gravity, Eighty-eight began to feel like home.

But when Eighty-eight approached a tangent to the hypothetical future orbit of E-M3, the company went back to maneuvering routine, watch on and watch off, with the captain living on black coffee and catching catnaps in the plotting room.

Libby was assigned to the ballistic calculator, three tons of thinking metal that dominated the plottting room. He loved the big machine. The chief fire controlman let him help adjust it and care for it. Libby subconsciously thought of it as a person—his own kind of person.

On the last day of the approach, the shocks were more frequent. Libby sat in the right-hand saddle of the calculator and droned out the predictions for the next salvo, while gloating over the accuracy with which the machine tracked. Captain Doyle fussed around nervously, occasionally stopping to peer over the navigator's shoulder. Of course, the figures were right, but what if it didn't work? No one had ever moved so large a mass before. Suppose it plunged on and on—and on. Nonsense! It couldn't. Still he would be glad when they were past the critical speed.

A marine orderly touched his elbow. "Helio from the flagship, sir."

"Read it."

"Flag to Eighty-eight; private message, Captain Doyle; am lying off to watch you bring her in—Kearney."

Doyle smiled. Nice of the old geezer. Once they were on station, he would invite the Admiral to ground for dinner and show him the park.

Another salvo cut loose, heavier than any before. The room trembled violently. In a moment the reports of the surface observers commenced to trickle in. "Tube nine, clear!" "Tube ten, clear!"

But Libby's drone ceased.

Captain Doyle turned on him. "What's the matter, Libby? Asleep? Call the polar stations. I have to have a parallax."

"Captain—" The boy's voice was low and shaking.

"Speak up, man!"

"Captain—the machine isn't tracking."

"Spiers!" The grizzled head of the chief fire controlman appeared from behind the calculator.

"I'm already on it, sir. Let you know in a moment."

He ducked back again. After a couple of long minutes he reappeared. "Gyros tumbled. It's a twelve-hour calibration job, at least."

The captain said nothing, but turned away, and walked to the far end of the room. The navigator followed him with his eyes. He returned, glanced at the chronometer, and spoke to the navigator.

"Well, Blackie, if I don't have that firing data in seven minutes, we're sunk. Any suggestions?"

Rhodes shook his head without speaking.

Libby timidly raised his voice. "Captain—"

Doyle jerked around. "Yes?"

"The firing data is tube thirteen, seven point six three; tube twelve, six point nine oh; tube fourteen, six point eight nine."

Doyle studied his face. "You sure about that, son?"

"It *has* to be that, Captain."

Doyle stood perfectly still. This time he did not look at Rhodes but stared straight ahead. Then he took a long pull on his cigarette, glanced at the ash, and said in a steady voice, "Apply the data. Fire on the bell."

Four hours later, Libby was still droning out firing data, his face gray, his eyes closed. Once he had fainted but when they revived him he was still muttering figures. From time to time the captain and the navigator relieved each other, but there was no relief for him.

The salvos grew closer together, but the shocks were lighter.

Following one faint salvo, Libby looked up, stared at the ceiling, and spoke.

"That's all, Captain."

"Call polar stations!"

The reports came back promptly, "Parallax constant, sidereal-solar rate constant."

The captain relaxed into a chair. "Well, Blackie, we did it—thanks to Libby!" Then he noticed a worried, thoughtful look spread over Libby's face. "What's the matter, man? Have we slipped up?"

"Captain, you know you said the other day that you wished you had earth-normal gravity in the park?"

"Yes. What of it?"

"If that book on gravitation you lent me is straight dope, I think I know a way to accomplish it."

The captain inspected him as if seeing him for the first time. "Libby, you have ceased to amaze me. Could you stop doing that sort of thing long enough to dine with the Admiral?"

"Gee, Captain, that would be swell!"

The audio circuit from Communications cut in.

"Helio from flagship: 'Well, done, Eighty-eight.'"

Doyle smiled around at them all. "That's pleasant confirmation."

The audio brayed again.

"Helio from flagship: 'Cancel last signal, stand by for correction.'"

A look of surprise and worry sprang into Doyle's face—then the audio continued:

"Helio from flagship: 'Well done, E-M3.'"

Genius

by POUL ANDERSON

Approach this story with caution for there's more to it than meets the eye—and in more ways. This is a long look into the future of the human race, and a very interesting summing up of the past. The unleashed giant here is truly enormous—— But when you reach the end, compare it with the giant of the next story.

"THE EXPERIMENT HAS been going on for almost fifteen hundred years," said Heym, "and it's just starting to get under way. You can't discontinue it now."

"Can and will," replied Goram, "if the situation seems to justify it. That's what I'm going to find out."

"But—one planet! One primitive planet! What sort of monsters do you think live here? I tell you, they're people, as human as I—" Heym paused. He had meant to add—"and you," but couldn't quite bring himself to it. Goram seemed less than human, an atavistic remnant of past ages, an ape in uniform. "—as I am," finished Heym.

The hesitation seemed lost on Goram. The marshal stood regarding the psychologist out of little black eyes, blocky form faintly stooped, long arms dangling, prognathous jaw thrust ahead of the broad flat-nosed countenance. The fluorotubes gleamed down on his shining shaven bullet skull. The black gold-braided uniform fitted him closely with a military neatness and precision that was in its way the most primitive characteristic of all.

He said in his hoarse bass: "So are the rebels. So are barbari-

185

ans and pirates. So are serfs and slaves and criminals and the insane. But it's necessary to suppress all of them. If Station Seventeen represents a menace, it must be suppressed."

"But what conceivable danger—one barbarian planet—under constant surveillance throughout its history! If that can menace an empire of a hundred thousand star systems, we're not safe from anything!"

"We aren't. For three thousand years of history, the Empire has been in danger. You have to live with it, as we soldiers do, to realize how ultimately unstable the stablest power in history really is. Oh, we can smash the peripheral barbarians. We can hold the Taranians and the Comi and Magellanics in check." The marshal's heavy-ridged eyes swept contemptuously up and down the scientist's long weedy form. "I'm in no danger from you. I could break you with my bare hands. But a dozen viruses of Antaric plague, entering my body and multiplying, would paralyze me in agony and rot the flesh off my bones and probably empty this ship of life."

The office quivered, ever so faintly. The muffled throb of the great engines was vibrant in its walls and floor and ceiling, in the huge ribs and plates of the hull, in guns that could incinerate a continent, and in the nerves and bones of the two thousand men manning that planetoidal mass. The ship drove through a night of mind-cracking empty distances, outpacing light in her furious subdimensional quasivelocity. And a dozen blind half-living protein molecules could kill her.

Heym nodded stiffly. "I know what you mean," he said. "After all"—deliberate snobbery edging his voice—"applied psychological science is the basis of the Empire. Military power is only one tool for—us."

"As you will. But I am not a researcher's tool, I belong to practical men. If I report Station Seventeen potentially dangerous, they will order me to destroy it. If I decide it is already dangerous, I have the authority to order it destroyed myself."

Heym kept his gaunt face impassive, but for a moment he felt physically ill. He looked across the sparsely furnished office at the marshal's simian form, saw the barely suppressed triumph in the heavy visage, and a wave of revulsion swept over him.

He thought wearily: *Fifteen hundred years . . . patience, work, worry, heartbreak, and a gathering dawn . . . generation after generation, watching from the skies, learning, pouring their whole lives into the mighty project— As if I didn't know the danger, the fear which is the foundation and the reason for the Empire . . . and here we have the first glimmerings of what may be a way out of the rattrap which history has become . . . and it's now all dependent on him! On the whim of a two-legged animal who will strike out in blind fear to destroy whatever he doesn't understand . . . or even understanding, will destroy just for the satisfaction of watching better men squirm in pain.*

Calmness came, a steadiness and an icy calculation. After all, he thought, he was a psychologist and Goram was a soldier. It should be possible for him to handle the creature, deftly convince him that he himself wanted what Heym wanted and had in fact thought of it himself and had to argue the scientist into agreement.

Yet—slow, easy, careful. He, Sars Heym, was a research man, not a practicing psychotechnician. He wasn't necessarily able to handle the blind irrationality of the man, any more than a physicist was ordinarily capable of solving an engineering problem. And so much depended on the outcome . . . For Station Seventeen was the key to the next phase of history—of that Heym was certain.

He shook himself, as if to get rid of a clinging burden, and with an effort forced coolness on himself.

"I understand your position, of course," said Heym, "even if I do not agree. I am sure that a glance at our records will convince you there is no danger."

"I'm not interested in records," said the marshal. "I could have had all that transvised to me at Sol if I wanted to see it. But that's the psychologists' department. I want to make a personal inspection."

"Very well. Though we could just as well have transvised the scenes revealed on the spy devices from our headquarters to Sol."

"I'm not interested in telescreen images either. I want to land on the planet, see its people with my own eyes, hear them talk, watch them at work and play. There's a *feel* to a race you can only get by direct observation." Goram's bulldog face thrust aggressively forward. "Oh, I know your fancy theories don't include that—you just watch from afar and write it all down in mathematical symbols nobody can read without twenty years of study. But I'm a practical man, I've dealt with enough barbarians to have an instinct for them."

Superstition! thought Heym bitterly. *Typical primitive mind reaction—magnifying his own ignorant guesses and impulses into an "instinct." No doubt he also believes hair turns gray from fear and drowned men always float face down. Behold the "practical man"!*

It was surprisingly hard to lie, after a lifetime's training in the honesty of science and the monastic community of observers at the station. But he said calmly enough: "Well, that's very interesting, Marshal Goram. We've often noticed curious talents—precognition, telepathy, telekinesis, and the rest, appearing sporadically among people who have some use for them, but we've never been able to pin them down. It's as if they were phenomena inaccessible to the ordinary scientific method. I see your point."

And I flatter myself that's good flattery—not too obviously in agreement, but still hinting that he's some kind of superman.

"Haven't you ever landed at all?" asked Goram.

"Oh, yes, fairly often—usually invisible, of course. However, we can generally see quite enough through the strategically planted recording televisors and other spy devices."

"A planet is mighty big. How do you know what they're cooking up in places your gadgets don't see?"

Heym was unable to keep all the weariness and disgust out of his voice. "Because history is a unity," he said. "The whole can be inferred from the part, since the part belongs to the whole. Why should the only unwarlike people in the Galaxy suddenly start building weapons?"

"Oh, we don't fear their military power—yet," replied Goram. "I should think you, as a psychologist, would know what sort of a danger Station Seventeen represents—a danger that can wreck civilization. They can become a *disrupting factor*— the worst in all history."

"Progress is disruption."

"Maybe. But the Empire is based on stasis. It's sacrificed progress for—survival."

"True—but here we may have a clue to controlled progress, safe advancement. Even stasis isn't safe, as we well know. It's a poor makeshift, intended to keep civilization alive while something else is worked out. Well—we're working it out at Station Seventeen."

Goram grunted again, but remained silent.

Valgor's Star lay a good hundred parsecs from Sol, not far from the Empire's border, though sufficiently within the garrisoned marches to be protected from barbarian raids. The early researchers, looking for an uninhabited earth-like planet, had found the obscure GO-type sun far off the regular space lanes; an ancient planetographic expedition had stopped briefly there, recording that the third world was practically terrestrial, but this whole galactic sector was so isolated and unprofitable that there had been no further visits, and the old report lay for centuries in the Imperial files before the Psychotechnic Foundation resurrected it. Fifteen hundred years ago. . . .

At an easy cruising speed, the battleship used three days going from Sol to Valgor's Star. Sars Heym spent most of that time getting on the right side of Tamman Goram. It involved listening to endless dreary reminiscing of border warfare and the consummate ability required to rise from simple conscript to Imperial Marshal, but the price was small if it could save Station Seventeen.

"Nobody appreciates the border garrisons who hasn't served in them," declared Goram, "but I tell you, if it weren't for them the Empire wouldn't last a year. The barbarians would sweep in, the rival empires would gobble up all they could hold and go to war over the spoils. The Spirit alone knows what the Magellanics would do—but it wouldn't be pleasant—and the whole structure would disintegrate—three thousand years of stability might as well never have been!"

A high official would be used to open flattery. Heym disagreed just enough to seem sincerely to agree on all important points. "We couldn't do without the border patrols," he said, "but it's like any organism, requiring all its parts to live—we couldn't dispense with internal police either, and certainly not with the psychotechnicians who are the government."

"Spirit-damned bureaucrats," snorted Goram. "Theoreticians —what do they know of real life? Why, d'you know, I saw three stellar systems lost once to the barbarians because we didn't have enough power to stand them off. There was a horde of them, a dozen allied suns, and we had only three garrisoned planets. For months we begged—wrote to Antares and Sirius and Sol itself *begging* for a single Nova-class battleship. Just one, and we could have beaten off their fleet and carried the war to them. But no, it was 'under consideration' or 'deferred for more urgent use'—three suns and a hundred thousand men lost because some soft-bellied psychotechnician mislaid a file."

"Robot-checked files don't get mislaid," said Heym softly. "I have friends in administration, and I've seen them weep at some of the decisions they had to make. It isn't easy to abandon an army to its fate—and yet the power that could have saved them is needed elsewhere, to drive off a larger invasion or to impress the Taranians or to take a star cluster of strategic value. The Empire has sacrificed a lot for sheer survival. Humanness in government is only one thing lost.

"And it isn't only in the military field," he went on. "After all, you know the Empire isn't interested in further expansion. It wants to keep civilization alive on the planets where it exists, and keep the non-human imperia out. Ever since the Founder, our military policy has been basically defensive— because we can't handle more than we have. The border is always in a state of war and flux, but the Empire is at peace, inside the marches.

"Yes—how long would the Empire last, even assuming no hostile powers outside, without the most rigid form of psychotechnocratic government? There are roughly three times ten to the fourteenth power humans in the Solarian Empire. The nonhuman aborigines have been pretty thoroughly exterminated, assimilated as helots, or otherwise rendered harmless, but there are still all those humans, with all the terrific variations and conflicting desires inherent in man and intensified by radically different planetary and consequently social environments. Can you imagine a situation where three hundred trillion humans went their own uncoordinated ways—with atomic energy, biotoxic weapons, and interstellar spaceships to back up their conflicting demands?"

"Yes, I can," said Goram, "because after all it has happened —for nearly a thousand years before the Empire, there was virtual anarchy. And"—he leaned forward, the hard black glitter of his eyes nailing Heym—"that's why we can't take chances, with this experiment of yours or anything else—anything at all. In the anarchic centuries, with a much smaller population, there was horror—many planets were blasted back to savagery, or wiped out altogether. Have you seen the dead worlds? Black cinders floating in space, some still radioactive, battlegrounds of the ancient wars. The human barbarians beyond the Imperial borders are remnants of that age—some of them have spaceships, even a technology matching our own, but they think only of destruction—if they ever got past the marches, they'd blast and loot and fight till nothing was left. Not to mention the nonhuman border barbarians, or the rival empires always watching their chance, or the Magellanics sweeping in every century or so with weapons such as we never imagined. Just let any disrupting factor shake the strength and unity of the Empire and see how long it could last."

"I realize that," said Heym coldly. "After all, I am a psychologist. I know fully what a desperate need the establishment of the Empire filled. But I also know that it's a dead end—its purpose of ultimate satisfied stasis cannot be realized in a basically dynamic cosmos. Actually, Imperial totalitarianism is simply the result of Imperial ignorance of a better way. We can only find that better way through research, and the project at Station Seventeen is the most promising of all the Foundation's work. Unless we find some way out of our dilemma, the Empire is doomed—sooner or later, something will happen and we'll go under."

Goram's eyes narrowed. "That's near lese majesty," he murmured.

Heym laughed, and gave the marshal a carefully gauged you-

and-I-know-better-don't-we look, as he went over to the wall of the officers' lounge and touched a button. The telescreen sprang to life with a simulacrum of the outside view. An uncounted host of stars blazed against the infinite blackness, a swarming magnificent arrogance of unwinking hard jewels strewn across the impassive face of eternity. The Milky Way foamed around the sky, the misty nebulae and star clusters wheeled their remote way around heaven, and the other galaxies flashed mysterious signals across the light-years and the centuries. As ever, the psychologist felt dwarfed and awed and numbed by the stupendous impact.

"It was a great dream," he whispered. "There never was a higher dream than man's conquest of the universe—and yet like so many visions, it overleaped itself and shattered to bits on the rocks of reality—in this case, simple arithmetic defeated us. How reconcile and coordinate a hundred thousand stars except by absolutism, by deliberate statism—by chaining ourselves to our own achievements? What other answer is there?"

He turned around to Goram. The soldier sat unmoving, face stone-hard, like a primitive idol. "We're looking for a new day," said Heym. "We think we're finding it, at Station Seventeen. It's the first hope in four thousand years."

The planet might almost have been earth, a great blue spheroid swinging majestically against the incredible spatial sky with a softly shining moon for a companion. Auroras wavered over the ice-capped poles, and cloud masses blurred the greenish brown continents. They were storms, those clouds, snow and rain and wind blowing out of a living heaven over broad fair fields and haughty mountains; and looking down from the sterile steel environment of the ship, remembering the world city sprawling over earth and the cold, hard mechanized pattern of all Imperial life, Heym felt a brief wistfulness. All at once, he envied his experimental animals, down there on the young green planet. Even if they were to be destroyed, they had been more fortunate than their masters.

But they wouldn't be destroyed. They mustn't be.

"Where is your observation post?" asked Goram.

"On an asteroid well away from here and rendered invisible."

"Why not on the satellite? It'd be a lot closer."

"Yes, but distance doesn't mean anything to a transvisor. Also, if—when—the colonists learn the means of interplanetary travel, we'd have had to move off the moon, while we can remain hidden indefinitely on the invisible planetoid."

"I'd say 'if' rather than 'when'," amended Goram grimly. "It was your report that the inhabitants were experimenting with rockets that alarmed the rulers enough to order me here to see if it weren't best simply to sterilize the planet."

"I've told you before, there's no need for alarm," protested Heym. "What if the people do have a few rocketships? They have no reason to do more than visit the other worlds of this system, which aren't habitable—certainly no reason to colonize, with their own planet still practically uninhabited. The present population is estimated at only some eight hundred million."

"Nevertheless, as soon as they have a whole system to move about in they'll be dangerous. It'll no longer be possible to keep track of everything of importance they may do. They'll be stimulated by this success to perfect an interstellar drive—and even you will agree that that cannot be permitted. That engine may be developed without our knowledge, on some remote world of this system—and once even a few of them are running loose between the stars we'll have no further control—and the results may well be catastrophic! Imagine a pure-bred line of geniuses allied with the barbarians!"

"I tell you, they're not warlike. They haven't had a single war in all their history."

"Well, then they'll try to innovate within the Empire, which would be just as bad if not worse. Certainly they won't be satisfied with the status quo—yet that status quo means survival to us."

"They can be co-ordinated. Good Spirit, we have plenty of geniuses in the Galaxy today! We couldn't do without them. They are the very ones who run the Empire. Advancement is on a strict merit basis simply because we must have the best brains of mankind for the gigantic job of maintaining the social order."

"Sure—everyone's strictly brought up to accept the Empire, to identify its survival with his own. We have plenty of tame geniuses. But these are wild—a planetful of undomesticated intellects! If they can't be tamed, they must be killed."

"They can be tamed," insisted Heym. "Rather, they can become the leaders to get us out of status quo safely—if not directly, then indirectly through knowledge gained by observing them. Already administrative techniques have been improved, within the last five hundred or so years, because by watching unhampered intellect at work we have l een able to derive more accurate psychomathematical expressions for the action of logic as a factor in society."

"I've heard it all before," said Goram wearily. "Now I want to go down there and look."

"Very well. I'll come along, of course. Do you wish to take anyone else?"

"Do I need to?"

"No, it's perfectly safe."

"Then I won't. Meet me at Lifeboat Forty in half an hour." Goram tramped off to give such orders as might be needed.

Heym stood for a while, chain-smoking and looking out the visiplate at the silently rolling planet. Like an ominous moon, the warship swung in an orbit just beyond the atmosphere. For all its Titanic mass, it was insignificant against the bulk of a world. Yet in guns and bombs and death-mists, gravitational beams and long-range disintegrators and mass-conversion torpedoes, in coagulative radiations and colloid-resonant generators, in the thousand hells man had made through all his tormented existence, lay the power to rip life off that surface and blanket the shuddering continents in smoke and flame and leave the blackened planet one great tomb under the indifferent stars.

No—no, that was wrong. The power did not lie in the ship, it was inert metal and will-less electronic intellect, a cosmic splinter that without man would spin darkly into eternity. The will, and hence the power, to destroy lay in men—in one man. One gorilla in uniform. One cave man holding a marshal's baton.

Screened by an invisibility field, the lifeboat spiraled down toward the surface. Goram let the robot-pilot handle the vessel, and spent most of his time peering through a field-penetrating visiscope.

"Not much sign of habitation," he said.

"No, I told you the population was still small," replied Heym. "After all, only a few thousand were planted originally and the struggle for existence was as hard as with any savages for the first few centuries. Only lately has the population really begun growing."

"And you say they have cities now—machines—civilization? It's hard to believe."

"Yes, it is. The whole result has been a triumphant confirmation of the psychotechnic theory of history, but nevertheless the sheer spectacular character of the success has awed us. I can understand it's a little frightening. One naturally thinks a race which can go from naked savages to mechanized civilization in fifteen hundred years is somehow demonic. Yet they're humans, fully as human as anyone else in the Galaxy, the same old earthly stock as all men. They've simply enjoyed the advantage of freedom from stupidity."

"How many stations are there?"

"About a hundred—planetary colonies, with colonists in ignorance of their own origin, where various special conditions are maintained. Different environments, for instance, or special human stocks. The progress of history is being observed on all of them, secretly, and invaluable data on mass-psychological processes are thereby gained. But Seventeen has been by far the most fruitful."

Goram wrinkled his low forehead. How like a typical militarist he looks, Heym thought, the brute riding mankind's back through all history—except on the one planet of Valgor's Star!

"I don't quite see the point," admitted the marshal. "Why spend all that time and money on creating artificial conditions that you'd never meet in real life?"

"It's the scientific method," said Heym, wondering at what elementary level he would have to begin his explanation. How stupid could one be and hold a marshal's position? "In order to find causal relationships, the scientist has to perform experiments in which he varies only one factor at a time, observing its effect—and, of course, running control experiments simultaneously. From these data he infers similar relationships in the real world. By means of theoretical analysis of observed facts he can proceed to predict new phenomena, and if these predictions are borne out by further observation, the theory is probably—though never certainly—right, and can be used as a guide in understanding and controlling the events of the real world."

In spite of himself, Heym was warming up to his subject. After all, it was his whole life.

"Hm-m-m." Goram looked out the visiscope. The boat was sweeping over a broad plain, yellow with ripening grain. A few primitive villages, houses built of stone and wood and brick, were scattered over the great landscape, a peaceful scene, reminiscent of civilization's dawn. "The planet looks backward enough," grunted Goram dubiously.

"It is," said Heym eagerly. "I assure you it is."

"Well . . . you were saying—" Goram didn't look at all sure of what Heym had been saying. "Get to the point."

"The early students of culture were struck by the similarity of development of different civilizations, as if man went along one inevitable historical path. And in a way he did—because one thing leads to another. The expanding units of a culture clash, there are ever fiercer wars, old fears and grudges intensify, economic breakdowns increase the misery. Finally, and usually unwittingly and even unwillingly, one nation overcomes all others to protect itself and found a 'universal state' which brings a certain peace of exhaustion but eventually decays and collapses of its own weaknesses or under the impact of alien invaders. That's exactly what happened to mankind as a whole, when he exploded into the Galaxy—only this time the fearful scale and resources of the wars all but shattered the civilization. Then the Solarian Empire took over and has lasted immensely longer than most preceding universal states, because its rulers have enough knowledge of mass-psychological processes to have a certain control over its hundred thousand planetary systems."

An ocean rolled beneath the boat, gray and green, showing

white mane on the restless horizon. "Swing northeast," said Heym. "The planet's greatest city lies that way, on a large island."

"Good. A city's a good place to observe a people. Can we go around incognito?"

"Naturally. I know the language well enough to pass for a traveler from some other part of the world. There's a lot of intercourse between continents. The cities are quite cosmopolitan."

"Well—go on. You've still not explained all this rigmarole of secrecy."

"I was laying the background," said Heym, unable to keep all the tiredness out of his voice. *Can I really talk this moron over? Can anyone? Reason is wasted on an ape.* "It's really very simple. Our military might can hold off the barbarians and the Magellanic raiders, and have sufficient power left over to police the three hundred trillion citizens.

"Yet our psychotechnology is primitive. On that vast scale, it can only deal with the simplest possible situations. It's all we can do to keep the Empire stable. We have trouble enough keeping industry and commerce flowing smoothly. If we permitted free invention and progress, there'd be an industrial revolution every year. Our carefully evolved techniques of control would become obsolete; there'd be economic anarchy, conflict, suffering, individuals rising to power outside the present social framework and threatening the co-ordinating authority— with planet-smashing power to back both sides and all our enemies on the watch for a moment's instability.

"That's only one example. It applies to any field. Science, philosophy—we can control known religions, channel the impulses to safe directions—but a new religion, rousing discontent, containing unknown elements—a billion fanatics going to war— No! We have to keep status quo, which we understand, at the cost of an uncontrollable advance into the unknown.

"The Empire really exists only to simplify the psychotechnic problem of co-ordination. Enforcement of population stability —good, we don't have to worry about controlling trillions of new births; there's no land hunger. Stable industry, ossified physical science, state religion, totalitarian control of the entire life span—good, we know exactly what we're dealing with and our decisions will be obeyed—imagine the situation if three hundred trillion people were free to do exactly as they pleased in the Galaxy!" Heym shrugged. "Why go on? You know as well as I do that the Empire is only an answer to a problem of survival—not a good answer, but the best our limited knowledge can make."

"Hah!" Goram's exclamation was triumphant. "And you want to turn a world of unpredictable geniuses loose in that!"

"If I thought for an instant there was any danger of this people's becoming a disrupting factor, I'd be the very first to advocate sterilization," said Heym. "After all, I want to live, too. But there's nothing to fear. Instead, there is—hope."

"What hope?" snorted Goram. "Personally, I can't see what you want, anyway. For three thousand years, we've kept man satisfied. Who'd want to change it?"

Heym bit back his temper. "Aside from the fact that the contentment is like death," he said, "history shows that universal states don't endure forever. Sooner or later, we'll face something that will overwhelm us. Unless we've evoked ourselves. But safe evolution is only possible when we know enough psychotechnics to keep the process orderly and peaceful—when our science is really quantitative. The stations, and especially Seventeen, are giving us the information we must have to develop such a science."

The island lay a few kilometers north of the great northern continent. A warm stream in the ocean made the climate equable, so that the land lay green in the gray immensity of sea, but polar air swept south with fog and rain and snow, storms roaring over the horizon and the sun stabbing bright lances down through a mightily stooping sky of restless clouds and galloping winds. Heym thought that the stimulating weather had as much to do as the favorable location along the northern trade routes with the islanders' leadership in the planet's civilization.

Many villages lay in the fields and valleys and on the edges of the forest that still filled the interior, but there was only one city, on an estuary not far from the southern coast. From the air, it was not impressive to one who had seen the world cities of

Sol and Sirius and Antares, a sprawling collection of primitive, often thatch-roofed dwellings that could hardly have housed more than a million, the narrow cobbled streets crowded with pedestrians and animal-drawn vehicles, the harbor where a few steam- or oil-driven vessels were all but lost in the throng of wind-powered ships, the almost prehistoric airport—but the place had the character, subtle and unmistakable, of a city, a community knowing of more than its own horizon enclosed and influencing events beyond the bounds of sight.

"Can we land without being detected?" inquired Goram.

Heym laughed. "An odd question for a military man to ask. This boat is so well-screened that the finest instruments of the Imperial Navy would have trouble locating us. Oh, yes, we observers have been landing from time to time all through the station's history."

"I must say the place *looks* backward enough," said Goram dubiously. "The existence of cities is certainly evidence of crude transportation."

"Well"—honesty forced Heym to argue—"not necessarily. The city, that is, the multi-purpose community, is one criterion of whether a society is civilized or merely barbaric, in the technical anthropological sense. It's true that cities as definite centers disappeared on earth after the Atomic Revolution, but that was simply because such closely spaced buildings were no longer necessary. In the sense of close relation to the rest of mankind and of resultant co-ordination, earth's people kept right on having cities. And today the older planets of the Empire have become so heavily populated that the crowded structures are reappearing—in effect, the whole world becomes one vast city. But I will agree that the particular stage of city evolution existing here on Seventeen is primitive."

Goram set the boat down in a vacant field outside the community's limits. "What now?" he asked.

"Well, I suppose you'll want to spend a time just walking around the place." Heym fumbled in a bag. "I brought the proper equipment, clothes and money of the local type. Planetary type, that is—since a universal coinage was established at the same time as a common language was adopted for international use, and nobody cares what sort of dress you wear." He unfolded the brief summer garments, shorts and sandals and tunic of bleached and woven plant fiber. "Funny thing," he mused, "how man has always made a virtue of necessity. The lands threatened with foreign invasion came to glorify militarism and war. The people who had to work hard considered idleness disgraceful. Dwellers in a northern climate, who had to wear clothes, made nudity immoral. But our colonists here are free of that need for compensation and self-justification. You can work, think, marry, eat, dress, whatever you want to do, just as you please, and if you aren't stepping on someone else's toes too hard nobody cares. Which indicates that intolerance is characteristic of stupidity, while the true intellectual is naturally inclined to live and let live."

Goram struggled awkwardly and distastefully into the archaic garments. "How about weapons?" he asked.

"No need to carry them. No one does, except in places where wild animals might be dangerous. In fact, arms are about the only thing in which the colonists' inventiveness has lagged. They never got past the bow and arrow. Aside from a few man-to-man duels in the early stages of their history, and now abandoned, they've never fought each other."

"Impossible! Man is a fighting animal."

Heym tried to find a reply which was not too obviously a slap at the whole military profession. "There's been war on all our other colonies," he said slowly, "and, of course, through all human history—yet there's never been any real, logical reason for it. In fact, at one stage of prehistoric man, the late neolithic, war seems to have been unknown—at least, no weapons were found buried with the men of that time. And your whole professional aim today is to maintain peace within the Empire, isn't it?

"It takes only one to make a quarrel unless the other lacks all spirit to resist—and a people like these are obviously spirited; in fifteen hundred years they've explored their whole planet. But suppose neither side wants to fight. Whenever two tribes met, in the history of Station Seventeen, they were all too intelligent to fight. So they didn't. It was as simple as that."

Goram snorted, whether in disbelief or contempt Heym didn't know. "Let's go," he said.

They stepped out of the boat and its invisibility screen into the field. Tall breeze-rippled grass tickled their bare legs, and the wind in their faces had the heady scent of green growing life brought over the many kilometers of field and forest across which it had rushed—incredible, that pulsing warm vitality after the tanked sterility of the ship, of the Empire. And up in the blue cloud-fleeced sky a bird was singing, rising higher and ever higher toward the sun, drunk with wind and light.

The two men walked across the field to a road that led city-ward. It was a narrow rutted brown track in the earth, and Goram snorted again. They walked along it. On a hill to the right stood a farm, a solid, substantial, contented-looking cluster of low tile-roofed stone buildings and the open fields, and ahead of the horizon was the straggling misty line of the city. Otherwise they were alone.

"Are all your colony planets this wild?" asked Goram.

"Just about," said Heym, "though the environments are often radically different—everything from a world that's barely habitable desert to one that's all jungle and swamp. That way, we can isolate the effects of environment. We even have one planet equipped with complex robot-run cities, to see how untutored humans will react. There are three control stations, earth-like planets where ordinary human types were left, and from them we're getting valuable information on the path which terrestrial history actually took. Then there are a number of worlds where different human types are planted—different races, different intelligence levels, and so on, to isolate the effects of heredity and see if there is any correlation of civilization with, say physiology. But only here on Seventeen, populated exclusively by geniuses, has progress been rapid. All the other colonies are still in the Stone Ages or even lower."

"And you mean you just dumped your subjects down on all these worlds?"

"Crudely put, yes. For instance, before colonizing Seventeen we—that is, the Foundation—spent several generations breeding a pure genius strain of man. On Imperial orders, the Galaxy's best brains were bred, and genetic control and selection were applied, until a stock had been developed whose members had only genius in the intellectual part of their heredity. Barring mutation or accident, both negligible, the people here and their children can only be geniuses. Then the few thousand adult end-products, who had naturally not been told what was in store for them, were seized and put under the action of memory erasers which left them able to walk and eat and little else. Then a couple of hundred were planted in each climatic region of this planet, near strategically placed invisible spy devices, and the observers sat back on their asteroid to see what would happen. That was fifteen hundred-odd years ago, but even in the forty or so years I've been in charge the change here has been very noticeable."

Goram scowled. "So on that exponential advance, you can expect them to work out interplanetary travel in a matter of years," he said. "They'll know the principles of the star drive in a few more generations, and invent a faster-than-light engine almost at once. No—they aren't safe!"

It was strange to walk through the narrow twisting streets and among the high archaic façades of a city which seemed to belong to the almost forgotten past. To Goram, who must have visited uncivilized planets often, it could not be as queer as to Heym, and, also, the military mind would be too unimaginative to appreciate the situation. But even though Heym had spent the better part of his life watching this culture, it never failed to waken in him a dim feeling of dreamlike unreality.

Mere picturesqueness counted for little, though the place was colorful enough. Along those cobbled ways went the traffic of a world. There were fantastic-looking beasts, variations of the horned, hoofed genus which the colonists had early tamed to ride and load with their burdens, and still more exotic pets; and steering cautiously between them came trucks and passenger vehicles which for all their crudeness of material and principle had a cleanness of design, all the taut inherent beauty of the machine, that only Imperial mechanisms matched. More significant were the people.

There was nothing marking them out as obviously different. Many physical types were in evidence here, from the tall fair islanders to the stocky arctic dwellers or the sun-burned southern folk; and costumes varied accordingly, though even strangers tended to wear some form of the light local summer dress.

If perhaps a tendency toward higher foreheads and more clean-cut features than the Galactic average existed, it was not striking, and there was as wide deviation from it as could be found anywhere. The long hair of both sexes and the full beards worn by many men screened any intellectuality of appearance behind a hirsute veil associated with the peripheral barbarians.

No—the difference from any other world in the Galaxy was real and unmistakable, but it wasn't physical. It was in the clear air of the city, where all chimneys were smokeless, and in the clean-swept streets. It was in the orderliness of traffic, easy movement without jostling and confusion. It was in the clean bodies and soft voices of the people, in the casually accepted equality of the sexes even at this primitive level of technology. It was negative, in the absence of slums and jails, and positive, in the presence of parks and schools and hospitals. There were no weapons or uniforms in sight, but many in the street carried books or wore chemical-stained smocks. There were no ranting orators, but a large group sat on the grass of one park and listened to a lecture on ornithology. Laughter was quiet, but there was more of it than Heym had heard elsewhere in the Empire.

Goram muttered once: "I seem to hear quite a few languages here."

"Oh, yes," replied Heym. "Each region naturally developed its own tongue and generally sticks to it for sentimental reasons and also because the thoughts of a people are best expressed in the speech they themselves developed. But as soon as contact between the lands became common, an international language was worked out and learned by all concerned. In fact, only about fifty years ago a completely new world language was adopted, one correct according to the newly established principles of semantics. That's more than the Empire has yet done. We can talk Terrestrial safely enough, it'll pass for some local dialect, and I can do the talking for both of us with the natives."

"Still"—Goram scowled—"I don't like it. Everybody here has a higher I.Q. than myself—that's not right for a bunch of barbarians. I feel as if everyone was looking at me."

"Most of them observe us, yes, geniuses being naturally observant," said Heym. "But we aren't conspicuous in any way.

Our men have often been on the planet in person without attracting attention."

"Didn't you say you'd appeared openly?"

"Yes—a few times, some centuries back, we made the most awe-inspiring possible descents, coming down through the air on gravibeams in luminous clothes and performing seeming miracles. You see, even the primitive tribes had shown no signs of organized religion beyond the usual magical rites which they soon outgrew. We wanted to see if god-worship couldn't be induced." Heym smiled wryly. "But after the generation which had actually seen us, there was no sign of our manifestation. I suppose the young, being of independent mind, simply refused to believe their elders' wild stories. Not that the people are without religious sense. There is a high proportion of unbelievers, but there is also a large philosophical and even devotional literature. But nobody founds a school of thought, rather everybody reaches his own conclusions."

"I don't see how progress is possible then."

You wouldn't, thought Heym contemptuously, but he only smiled and said, "Apparently it is."

An aircraft roared low overhead, and a wagon driver fought to control his suddenly panicky animals. Goram said: "The biggest paradox here is the anachronism. Sailships and oilburners docked side by side, animal power in the same street with chemical engines, stone and wood houses with efficient smoke precipitators—how come?"

"It's partly a matter of the extremely rapid progress," declared Heym. "A new invention appears before the economy has become geared to it. There won't be many machines until mass-production factories are set up to produce them in quantity, and that will have to wait till mechanical knowledge is sufficiently advanced to develop factories almost entirely automatic—for few if any geniuses could stand to work on an assembly line all day. Meanwhile, the people are in no hurry to advance their standard of living. Already they have sufficient food, clothing, and other necessities for all, as well as abundant free time— why strain themselves to go beyond that?"

Goram was silent for a while, then at last a blurted protest: "But they're working on rockets!"

"Oh, yes—but there's a difference between exploration and exploitation. The social system here is unique, and doesn't lend itself to imperialism. The Empire doesn't have to fear Station Seventeen."

"I've told you before I'm not worried about their military power," snarled Goram.

Heym fell silent, for he felt the sudden sickening fear that the marshal might, without reason or provocation, decide to annihilate the colony—destroy it out of pique with the psychologists and their dominion over the soldiers. With a growing desperation, he looked around at the people—the fortunate children of an open sky, quiet, urbane, and strong with the unconquerable strength of intelligence. Here was truly Homo sapiens, man the wise—man who had plucked fire from the mouth of a volcano, far back in the lost ages of the ice, and started on a long journey into darkness. He had come far since then, but he had ended in a blind alley. Only here, on this one insignificant world of the countless millions swarming around the stars, only here was the old quest being renewed, the path of hope being trodden.

The psychologist said, with desperation raw in his voice, "Goram—Marshal Goram—surely you can see the experiment is harmless. More than that, it's the most beneficial thing that has yet happened in all human history. The mere absence of war shows that. I can list supporting evidence. The social system here has achieved the miracle of combining progress and stability. Just give the Foundation a chance to learn from these people—or even, if they do work out an interstellar drive, give them a chance to teach us themselves. They're the most reasonable race in the universe—they'll be on the side of civilization, and even while overhauling it they'll be better able to preserve it than we ourselves."

"Let a bunch of barbarians take over the holy throne?" muttered Goram.

Heym closed his mouth, and a gathering determination tightened his gaunt face. He looked around the pulsing city, and a vast tenderness and pity welled up in him—poor geniuses, poor helpless unwitting supermen—and answering it came an implacable resolve.

There was too much at stake to let his own personal fate matter. Certainly a mindlessly destructive atavist could not be allowed to block history. He would keep trying, he'd do his best to talk Goram over, because the alternative was fantastically risky for the station and against all his own training and principles—including elementary self-preservation.

But if he failed, if Goram remained obdurate, then he'd have to apply the same primitive methods as the soldier. Goram would have to die.

Rain clouds came out of the west with sunset, thunder rolling over the sky and a cool wet wind blowing from the sea. Goram and Heym finished a primitive but satisfying meal in a small restaurant and the psychologist said: "We'd better look for a place to stay tonight. Will you be in this city tomorrow?"

"Don't know," answered Goram curtly. He had been silent and withdrawn during the day's tour of the metropolis. "I have to think over what I've seen today. It may be enough basis for a decision, or I may want to see more of the planet."

"I'll pay the score," offered Heym. He fought to keep his voice and face blank. "And I'll ask the waiter to recommend a tavern."

He followed the man toward the kitchen. "Please," he said in the common tongue, "I wish to pay the check."

"Very well," answered the native. He was a tall young fellow with the faintly weary eyes of a scholar—probably a student, thought Heym, doing his stint here and getting his education free. He took the few coins casually.

"And—is there a place to stay overnight near here?"

"Right down the street. Stranger, I take it?"

"Yes. From Caralla on business. Oh—one other thing." It was a tremendous effort to meet that steady gaze. Heym was aware of his own clumsiness as he blurted the request: "I . . . uh . . . I've lost my knife and I need it to prepare some handicraft samples for display tomorrow. The stores are all closed now. I wonder if you have an extra one in the kitchen I could buy."

"Why—" The native paused. For an instant, Heym thought he was going to ask questions, and he braced himself as if to meet a physical impact. But on a world where crime was virtually unknown and lying hardly ever went beyond the usual polite social fibs, even so crude a fiction could get by. "Yes, I suppose we have," said the waiter. "Here, I'll get one."

"No . . . I'll come along . . . save you the trouble . . . choose one for my purpose if . . . uh . . . if you have several you can spare." Heym stuck close to the waiter's heels.

The kitchen was spotlessly clean, though it seemed incredible that cooking should still be done with fire. Heym chose a small sharp knife, wrapped it in a rag, and slipped it into his pocket. The waiter and chef refused his money. "Plenty where this one came from—a pleasure to help out a visitor."

"What were you out there for?" asked Goram.

Heym licked stiff lips. "The waiter was new here himself and went to ask the cook about hotels."

The first raindrops were falling as the two came out into the street. Lightning forked vividly overhead. Goram shuddered in the raw damp chill. "Foul place," he muttered. "No weather control, not even a roof for the city—uncivilized."

Heym made no reply, though he tried to unlock his jaws. The blade in his pocket seemed to have the weight of a world. He looked down from his stringy height at the soldier's squat massiveness. *I've never killed*, he thought dully. *I've never even fought, physically or mentally. I'm no match for him. It'll have to be a sneak thrust from behind.*

They entered the hotel. The clerk was reading a journal, the pages of which seemed purely mathematical symbols. He was probably a scientist of some kind in his main job. There was, luckily for Goram, no register to sign; the clerk merely nodded them casually toward their room.

"No system here," muttered Goram. "How can they keep track of anybody without registry?"

"They don't," said Heym. "And they don't have to."

The room was large and well-furnished. "I've slept in worse places," said the soldier grudgingly. He flopped into a chair. "But it's the first place I've seen where the hired help reads technical journals."

"That's easy enough to explain. Even though no high-grade mind could be put to the myriad routine and menial tasks essential to running a civilization, everything from garbage collection to government, someone must do the work. The present set-up is a compromise, in which everyone puts in a small proportion of his time at those jobs. He can do manual work, or teach, or run a public-service enterprise like a farm or restaurant —whatever he wishes. And he can work steadily at it for a few years and then have all his needs taken care of for the rest of his life, or else put in a few hours a day, two or three, over a longer period of time. The result is that needs and a social surplus are available for all, as well as education, health services, entertainment, or whatever else is considered desirable. The planet could, in fact, do without money, but it's more convenient to pay in cash than fill out credit slips.

"Incidentally, that's probably one reason there's no great interest in providing more material goods for all—it would mean that everyone would have to put in more time in the mines and factories and less on his chosen work. Which is apparently a price that genius is unwilling to pay. I don't think there'll be any great progress in applied science until the research project established some time back perfects the robots it's set for a goal."

"Uh-huh," muttered Goram. "And just let them expand into the Galaxy and find we have such robots—left unproduced since the Imperial populace has to be kept busy. They'd be able to wreck the whole set-up just by inventing and distributing robots."

"Can't you credit them with being smart enough to see the reasons for maintaining the status quo?" asked Heym. "They don't want the barbarians on their necks any more than we do. They'll help us maintain the Empire until they have developed a way to change conditions safely."

"Maybe." Goram's mouth was tight. "Still, they'll hold the balance of power, which is something no group except the Imperium can be permitted to do. Spirit! How do you even know they'll be on our side? They may decide their best advantage lies with our rivals. Or they may be irritated with our having used them so cavalierly all these centuries."

"They won't hold grudges," said Heym. "A genius doesn't."

"How do you know?" Goram sprang out of his chair and

paced the floor. His voice rose almost to a shout. "You've said all along that the genius is naturally peaceful and tolerant and unselfish and every other of the milk-and-water virtues. Yet, your own history is against you all the way. Every great military leader has been a genius. There've been sadistic geniuses, and bigoted geniuses, and criminal geniuses—yes, insane geniuses! Why, every one of the hundred billion or so important men in the Imperial Government is a genius—on our side—and more than half the barbarian chiefs are known to have genius intellect." He swung a red and twisted face on the psychologist. "How do you know this is a planet of saints? Answer me that!"

Heym took out a cigarette pack with fingers that shook. He held it out to Goram, who shook his heavy bullet head in angry refusal. The psychologist took time to bring one of the cylinders into his mouth and puff it into lighting. He drew smoke deeply into his lungs, fighting for steadiness.

It was his last real chance to convince Goram. If this failed, he'd just have to try to murder the soldier.

He said slowly: "To explain the theory of historical progress, I'd have to give you a fairly long lecture."

Goram sprawled back into his chair, crude and strong and arrogant. His little black eyes were drills, boring into the psychologist's soul. "I'm listening," he snapped.

"Well"—Heym walked up and down the floor, hands clasped behind his back—"it's evident from a study of history that all progress is due to gifted individuals. Always, in every field, the talented or otherwise fortunate few have led and the mass has dumbly followed. A republic is the only form of state which even pretends to offer self-government, and as soon as the population becomes any size at all the people are again led by the nose, their rulers struggling for power with money and such means of mass hypnotism as news services and other propaganda machines. And all republics become dictatorships, in fact if not in name, within a few centuries at most. As for art and science and religion and the other creative fields, it is still more obviously the few who lead.

"The ordinary man is just plain stupid. Perhaps proper mind training could lift him above himself, but it's never been tried. Meanwhile he remains immensely conservative, only occasional outbreaks of mindless hysteria engineered by some special group stirring him out of his routine.

"Yet it is society as a whole which *does*. History is a mass action process. Gifted individuals start it off, but it is the huge mass of the social group which actually accomplishes the process. A new invention or a new land to colonize or a new philosophy or any other innovation would have no significance unless everybody eventually adopted or exploited or otherwise made use of it. And society as a whole is conservative, or perhaps I should say, preservative. Civilization is ninety-nine per cent habit, the use of past discoveries or the influence of past events. Against the immense conservation of mankind in the mass, and in comparison to the tremendous accumulation of past accomplishment, the achievement of the individual genius or the small group is almost insignificant. It is not surprising that progress is slow and irregular and liable to stagnation or violent setbacks. The surprising thing is really that any event of significance can happen at all."

Heym paused. Goram stirred impatiently. "What are you leading up to?" he muttered.

"Simply this." Heym's hand fell into his pocket and closed on the smooth hard handle of the knife. Goram slumped in his chair, head lowered, staring sullenly at the floor. If the blade were driven in now, right into that bull neck, a paralyzing blow and then a swift slash across the jugular—

The intensity of the hatred welling up in him shocked Heym. He should be above the brutal level of his enemy.

Steady—steady— That move of desperation might not be necessary.

"Two factors control the individual in society," said Heym, and the detached calm of his voice was vaguely surprising to him.

"There is first the simple weight of social pressure. We all want to be approved by our fellows, within reasonable limits at least. It takes a really brave—and somewhat neurotic—individual to be different in any important respect. Many have paid with their lives for innovating. So a genius will be hampered in making original contributions.

"And, of course, this social pressure usually forces conformity even on reluctant individuals. A scientist may be naturally peaceful, for instance, but he will hardly ever refuse to engage in war research when so directed.

"The second hold on the individual is subtler and more effective. It is the mental conditioning induced by growing up in a society where certain conditions of living and rules of thought are accepted. A 'born' pacifist, growing up in a warlike culture, will generally accept war as part of the natural order of things. A man who might have been a complete skeptic in a science-based society will nearly always accept the gods of a theocracy if he has been brought up to believe in them. He may even become a priest and direct his logical talents toward elaborating the accepted theology—and help in the persecution of unbelievers. And so on. I needn't go into detail. The power of social conditioning is unbelievable—combined with social pressure, it is almost insuperable.

"And—this is the important point—the rules and assumptions of a society are accepted and enforced by the mass—the overwhelming majority, shortsighted, conservative, hating and fearing all that is new and strange, wishing only to remain in whatever basic condition it has known from birth. The genius is forced into the strait-jacket of the mediocre man's mentality. That he can expand any distance at all beyond his prison is a tribute to the supreme power of intellect."

Heym looked out at the empty street. Rain blew wildly across its darkened surface. "The Solarian Empire is nothing but the triumph of stupidity over intelligence. If every man could think for himself, we wouldn't need an empire."

"Watch yourself," muttered Goram. "The ruling class has a certain latitude of speech, but don't overstep it." And more loudly: "What does this mean in the case of Station Seventeen?"

"Why, it's a triumphant confirmation of the historical theory I was just explaining," said Heym. "We've isolated pure genius from mediocrity and left it free to work out its own destiny. The result has even exceeded our predictions.

"No doubt there are aggressive and conservative and selfish people born. But on this world the weight of social conditioning and social pressure is away from those tendencies, they don't get a chance to develop themselves.

"It seems"—Heym's voice rose—"that genius shows a qualitative distinction, due to quantitative differences, from mere human intelligence. The genius is basically a distinct type, just as the moron is on the other end of the scale. And here—on Seventeen—the new type has been set free."

He turned around from the window. Goram sat motionless, staring at the floor, and the slow seconds ticked away before he spoke.

"I don't know—" he murmured. "I don't know—"

Defeat and despair and a binding hatred rose into Heym's throat. *You don't know!* His mind screamed the thought, it seemed incredible that Goram should sprawl there, not moving, not hearing. *No, you don't know. Your sort never does, never has known anything but its own self-righteous rationalization of impulses that should have died ages ago! You'll destroy Seventeen, in spite of all reason, in sheer perversity—and you'll say you did it for the good of the Empire!*

The knife seemed to spring of its own accord into his hand. He was lunging forward before he realized it. He saw the blade gleam down as if another man were wielding it. The blow shocked back into his muscles and for an instant his mind wavered, it wasn't real—*what am I doing?*

No time to lose. Goram twisted around in his seat, yelling, grabbing for Heym. The knife was deep in his neck. Heym yanked at it—pull it loose, stick it in the throat, kill—

Something struck him from behind. The world shattered in a burst of stars, he crashed to the floor and rolled over. Through a haze of dizzy pain he saw men bending over Goram—men of the planet, rescuers for the monster who would annihilate them.

Words tumbled from the hotel clerk, anxious, shaken: "Are you hurt? Did you— Still, lie still, here comes a doctor—"

Pain curled Goram's lips back from his teeth, but he muttered a reply: "No . . . I'm all right . . . flesh wound—"

The doctor bent over his bloody form. "Deep," he said, "but it missed the important veins. Here, I'll just pull it out—"

"Go ahead," whispered Goram. "I've taken worse than this, though . . . I never expected it here."

Heym lay on the floor while they worked over the soldier. His ringing, whirling head throbbed toward steadiness, and slowly, with so tremendous an impact that it overloaded his nerves and entered his consciousness without emotional shock, the realization grew.

Goram had spoken to the natives—*in their own language.*

A man bent over the psychologist. "Are you all right?" he asked. "I'm sorry I had to hit you so hard. Here—drink this."

Heym forced the liquid down his throat. It coursed fierily through his veins, he sat up with an arm supporting him about his waist and held his head in his hands.

Someone else spoke, the voice seemed to come from across an abyss: "Did he hear?"

"I'm afraid so." Goram, his neck bandaged, spoke painfully. A rueful smile crossed his ugly face. "The excitement was too much for me, or I would have kept silent. This is going to be —inconvenient."

The men of the planet helped Heym into a chair. He began to revive, and looked dazedly across at the man he had tried to kill. The others stood around the chairs, tall bearded men in barbaric dress, watching him with alertness and a strange pity.

"Yes," said Tamman Goram very quietly, "the assistant Grand Marshal of the Solarian Empire is a native of Station Seventeen."

"Who else?" whispered Heym. "How and why? I tried to kill you because I thought you meant to order the planet sterilized."

"It was an act," said Goram. "I meant to concede at last that the station was harmless and could be safely left to the Foundation's observers. Coming from one who had apparently been strongly inclined to the opposite view, the statement would have been doubly convincing to Imperial officialdom. It was a powerful and suspicious minister who ordered the investigation, and I went to soothe his feelings. His successor will be one of our men, who will see that Station Seventeen drops into safe obscurity as an unimportant and generally unsuccessful experiment conducted by a few harmless cranks."

"But . . . aren't you . . . weren't you—"

"Oh, yes. My history is perfectly genuine. I was planted as an obscure recruit in the border guards many years ago, and since then my rise has been strictly in accord with Imperial principles. All our men in the Empire will bear the most searching investigation. Sometimes they come from families which have lived several generations on Imperial planets. Our program of replacing key personnel with our men is planned centuries ahead of time, and succeeds by the simple fact that on the average, over long periods of time, they are so much more capable than anyone else."

"How long—?"

"About five hundred years. You underestimated the capabilities of your experimental animals." Goram rested for a moment, then asked, "If human intelligence is qualitatively different from animal intelligence, and genius is different from ordinary reasoning power—then tell me, what about the equivalent of geniuses in a world where the average man is a genius by the usual standards?

"Pure genius strains kept right on evolving, more rapidly indeed than can be explained on any other basis than the existence of an orthogenetic factor in evolution. Supergenius—give it a different name, call it transcendence, since it is a different quality—has capabilities which the ordinary mind can no more comprehend than pure instinct can comprehend logic.

"Your spectacular god-revelations were not forgotten, they were treated discreetly. Later, when a theory of evolution was developed, it seemed strange that man, though obviously an animal, should have no apparent phylogenesis. The stories of the 'gods,' the theories of evolution and astronomy—we began to suspect the truth. With that suspicion, it was not hard for a transcendent to spot your masquerading psychologists. Kidnapping, questioning under drugs developed by psychiatry, and release of the prisoner with memory of his experience removed told us the rest. Later, disguised as other prisoners, with their knowledge, and his own intelligence to fill the gaps, one transcendent after another made his way to the observation asteroid—thence out into the Galaxy, where a little spying was sufficient to reveal the principles of the interstellar drive and the other mechanisms of the Empire."

Heym murmured: "The whole planet has been—acting?"

"Yes." Goram chuckled. "Rather fun for all concerned. You'd be surprised at the installations we have, out of spy-machine range. As soon as they are old enough to carry out the deception, our children are told the truth. It has actually made little difference to our lives except for those few million who are out in the Galaxy taking it over."

"Taking . . . it . . . over?" Heym's mind seemed to be turning over slowly, infinitely slowly and wearily.

"Of course." A strange blend of sternness and sympathy overlay Goram's harsh features. "One planet obviously cannot fight the Galaxy, nor do we wish to. Yet we cannot permit it to menace us. The only answer is—annexation."

"And . . . then?"

"I'm sorry." Goram's voice came slowly, implacably, "but I'm afraid you over-rated the good intentions of the pure genius strain. After all, Homo intelligens can no more be expected to serve Homo sapiens than early man to serve the apes.

"We're taking over barbarians and Empire alike. After that, the Galaxy will do as we wish. Oh, we won't be hard masters. Man may never know that he is being ruled from outside, and he will enter a period of peace and contentment such as he has never imagined.

"As for you—"

Heym realized with vague shock that he had not even wondered or cared what was to become of him personally.

"You are sympathetic to us—but your loyalty is to the Empire. You have thought of us only in relation to our usefulness to the Imperium. Perhaps we could trust you to keep our secret, perhaps not. We can't take the risk. You might even release the truth inadvertently. Nor can we erase your memory of this—it would leave traces that an expert psychiatrist could detect, and all high officials undergo regular psychoanalytical check-ups.

"I'll just have to report you as accidentally killed on the planet." Goram smiled. "I don't think you'll find life exile on this world, out of sight of the observers, uncongenial. And we might as well see about making your successor one of our men. It was about ready for that."

He added thoughtfully: "In fact, the Galaxy may be ready for a new Solarian Emperor."

Basic Right

by ERIC FRANK RUSSELL

There is no visible horizon beyond which the unleashed intellect cannot advance. But where is it
taking mankind? Compare the brutal complex-
ities of galactic conquest, as pictured here and in
Poul Anderson's Genius, with the possibility of
man's conquest of himself. This story provides
the perfect closing to our adventure in exploring
the enormous scope of man's intelligence and of
the universe he inhabits.

THEY CAME OUT of the starfield under the earth, from the region of a brilliant sun called Sigma Octantis. Ten huge copper-
colored ships. Nobody saw them land. They were astute enough
to sit awhile in the howling wastes of Antarctica, scout around
and seize all twenty members of the International South Polar
Expedition.

Even then the world did not take alarm. The newcomers,
who titled themselves Raidans, hazarded a guess that within a
fortnight earth would become curious about the fate of the
captured. But it didn't work out like that at all; contrary to ex-
pectations the Terran prisoners proved so submissive and co-
operative.

By signs and gestures the Raidans conveyed their cover-up order: "Send out reassuring messages."

The captives did it willingly, in straightforward manner, playing no tricks, well-nigh falling over themselves in eagerness to
please. Routine signals from the polar expedition continued to
be picked up by listening-posts in Australia, New Zealand, and

Chile. Nobody found reason to suspect that anything out of the ordinary had occurred down there within the ice barrier where blizzards raged throughout the long-drawn night.

Within the next eleven weeks the invaders learned the Terran language, devoting all their time to picking it up as fast and fluently as possible. This chore could have been avoided by insisting that the prisoners learn to speak Raidan but the tactic would have involved loss of conversational privacy. The Raidans preferred to do the work and keep their talk strictly to themselves.

In the twelfth week Zalumar, commander of the fleet, summoned Lakin, his personal aide. "Lakin, there is no need for us to waste any more hours upon this animal gabble. We can now speak it well enough to make ourselves properly understood. It is time to get out of this frozen place and assert ourselves in conditions of comfort."

"Yes, sire," agreed Lakin, heartened by the thought of coming sunshine and warmth.

"The leader of these prisoners is named Gordon Fox. I wish to speak with him. Bring him to me."

"Yes, sire." Lakin hastened out, returned shortly with the captive.

He was a tall, lean Terran, lank-haired, his face adorned with a polar beard. His gray eyes examined Zalumar, noting the broad shoulders, the long, boneless arms, the yellow eyes, the curious green fuzz overlying the skin. Zalumar found himself enjoying this inspection because it was made with a curious mixture of servility and admiration.

"I have something to say to you, Fox."

"Yes, sire?"

"Doubtless you've been wondering why we are here, what our intentions are, what is going to happen in the near future, eh?" Without waiting for a reply, he went on, "The answer is brief and to the point: we are going to take over your world."

He watched the other's face, seeking fear, shock, anger, any of the emotions normally to be expected. But he detected none of them. On the contrary, Fox seemed gratified by the prospect. There was no rage, no defiance, nothing but amiable complacency. Maybe the fellow had failed to grasp precisely what was meant.

"We are going to assume ownership of Terra lock, stock, and barrel," emphasized Zalumar, still watching him. "We are going to confiscate your world because the rewards of life belong to the most deserving. That is our opinion. We have the power to make it the only acceptable opinion. Do you understand me, Fox?"

"Yes, sire."

"The prospect does not annoy you?"

"No, sire."

"Why doesn't it?"

Fox shrugged philosophically. "Either you are cleverer than us or you aren't, one way or the other, and that is that. If you aren't, you won't be able to conquer this world no matter what you say or do."

"But if we are cleverer?"

"I guess we'll benefit from your rule. You can't govern us without teaching us things worth learning."

"This," declared Zalumar, with a touch of wonder, "is the first time in our history that we've encountered so reasonable an attitude. I hope all the other Terrans are like you. If so, this will prove the easiest conquest to date."

"They won't give you any bother," Fox assured.

"You must belong to an amazingly placid species," Zalumar offered.

"We have our own peculiar ways of looking at things, of doing things."

"They appear to be vastly different from everyone else's ways, so different as to seem almost contrary to nature." Zalumar put on a thin smile. "However, it is a matter of no importance. Very soon your people will look at everything in our way, do everything in our way. Alternatively, they will cease to exist."

"They're in no hurry to die," said Fox.

"Well, they're normal enough in that respect. I had you brought here to inform you of what we intend to do and, more importantly, to show you why your people had better let us do it without argument or opposition. I shall use you and your fellow captives as liaison officers, therefore it is necessary to convince you that your world's choice lies between unquestioning obedience or complete extermination. After that, it will be your duty to persuade Terran authorities to do exactly as we tell them. Lakin will take you to the projection room and show you some very interesting pictures."

"Pictures?"

"Yes, three-dimensional ones in full color. They will demonstrate what happened to Planet K14 whose people were stupid enough to think they could defy us and get away with it. We made an example of them, an object lesson to others. What we did to their world we can do to any planet including this one." He gave a careless wave of his hand. "Take him away and show him, Lakin."

After they'd gone he lay back in his seat and felt satisfied. Once again it was about to be demonstrated that lesser lifeforms are handicapped by questions of ethics, of morals, of right and wrong. They just hadn't the brains to understand that greed, brutality, and ruthlessness are nothing more than terms of abuse for efficiency.

Only the Raidans, it seemed, had the wisdom to learn and apply Nature's law that victory belongs to the sharp in tooth and swift in claw.

In the projection room Lakin turned a couple of switches, made a few minor adjustments to controls. Nearby a large grayish sphere bloomed to life. At its middle floated a tiny bead of intense light; near its inner surface swam a smaller, darker bead with one face silvered by the center illumination.

"Now watch!"

They studied the sphere. After a short while the dark outermost bead suddenly swelled and blazed into fire, almost but not quite rivaling the center one with the intensity of its light. Lakin reversed the switches. The two glowing beads disappeared, the big sphere resumed its dull grayness.

"That," said Lakin, having the grace not to smack his lips, "is the actual record of the expulsion from the stage of life of two thousand million fools. The cosmos will never miss them. They were born, they served their ordained purpose, and they departed—forever. Would you like to know what that purpose was?"

"If you please," said Fox, very politely.

"They were created so that their wholesale slaughter might knock some sense into their sector of the cosmos."

"And did it?"

"Beyond all doubt." Lakin let go a cold laugh. "On every planet in the vicinity the inhabitants fought each other for the privilege of kissing our feet." He let his yellow eyes linger speculatively upon the other. "We don't expect you to believe all this, not right now."

"Don't you?"

"Of course not. Anyone can fake a stereoscopic record of cosmic disaster. You'd be gullible indeed if you let us confiscate your world on the strength of nothing better than a three-dimensional picture, wouldn't you?"

"Credulity has nothing to do with it," assured Fox. "You want to take us over. We're glad to be taken over. That's all there is to it."

"Look, we can back up our pictures with proof. We can show your own astronomers upon their own star maps exactly where a minor sun has become a binary. We can name and prove the date on which this change took place. If that doesn't satisfy them, we can convert to a ball of flaming gas any petty satellite within this system that they care to choose. We can show them what happens and demonstrate that we made it happen." He stared at Fox, his expression slightly baffled. "Do you really mean to say that such proof will not be required?"

"I don't think so. The great majority will accept your claims without argument. A few skeptics may quibble but they can be ignored."

Lakin frowned in evident dissatisfaction. "I don't understand this. One would almost think your kind was eager to be conquered. It is not a normal reaction."

"Normal by whose standards?" asked Fox. "We are aliens, aren't we? You must expect us to have alien mentalities, alien ways of looking at things."

"I need no lecture from you about alien mentalities,"

snapped Lakin, becoming irritated. "We Raidans have handled a large enough variety of them. We've mastered more life-forms than your kind can imagine. And I still say that your attitude is not normal. If Terra reacts in the way you seem to think it will, without proof, without being given good reason to fear, then everyone here must be a natural-born slave."

"What's wrong with that?" Fox countered. "If Nature in her wisdom has designed your kind to be the master race, why shouldn't she have created my kind as slaves?"

"I don't like the way you gloat about your slavery," shouted Lakin. "If Terrans think they can outwit us, they've another think coming. Do you understand?"

"Most certainly I understand," confirmed Fox, as soothingly as possible.

"Then return to your comrades and tell them what you have seen, what you've been told. If any of them wish for further evidence, bring them here immediately. I will answer their questions, provide any proof for which they may ask."

"Very well."

Sitting on the edge of the table, Lakin watched the other go out. He remained seated for ten tedious minutes. Then he fidgeted for five more, finally mooched several times around the room. Eventually Fox looked in.

"They are all willing to take my word for it."

"Nobody desires to learn more?" Lakin showed his incredulity.

"No."

"They accept everything without question?"

"Yes," said Fox. "I told you they probably would, didn't I?"

Lakin did not deign to answer that one. He made a curt gesture of dismissal, closed the projection room, went back to the main cabin. Zalumar was still there, talking to Heisham, who was the fleet's chief engineer.

Breaking off the conversation, Zalumar said to Lakin, "What happened? Did the bearded low-life get the usual fit of hysterics?"

"No, sire. On the contrary, he appears to enjoy the prospect of his world being mastered."

"I am not at all surprised," commented Zalumar. "These Terrans are philosophical to the point of idiocy." His sharp eyes noted the other's face. "Why do you look so sour?"

"I don't like the attitude of these aliens, sire."

"Why not? It makes things easy for us. Or do you prefer to get everything the hard way?"

Lakin said nothing.

"Let us congratulate ourselves upon our good fortune," encouraged Zalumar, oozing oily self-confidence. "Victory without battle comes far cheaper than one paid for in blood. A planet mastered is worth infinitely more than a world destroyed."

Speaking up with sudden resolve, Lakin said, "According to the books we've found here, and according to our own preliminary observations, these Terrans have a civilization only a couple of jumps behind our own. They have short-range spaceships on regular runs to their outer planets. They've even got that small colony we noticed on the system of their nearest star. All that has to be born of and supported by a technology that cannot be the creation of imbeciles."

"I agree," chipped in Heisham, with the enthusiasm of an engineer. "I've been studying the details of their ships. These Terrans are supposed to be about twenty thousand years younger than we—but technically they're nothing like as far behind. Therefore they must—"

"Quiet!" roared Zalumar. He paused to let ensuing silence sink in, then continued in lower tones. "All species are afflicted by what they consider to be virtues. We know that from our own firsthand experience, don't we? The disease of goodness varies as between one life form and another. This happens to be the first world we've discovered on which the prime virtue is obedience. They may have a modicum of brains but they've all been brought up to respect their betters." He threw his listener a sardonic glance. "And you, an experienced spacewarrior, permit it to surprise you, allow it to worry you. What is the matter with you, eh?"

"It is only that their submissive attitude runs contrary to my every instinct."

"Naturally, my dear Lakin, naturally. We submit to nobody. But surely it is self-evident that Terrans are not Raidans, never have been, never will be."

"Quite right," approved Heisham.

Now under double-fire, Lakin subsided. But deep down within himself he wasn't satisfied. Within this peculiar situation was something sadly and badly out of kilter, his sixth sense told him that.

The move was made next day. Ten ships rose from the barren land bearing with them the twenty members of the I. S. P. Expedition. In due time they landed upon a great spaceport just beyond the environs of a sprawling city which, Fox had assured, was as good a place as any in which to tell the world of the fate that had come upon it from the stars.

Zalumar summoned Fox, said, "I do not go to native leaders. They come to me."

"Yes, sire."

"So you will fetch them. Take all your comrades with you so that if necessary they may confirm your story." He eyed the other, his face hard. "With what we've got we do not need hostages. Any treacherous attack upon us will immediately be answered a hundredfold without regard for age or sex. Do you understand?"

"Yes, sire."

"Then get going. And you won't take all day about it if you're wise."

He strolled to the rim of the flagship's air lock door and watched the twenty make off across the hot concrete, hurrying toward the city. They were still hairy-faced and wearing full polar kit under the blazing sun. Four clean-shaven Terrans in neat, cool uniforms drove up and braked at the bottom of the ladder. One got out of the car, shaded his eyes as he looked upward at the alien figure framed in the lock.

With total lack of amazement, this newcomer called, "You sent no beam warning of arrival. We've had to divert two ships to another port. Carelessness like that makes accidents. Where are you from?"

"Do you really expect me to know your language and be familiar with your rules and regulations?" asked Zalumar, interestedly.

"Yes, for the reason that you had twenty Terrans with you.

They know the law even if you don't. Why didn't you beam a warning?"

"Because," said Zalumar, enjoying himself, "we are above your laws. Henceforth they are abolished so far as we are concerned."

"Is that so?" gave back the other. "Well, you're going to learn different mighty soon."

"On the contrary," retorted Zalumar, "it is you who will learn, we who shall teach." With that he returned to his cabin, smiled to himself, fiddled around with a thick file of papers. Three hours later he was called to the lock door by a crewman. He went there, looked down upon the same uniformed quartette as before.

Their spokesman said, blankly and unemotionally, "I'm ordered to apologize to you for questioning your right to land without warning. I am also instructed to inform you that certain persons whom you wish to see are now on their way here."

Acknowledging this with a sniff of disdain, Zalumar went back to his desk. A multijet plane screamed far overhead and he ignored it. Doubtless some of the crew were leaning out the locks and nervily watching lest something long, black, and lethal drop upon them from the sky. But he couldn't be bothered himself. He had these Terrans weighed up—they just wouldn't dare. He was dead right, too. They didn't dare. The shrill sound died over the horizon and nothing happened.

Some time later Fox appeared with two other I.S.P. members named McKenzie and Vitelli. They conducted a bunch of twelve civilians into the cabin. The dozen newcomers lined up against a wall, studied the Raidan commander with frank curiosity but no visible enmity.

Fox explained, "These, sire, are twelve of Terra's elected leaders. There are thirty more scattered around, some in far places. I regret that it is not possible to trace and bring them here today."

"No matter." Zalumar lay back in his chair and surveyed the dozen with suitable contempt. They did not fidget under his gaze nor show any signs of uneasiness. They merely gazed back steadily, eye for eye, like a group of impassive lizards. It occurred to him that it was well-nigh impossible to discern what they were thinking. Oh, well, the time-honored tactic was to start by kicking them right in the teeth.

"Let's get something straight," harshed Zalumar at the twelve. "So far as we are concerned, you are animals. Lower animals. Cows. My cows. When I order you to produce milk you will strain to produce it. When I order you to moo you will promptly moo, all together, in concert with the other thirty who are absent."

Nobody said anything, nobody got hot under the collar, nobody appeared to care a solitary damn.

"If any one of you fails to obey orders or shows lack of alacrity in doing so, he will be jerked out of mundane existence and replaced with a good, trustworthy, and melodious mooer."

Silence.

"Any questions?" he invited, feeling a little irritated by their bland acceptance of racial inferiority. A scowl, just a frightened half-concealed scowl from any one of them would have given him much inward pleasure and enabled him to taste the full, fruity flavor of conquest. As it was, they made victory seem appallingly insipid; a triumph that was no triumph at all because there had been nothing to beat down.

They didn't so much as give him the satisfaction of meeting their queries with a few devastating retorts, of crushing them with responses calculated to emphasize their individual and collective stupidity. Still in line against the wall, they posed silently, without questions, and waited for his next order. Looking at them, he got the weird feeling that if he'd suddenly bawled, "Moo!" they'd have all mooed together, at the tops of their voices—and in some mysterious, elusive way the laugh would be on him.

Snatching up the intercom phone, he called Captain Arnikoj and when that worthy arrived, said, "Take these twelve simpletons to the registry on Cruiser Seven. Have them thoroughly recorded from toenails to hair. Extract from them all the details you can get concerning thirty others who have yet to arrive. We shall want to know who the culprit is if one of them fails to turn up."

"As you order, sire," said Arnikoj.

"That's not all," continued Zalumar. "When you've finished I want you to select the least cretinous specimen and return him to this ship. He will be retained here. It will be his duty to summon the others whenever I require them."

"It shall be done, sire."

Zalumar now switched attention back to the twelve. "After you have been registered you may go back to your posts in the city. Your first act will be to declare this spaceport the sole and exclusive property of the Raidan fleet now occupying it. All Terran officials will be removed from the port, none will be allowed to enter except with my permission."

They received that in the same silence as before. He watched them go out, moving dully along one behind the other, following Arnikoj's lead. Great God in Heaven, what witless animals they were!

Zalumar now stared querulously at Fox, McKenzie, and Vitelli. "Where are the other seventeen members of your expedition?"

"They remained in the city, sire," explained Fox.

"Remained? Who said they could remain? They are required here, *here!*" He slammed an angry fist upon the desk top. "They have not the slightest right to stay behind without an order to that effect. Who do they think they are? I shall swiftly show them how we deal with those who think they can do as they like. I shall—"

"Sire," chipped in Fox, cutting short the tirade, "they asked if they might stay a short while to clean up and change into more suitable clothing. I told them I felt sure you would approve of them looking more presentable. It didn't seem reasonable to suppose that you might resent their efforts to please you."

A momentary confusion afflicted Zalumar's mind. If a trooper goes AWOL solely to fetch his commanding officer a gold medal, what does the latter do about it? For the first time he sensed a vague touch of the indefinable something that was troubling the uneasy Lakin. All was not quite as it should be. This Fox fellow, for instance, was twisting his arm in front of two witnesses and there was nothing much he could do about it.

Determined to concoct a gripe, he growled, "All right, let us accept that their concern for my pleasure is praiseworthy and therefore excusable. Why have you and these other two not shown the same desire to gratify me? Why have you returned in those shapeless and filthy clothes, your faces still covered with bristles? Are you telling me that seventeen care but three do not?"

"No, sire," said Fox, busily polishing apples that might prove to be scoot-berries. "Someone had to come back. We hope that when the seventeen return you might graciously permit us to go and get cleaned up in our turn."

"You had better do that," conceded Zalumar. "We can recognize animals with no trouble at all. Therefore it isn't necessary for you to look like them, smell like them."

He watched the other carefully, seeking a hint of hidden anger such as a slight narrowing of the eyes or a tightening of the jaw muscles. Fat lot of good it did him. Fox's features remained wooden behind his polar mask of hair. McKenzie acted like he was stone-deaf. Vitelli wore the same unctuous smile that never left his moonlike face.

"Get out," he ordered. "Report to Arnikoj. Tell him you have my permission to visit the city after the others have returned. Be back by nightfall."

"And after that, sire?"

"You will remain under Arnikoj's personal command. I will send for you whenever I want you."

When they had gone he strolled to the nearest port, gazed out at the great city. Slowly and with miserly lovingness he took in its towers, spires, skyways, and bridges. Mine, he thought, all mine. A worthy prize for the worthy. The battle to the strong, the spoils to the bold and brave.

Lakin mooched in, said hesitantly, "I have been thinking, sire. We're sort of all bunched up together. Ten ships practically standing side by side. Might it not be better if we spread ourselves a little? Couldn't we keep, say, four ships here and place three each in two other spaceports?"

"Why?"

"We don't yet know what their best weapons are like—but

we do know that one well-placed bomb could vaporize the lot of us."

"So could three bombs. So what have we to gain by splitting up?"

"Unless they dropped them simultaneously, the first blow would warn the rest. Some of us could escape and hit back."

"If they can summon up the nerve to drop any at all," said Zalumar, "you can bet your life they'll drop them together. It's all or nothing so far as they're concerned. Probably they would do their best to wipe us out if they thought for one moment that it would do them any good. They know it won't. They know it would bring retaliation from the Raidan Imperial Forces. We would be avenged."

"Not yet we wouldn't," Lakin contradicted. "To date Raidan hasn't the faintest notion of where we are or what we're doing. I have just asked Shaipin whether he had yet beamed our official report. He hasn't. Until he does so, and receives Raidan's acknowledgment, we are just another task force lost in the mist of stars."

Zalumar gave a grim smile. "My dear Worryguts Lakin, only we know that we're out of contact. The Terrans don't know it. They're not going to take the risk of enticing a full-scale attack that will cremate the lot of them. Like everything else, they have a natural desire to survive. They value their skins, see?"

"I asked Shaipin why he hasn't yet signaled our whereabouts," Lakin persisted. "He said he'd not yet received the order from you. Do you wish me to tell him to beam our report?"

"Certainly not." Turning his back upon him, Zalumar again absorbed the glorious vision of the city.

"Sire, regulations require us to report immediately we have overcome opposition and taken complete command."

Swinging around, Zalumar spat at him. "Do you think I, the commander, am ignorant of regulations? Shaipin will send the necessary signals when I say so, and not before. I am the sole judge of the proper moment."

"Yes, sire," agreed Lakin, taken aback.

"And the proper moment is not yet."

He said it as though it might never come.

Zalumar was quite a prophet.

Shaipin still had not been given the order a month later. Nor three months later, nor six. It never occurred to him to query the omission or, if it did, he preferred to keep his mouth shut. As for Lakin, he had tactfully refrained from mentioning the matter again. To his mind, Zalumar had staked his claim to full responsibility for everything done or not done—and he was welcome to stay stuck with it.

Through the many weeks events had shaped themselves beautifully. The Terrans co-operated one hundred per cent, displaying no visible enthusiasm but functioning with quiet efficiency.

Whenever Zalumar felt like larruping the leadership he ordered the entire snollygoster to parade before him and forty-two of them came on the run. His word was their command, his slightest whim had the status of a law. He did not doubt that if he'd beeen capable of sinking to such childishness he could have made them worship the ground on which he trod and kiss every footprint he left in the dirt. It was a wonderful exhibition of what can be done when the choice is the simple one of obey or burn.

One result of all this was that he, Zalumar, had fled the confines of a warship for the first time in more years than he'd care to count. He was no longer encased in metal, like a canned *rashim*. The tactic had been the easiest ever, requiring not even the chore of waving a magic wand. All he'd had to do was ask and it shall be given unto you. No, not ask, *tell*.

"You will confiscate and assign solely to me this world's most imposing palace. Whoever occupies it at present will be thrown out. All necessary repairs will be tended to without delay. The palace will be decorated and refurnished in sumptuous style suitable to my position as Planetary Governor. You will provide a full quota of trained servants. I'll inspect the place immediately everything is ready—and for your own good you'd better make sure that it meets with my approval!"

They made sure all right. Even on Raidan nobody had it half so magnificent or a third as luxurious. He could think of many military contemporaries who'd grind their teeth with envy to see Nordis Zalumar, a mere ten-ship commander, making like a natural-born king. Nay, an emperor.

The palace was enormous. The center portion alone came

close to being an international monument in its own right, without considering the vast expanse of east and west wings. Even the servants' quarters were about the size of a large hotel. The grounds around the palace numbered four thousand acres, all carefully landscaped, complete with a lake filled with multi-colored fish and ornamental water-fowl.

It was evident that the place had been prepared with a lavishness that had no regard for cost. A world had been looted to gratify the one who could vaporize it from poles to core. Three thousand million animals had combined to pay the heavy premium on a fire-insurance policy.

Zalumar approved; even he could not dig up a lordly quibble. There was only one snag: The palace lay two thousand miles from the spaceport, the city, the seat of world-government. There was only one solution: he ordered a new spaceport built on the fringe of his estate. This was done and his ten-ship fleet moved to the new location.

Next, he commanded the entire world leadership to set up home immediately outside his guarded gates. Nobody moaned, groaned, raised objections, or so much as favored him with a disapproving frown. There was a rush of prefabricated buildings to the designated spot, and a new township sprang into being complete with a huge web of telephone wires and a powerful radio station.

Meanwhile Zalumar had taken possession of his property. The transfer was made without ceremony; he merely stalked in at the front door as becomes one who literally owns the earth. His first move was to assign apartments in the west wing to his senior officers, inferior ones in the east wing to his twenty-one Terran stooges. This tactic helped populate a great emptiness, provided company, ensured a constant supply of adulation or, at least, dumb agreement.

"Aie!" he sighed with pleasure. "Is this not better than squatting in a hot can and being hammered day after day for the greater glory of others but never of ourselves?"

"Yes, sire," dutifully approved Heisham.

Lakin said nothing.

"We shall now reap the rewards of our virtues," continued Zalumar. "We shall live the life of . . . of—" He felt around in his jacket, produced a small pocket book and consulted it. "A character named Reilly."

"I have heard him mentioned by the Terrans," said Heisham. "And I imagine this is just the sort of place he'd have." He let admiring eyes survey the room, finished, "I wonder who did own it and what has happened to him."

"We can soon learn," Zalumar answered. "A Terran has just crossed the hall. Go get him and bring him here."

Heisham hastened out, came back with Vitelli.

"To whom did this place belong?" demanded Zalumar.

"To nobody." Vitelli favored him with his usual oily smile. "Nobody?"

"No, sire. Previously this was the world's largest and latest international hospital.'

"And just what is a hospital?"

The smile faded away, Vitelli blinked a couple of times and told him.

Zalumar listened incredulously, said, "An individual who is sick or injured is either capable or incapable of recovering. He can regain his efficiency or he is permanently useless. One thing or the other—there is no third alternative. That is logical, isn't it?"

"I suppose so," responded Vitelli, with reluctance.

"You don't suppose anything," Zalumar contradicted in louder tones. "You know for a fact that it is logical because I have said that it is. And say 'sire' when you answer me!"

"Yes, sire."

"If an individual can recover, he should be left to do it as best he can; he has every inducement to succeed, knowing the penalty of failure. If he cannot do it, he should be got rid of in the orthodox way; he should be gassed and cremated. It is sheer waste of time and effort for the fit to coddle the unfit."

He stared hard at Vitelli who offered no remark.

"It is contrary to natural law for the efficient to assist the inefficient who should be left to stew in their own juice. How many defective bodies were being pampered in this . . . uh . . . hospital?"

"About six thousand," informed Vitelli, again forgetting the "sire."

"Where are they now?"

"They were transferred to other hospitals. It has meant a little overcrowding in some places but I guess things will be straightened out in due time."

"So!" Zalumar thought a bit, looked as though about to voice something drastic, changed his mind and said, "You may go." After Vitelli had departed, Zalumar commented to the others, "I could order the prompt destruction of all this defective rubbish. But why should I bother? The chore of tending a horde of mental or physical cripples keeps Terran hands busy. Things remain orderly and peaceful when everyone is fully occupied. It is a world with time on its hands that makes itself a dangerous nuisance."

"Yes, sire," agreed Heisham, admiring him.

"Well, we now know something more," Zalumar went on. "In addition to being cowardly and stupid they are also soft. They are soft and yielding, like this stuff they call putty."

Lakin said in the manner of one meditating aloud, "How far does one get by plunging a sword into a barrel of putty? How much does one really cut, stab or destroy?"

Studying him blank-faced, Zalumar harshed, "Lakin, you will cease annoying me with senseless remarks."

Everything worked smoothly for another two years. In between regal jaunts around his planetary property Zalumar lurked in his palace like a spider in the center of its web. Terra remained utterly and absolutely his to command, ran itself according to his directions. There had been no trouble other than that attributable to ordinary misunderstandings. In nobody's history had anyone sat more securely upon the throne than had the Emperor Nordis Zalumar.

At his command three groups of Raidan officers had gone on a tour of inspection of Terran colonies on Venus, Mars, and Callisto. No crude frontiersman would risk cutting their throats; the home-world remained hostage for their safety. They were due back most any time.

A fourth bunch had gone to look at a small settlement in the Centauri group, earth's first foothold in another system. They'd not return for quite a piece. None of these groups had sailed in a Raidan warship; they'd all been taken in Terran spaceliners, traveling in utmost comfort as was proper for a higher form of life.

Of the sixteen hundred Raidans composing the original task force, less than two hundred continued on military duty. A hundred formed the permanent palace guard. Eighty kept watch on the ships. All the rest were touring Terra, going where they pleased, at no cost whatsoever. Every man a prince and Zalumar the king of kings.

Yes, every man a prince—that was no exaggeration. If any of them saw something he fancied behind a shop window he walked inside, demanded it, and it was handed over. An expensive camera, a diamond pendant, a racing motor-bike, a streamlined moon-boat, one had only to ask to be given.

Thus two junior navigators owned a subtropic island on which stood a magnificent mansion. They'd seen it from a confiscated amphibian, landed, marched in, and said to the owners, "Get out." They'd said to the servants, "You stay." So the owners had gone posthaste and the servants had remained. Similarly, twenty grease monkeys were touring the world on a two-thousand-ton luxury yacht, having ambled aboard, ordered all passengers ashore, and commanded the crew to raise anchor.

It seemed impossible that in such circumstances any Raidan could be discontented. Yet here again was that whining nuisance Lakin with a further batch of moans and groans. Some folk evidently would gripe even if given the cosmos on a platter.

"It can't go on forever," opined Lakin.

"It isn't intended to," Zalumar gave back. "We aren't immortal and more's the pity. But so long as it lasts our lifetimes we have every reason to be satisfied."

"Our lifetimes?" Lakin's expression showed that a deep suspicion had been confirmed. "Do you mean that Raidan is to be left in ignorance of this conquest and that contact with our home forces is never to be made?"

Zalumar settled himself deeper in his chair which resembled a cunning compromise between a bed and a throne. He folded hands across an abdomen that was becoming a little more prominent, more paunchy with every passing month.

"My dear witless Lakin, an official report should have been sent more than two and a half years ago. If, like these Terran animals, we had been dumbly obedient and beamed that report where would we be now?"

"I haven't the slightest idea," admitted Lakin.

"Neither have I. But one thing is certain: we would not be here. By this time a consolidating expedition would have arrived and off-loaded the usual horde of desk-bound warriors, non-combatant officials, overseers, exploiters, slave drivers, form fillers, and all the other parasites who squat all day and guzzle the spoils that space roamers have grabbed for them."

Lakin stayed silent, finding himself unable to contradict an unpleasant truth.

"As for us, we'd be summarily ordered back into our metal cans and told to go find yet another snatch. Right now we'd be somewhere out there in the sparkling dark, hunting around as we've been doing for years, taking risks, suffering continual discomfort, and knowing the nature of our ultimate reward." He pursed his lips and blew through them, making a thin slobbering sound. "The reward, my dear fatheaded Lakin, will be a row of medals that one can neither eat nor spend, a modest pension, a ceremonial mating, a shower of kids, old age, increasing feebleness and, finally, cremation."

"That may be so, sire, but—"

Waving him down, Zalumar continued, "I am of a mind to let the parasites seek their own prey and thus justify their own existence. Meanwhile we'll enjoy the prize we have gained for ourselves. If greed and ruthlessness are virtues in the many, they are equally virtues in the few. Since arriving on Terra I have become exceedingly virtuous and I advise you to do likewise. Remember, my dear belly-aching Lakin, that on our home-world they have an ancient saying." He paused, then quoted it with great relish. "Go thou and paint the long fence, Jayfat, for I am reclining within the hammock."

"Yes, sire, but—"

"And I am very comfortable," concluded Zalumar, hugging his middle.

"According to regulations, not to send a prompt report is

treachery, punishable by death. They will gas and burn the lot of us."

"If they find us, *if* they ever find us." Zalumar closed his eyes and smiled sleepily. "With no report, no signal, no clue of any sort, it will take them at least a thousand years. Possibly two thousand. When they rediscover this planet, if ever they do, we shall be gone a long, long time. I am splendidly indifferent about how many officials go purple with fury several centuries after I am dead."

"The men think that a report to Raidan has been postponed for strategic reasons known to the senior officers," Lakin persisted. "If ever they learn the truth, they won't like it."

"Indeed? Why shouldn't they like it? Are they so crammed with patriotic zeal that they prefer to be bounced around on a tail of fire rather than stay here living the life they have earned and deserve?"

"It isn't that, sire."

"Then what is it?"

"A quarter of them are nearing the end of their term of service."

"They have reached it already," Zalumar pointed out. "*All* of us have reached it." He let go the sigh of one whose patience is being tried. "We are in retirement. We are enjoying the Terran pension which is on a scale far more lavish than anything Raidan offers to its conquering heroes."

"That may be—but I fear it won't prove enough."

"What more do they want?"

"Wives and children, homes of their own among their own kind."

"Pfah!"

"We can mate only with our own species," Lakin went on. "Men detained here beyond their term of service are going to be denied that right. It is no satisfactory substitute to have absolute claim on this world's treasures. Anyway, one soon loses appreciation of the value of something gained for nothing, one becomes bored by getting it for the mere asking."

"I don't," assured Zalumar. "I like it, I love it."

"Every day I see windows full of gold watches," said Lakin. "They tire me. I have a gold watch which I obtained by demanding it. I don't want fifty gold watches. I don't even want two of them. So what use are all the others to me?"

"Lakin, are you near the end of your term?"

"No, sire. I have another twelve years to serve."

"Then you are not yet entitled to be mated. As for those who soon may be entitled, that is their worry and not yours."

"It will be our worry, sire, if they cause trouble."

Zalumar's yellow eyes flared. "The first mutineers will be slaughtered as a warning to the rest. That is established space-discipline which I, as commander, am entitled to order. Be assured that I shall have no hesitation in ordering it should the need arise."

"Yes, sire, but—"

"But what?"

"I am wondering whether we can afford to take such action."

"Speak plainly, Lakin, and cease to talk in riddles."

"Three years ago," responded Lakin, with a sort of gloomy desperation, "there were sixteen hundred of us. There are less today."

"Go on."

"Forty-two died in that epidemic of influenza to which they had no natural resistance. Eighteen killed themselves joyriding in a commandeered plane. Twenty-three have expired from sheer overeating and indolence. Two vanished while exploring under the seas. This morning three met death by reckless driving in a powerful sports car which the Terrans had built to their order. About forty more have come to their end in forty different ways. We're being thinned down slowly but surely. If this goes on long enough, there'll be none of us left."

"My poor foolish Lakin, if life goes on long enough there will be none of us left no matter where we are, here or on Raidan."

"On Raidan, sire, our passing would not be tantamount to defeat for us and victory for these Terrans."

Zalumar favored him with an ugly grin. "In death there is neither victory nor defeat." He made a gesture of dismissal. "Go thou and paint the long fence . . ."

When the other had departed Zalumar summoned his chief signals officer. "Shaipin, I have just heard that some of our men are getting restless. Do you know anything of this?"

"Somebody is always ready to gripe, sire. Every military force has its minority of malcontents. It is best to ignore them."

"You have six beam-operators per ship, making sixty in all. Are any of these among the grouchers?"

"Not that I am aware of, sire."

"More than two years ago I ordered you to put all the beam-transmitters out of action just sufficiently to prevent them from being repaired and used in secret. Are they still immobilized? Have you checked them lately?"

"I examine them every seventh day, sire. They remain unworkable."

"You swear to that?"

"Yes," said Shaipin, positively.

"Good! Could any one of them be restored in less than seven days? Could it be made to function in between your regular checks?"

"No, sire. It would take at least a month to repair any one of them."

"All right. I continue to hold you personally responsible for seeing to it that nobody interferes with these transmitters. Anyone caught trying to operate one of them is to be killed on the spot. If you fail in this, you will answer for it with your head." The look he threw the other showed that he meant it. "Is Heisham around or is he vacationing some place?"

"He returned from a tour three or four days ago, sire. Probably he will be in his apartment in the west wing."

"Tell him I want to see him immediately. While you're at it, find Fox and send him here also."

Heisham and Fox arrived together, the former wearing a broad grin, the latter impassive as usual.

Zalumar said to Heisham, "You are in charge of the nominal roll. What is our present strength?"

"Fourteen hundred seventy, sire."

"So we're down one hundred thirty, eh?" observed Zalumar, watching Fox as he said it but getting no visible reaction.

"Yes, sire," agreed Heisham, too well-pleased with himself to be sobered by statistics.

"A self-satisfied smirk is at least a pleasant change from La-

kin's miserable features," commented Zalumar. "What has made
you so happy?"

"I have been awarded a Black Belt," informed Heisham, swell-
ing with pride.

"You have been awarded it? By whom?"

"By the Terrans, sire."

Zalumar frowned. "There can be no worth-while award on a
world where anything may be confiscated."

"A Black Belt means nothing if merely grabbed," explained
Heisham. "Its value lies in the fact that it must be won. I got
mine at the risk of my neck."

"So we're down one-thirty and you've been trying to make it
one-thirty-one. No wonder the men get careless when senior
officers set such a bad example. What is this thing you have
won?"

"It's like this, sire," said Heisham. "Over a year ago I was telling a bunch of Terrans that we warriors are raised like warriors.
We don't play silly games like chess, for instance. Our favorite
sport is wrestling. We spend a lot of our childhood learning how
to break the other fellow's arm. The natural result is that every
Raidan is a first-class wrestler and hence an efficient fighting-
machine."

"So—?" prompted Zalumar.

"A medium-sized Terran showed great interest, asked what
style of wrestling we used. I offered to show him. Well, when I
recovered consciousness—"

"Eh?" ejaculated Zalumar.

"When I recovered consciousness," Heisham persisted, "he
was still there, leaning against the wall and looking at me. A lot
of witnesses were hanging around, all of them Terrans, and in
the circumstances there was nothing I could do about this
fellow except kill him then and there."

"Quite right," approved Zalumar, nodding emphatically.

"So I snatched him in dead earnest and when they'd picked
me off the floor again I asked—"

"Huh?"

"I asked him to show me how he'd done it. He said it would
need a series of lessons. So I made arrangements and took the les-

sons, every one of them. I passed tests and examinations and persisted until I was perfect." He stopped while he inflated his chest to suitable size. "And now I have won a Black Belt."

Zalumar switched attention to Fox. "Did you have any hand in this matter?"

"No, sire."

"It is just as well. Folly is reprehensible enough—I would not tolerate Terran encouragement of it." He turned back to Heisham. "Nobody has anything to teach us. But you, a senior officer, consent to take lessons from the conquered."

"I don't think it matters much, sire," offered Heisham, unabashed.

"Why doesn't it?"

"I learned their technique, mastered it, and applied it better than they could themselves. To win my prize I had to overcome twenty of them one after the other. Therefore it can be said that I have taught them how to play their own game."

"Humph!" Zalumar was slightly mollified but still suspicious. "How do you know that they didn't *let* you throw them?"

"They didn't appear to do so, sire."

"Appearances aren't always what they seem," Zalumar said, dryly. He thought a bit, went on, "How did it happen that the medium-sized Terran mastered you in the first place?"

"I was caught napping by his extraordinary technique. This Terran wrestling is very peculiar."

"In what way?"

Heisham sought around for an easily explainable example, said, "If I were to push you it would be natural for you to oppose my push and to push back. But if you push a Terran he grabs your wrists and pulls the same way. He *helps* you. It is extremely difficult to fight a willing helper. It means that everything you try to do is immediately taken farther than you intended."

"The answer is easy," scoffed Zalumar. "You give up pushing. You pull him instead."

"If you change from pushing to pulling, he promptly switches from pulling to pushing," Heisham answered. "He's still with you, still helping. There's no effective way of controlling it except by adopting the same tactics."

"It sounds crazy to me. However, it is nothing unusual for aliens to have cockeyed ways of doing things. All right, Heisham, you may go away and coddle your hard-won prize. But don't encourage any of the others to follow your bad example. We are losing men too rapidly already."

He waited until Heisham had gone, then fixed attention on Fox.

"Fox, I have known you for quite a time. I have found you consistently obedient, frank and truthful. Therefore you stand as high in my esteem as any mere Terran can."

"Thank you, sire," said Fox, showing gratitude.

"It would be a pity to destroy that esteem and plunge yourself from the heights to the depths. I am relying upon you to give me candid answers to one or two questions. You have nothing to fear and nothing to lose by telling the absolute truth."

"What do you wish to know, sire?"

"Fox, I want you to tell me whether you are waiting, just waiting."

Puzzled, Fox said, "I don't understand."

"I want to know whether you Terrans are playing a waiting game, whether you are biding your time until we die out."

"Oh, no, not at all."

"What prevents you?" Zalumar inquired.

"Two things," Fox told him. "Firstly, we suppose that other and probably stronger Raidan forces will replace you sometime. Obviously they won't leave you here to the end of your days."

Hah, won't they? thought Zalumar. He smiled within himself, said, "Secondly?"

"We're a Raidan colony. That means you're stuck with the full responsibilities of ownership. If anyone else attacks us, you Raidans must fight to keep us—or let go. That suits us quite well. Better the devil we know than the devil we don't."

It was glib and plausible, too glib and plausible. It might be the truth—but only a tiny fragment of it. For some reason he couldn't define Zalumar felt sure he wasn't being told the whole of it. Something vital was being held back. He could not imagine what it might be, neither could he devise an effective method of forcing it into the open. All that he did have was this vague uneasiness. Maybe it was the after-effect of Lakin's persistent morbidity. Damn Lakin, the prophet of gloom.

For lack of any better tactic he changed the subject. "I have an interesting report from one of our experts named Marjamian. He is an anthropologist or a sociologist or something. Anyway, he is a scientist, which means that he'd rather support an hypothesis than agree with an idea. I want your comments on what he has to say."

"It is about we Terrans?"

"Yes. He says your ancient history was murderous and that you came near to exterminating yourselves. In desperation you reached accord on the only item about which everyone could agree. You established permanent peace by mutually recognizing the basic right of every race and nation to live its own life in its own way." He glanced at his listener. "Is that correct?"

"More or less," said Fox, without enthusiasm.

"Later, when you got into free space, you anticipated a need to widen this understanding. So you agreed to recognize the basic right of every *species* to live its own life in its own way." Another glance. "Correct?"

"More or less," repeated Fox, looking bored.

"Finally, we arrived," continued Zalumar. "Our way of life is that of ruthless conquest. That must have put you in a mental and moral dilemma. All the same, you recognized our right even at great cost to yourselves."

"We didn't have much choice about it, considering the alternative," Fox pointed out. "Besides, the cost isn't killing us. We have been keeping a few hundred Raidans in luxury. There are three thousand millions of us. The expense works out at approximately two cents per head per annum."

Zalumar's eyebrows lifted in surprise. "That's one way of looking at it."

"For which price," added Fox, "the planet remains intact and we get protection."

"I see. So you regard the situation as mutually beneficial. We've got what we want and so have you." He yawned to show the interview was over. "Well, it takes all sorts to make a cosmos."

But he did not continue to yawn after Fox had gone. He sat and stared unseeingly at the ornamental drapes covering the distant door, narrowing his eyes occasionally and striving within his mind to locate an invisible Terran tomahawk that might or might not exist.

He had no real reason to suppose that a very sharp hatchet lay buried some place, waiting to be dug up. There was nothing to go on save a subtle instinct that stirred within him from time to time.

Plus unpleasant tinglings in the scalp.

Another three and a half years, making six in all. Suddenly the hatchet was exhumed.

Zalumar's first warning of the beginning of the end came in the form of a prolonged roar that started somewhere east of the palace and died away as a shrill whine high in the sky. He was abed and in deep sleep when it commenced. The noise jerked him awake, he sat up, unsure whether he had dreamed it.

For a short time he remained gazing toward the bedroom's big windows and seeing only the star-spangled sky in between small patches of cloud. Outside there was now complete silence, as though a slumbering world had been shocked by this frantic bellowing in the night.

Then came a brilliant pink flash that lit up the undersides of the clouds. Another, another, and another. Seconds later came a series of dull booms. The palace quivered, its windows rattled. Scrambling out of bed he went to the windows, looked out, listened. Still he could see nothing, but clearly through the dark came many metallic hammerings and the shouts of distant voices.

Bolting across the room he snatched up his bedside phone, rattled it impatiently while his eyes examined a nearby list of those on duty tonight. Ah, yes, Arnikoj was commander of the palace guard. He gave the phone another shake, cursed under-breath until a voice answered.

"Arnikoj, what's going on? What's happening?"

"I don't know, sire. There seems to be some sort of trouble at the spaceport."

"Find out what's the matter. You have got a line to the port, haven't you?"

"It is dead, sire. We cannot get a reply. I think it has been cut."

"Cut?" He fumed a bit. "Nonsense, man! It may be accidentally broken. Nobody would dare to cut it."

"Cut or broken," said Arnikoj, "it is out of action."

"You have radio communication as well. Call them at once on your transmitter. Have you lost your wits, Arnikoj?"

"We have tried, sire, and are still trying. There is no response."

"Rush an armed patrol there immediately. Send a portable transmitter with them. I must have accurate information without delay."

Dropping the phone, he threw on his clothes as swiftly as possible. A dozen voices yelled in the garden not a hundred yards from his windows. Something let go with a violent hammering. He made a jump for the door but the phone shrilled and called him back.

He grabbed it. "Yes?"

Arnikoj screamed at him, "It is too late, sire. They are already—" A loud br-r-op-op interrupted him, his voice changed to a horrid gurgling that receded and slowly ceased.

Zalumar raced out the room and along the outer passage. His mind seemed to be darting forty ways at once. "They," who are "they"? Another Raidan expedition that had discovered this hide-out of renegades? Unknown and unsuspected Terran allies at long last come to the rescue? Mutineers led by Lakin? Who?

He rounded a corner so fast that he gave himself no chance to escape three armed Terrans charging along the corridor. They grabbed him even as he skidded to a stop. This trio were big, brawny, tough-looking, wore steel helmets, were smothered in equipment and bore automatic guns.

"What is meant by this?" shouted Zalumar. "Do you realize—"

"Shut up!" ordered the largest of the three.

"Somebody will pay for—"

"I said to shut up!" He swung a big hand, slapped Zalumar

with force that rattled his teeth and left him dazed. "See if he's clean, Milt."

One of the others ran expert hands over Zalumar's person. "Nothing on him, not even a loaded sock."

"O.K. Toss him in that small room. You stand guard, Milt. Beat his ears off if he gets uppish."

With that, two of them hustled around the corner, guns held ready. Twenty more similarly armed Terrans appeared and chased after the first two, none of them bothering to give the captive a glance in passing. Milt opened a door, shoved Zalumar's shoulder.

"Get inside."

"To whom do you think you're—"

Milt swung a heavy, steel-tipped boot at the other's tail and roared, "Get inside when you're told!"

Zalumar got in. The small room held a long, narrow table and eight chairs. He flopped into the nearest chair and glowered at Milt who leaned casually against the wall by the door. A minute later someone opened the door and slung Lakin through. Lakin had a badly discolored face and a thin trickle of blood along the jawline.

"Arnikoj is dead," said Lakin. "Also Dremith and Vasht and Marjamian and half the palace guard." He touched his features tenderly. "I suppose I'm lucky. They only beat me up."

"They will pay dearly for this," promised Zalumar. He studied the other curiously. "I suspected you of disloyalty to me. It seems that I was wrong."

"One can foresee trouble without having to take part in it. I've known for long enough that Heisham was brewing something. It was obvious that sooner or later—"

"Heisham?"

"Yes. His term of service ended two years ago—and he was still here. He is not the kind to sit around and do nothing about it. So he waited his chance."

"What chance?"

"We maintain a permanent ships' guard of eighty men. Everyone serves in rotation. Heisham needed only to bide his time until he and a bunch of sympathizers were selected for guard duty. The ships would then be his to do with as he pleased."

"That would be of no use. He couldn't take away ten cruisers with a mere eighty men."

"He could make off with two ships, each with a skeleton crew of forty," said Lakin.

"The fellow is stark, staring mad," declaimed Zalumar. "Immediately he shows his face on Raidan, he and all those with him will have to undergo interrogation, with torture if necessary. And when they've given up every item of information they'll be executed as traitors."

"Heisham doesn't think so," Lakin responded. "He is going to put all the blame on you. He's going to tell them that you prohibited the sending of a report because you wanted all the spoils and the glory for yourself."

"They won't take his unsupported word for that."

"There are eighty men with him and they'll all say the same. They've got to—they're in the same jam. Besides, he has persuaded the Terrans to confirm his story. When a Raidan commission arrives to check up the Terrans will give evidence in Heisham's favor. He's quite confident that this tactic will not only save his life but also gain him honor."

"How do you know all this?" demanded Zalumar.

"He told me of his plans. He invited me to come in with him."

"Why didn't you?"

"I didn't share his optimism. Heisham always was too cocksure for my liking."

"Then why didn't you inform me of this plot?"

Lakin spread hands to indicate helplessness. "What was the use? You'd have taxed him with treachery and he'd have denied it, knowing full well that you were already tired of my warnings. Would you have believed me?"

Letting that awkward question pass unanswered, Zalumar buried himself in worried thought, eventually said, "The Terrans will not support his tale. They have nothing to gain by doing so. It is of total indifference to them whether Heisham's gang live or die."

"The Terrans have agreed to confirm everything he says—for a price."

Leaning forward, Zalumar asked in tones of suppressed fury, "What price?"

"The eight ships Heisham could not take."

"Intact and complete with their planet-busting equipment?"

"Yes," Lakin brooded a moment, added, "Even Heisham would have refused such payment had the Terrans any idea of where Raidan is located. But they don't know. They haven't the slightest notion."

Taking no notice, Zalumar sat breathing heavily while his features changed color. Then suddenly he shot to his feet and yelled at the guard.

"You piece of filth! You dirty, lowdown animal!"

"Now, now!" said Milt, mildly amused. "Take it easy."

The door opened. Fox entered along with McKenzie and Vitelli. The latter bestowed on Zalumar the same unctuous smile that had not varied in six long years.

All three wore uniform and carried guns. Thus attired they looked much different; they'd acquired a hardness not noticed before. It wasn't quite like Raidan hardness, either. There was something else, a sort of patient craftiness.

Zalumar still had an ace up his sleeve; without giving them time to speak, he played it. "The ships won't do you any good. We shall never tell you where Raidan is."

"There's no need to," said Fox, evenly. "We know."

"You're a liar. None of my men would give you that information, not even a self-seeking swine like Heisham."

"Nobody did tell us. We found out from what they did not tell."

"Don't give me that! I—"

"It was a long and tedious task but finally we made it," Fox chipped in. All your wandering, sight-seeing tourists were willing to talk, being lonesome and far from home. We chatted with them at every opportunity. Not one would say just where he came from but every one of them readily admitted he did not come from some other place. We have analyzed records of eighty thousand conversations spread across six years. By simple process of elimination we've narrowed it down to the system of Sigma Octantis."

"You're wrong," asserted Zalumar, straining to hold himself in check. "Dead wrong."

"Time will show. There won't be much of it, either. Maybe we could build a super-fleet by combining the virtues of your ships and ours. But we're not going to bother. It would take too long. We'll have learned how to operate your vessels before another day has passed."

"Eight ships against Raidan's thousands?" Zalumar indulged in a harsh laugh. "You haven't a hope of victory."

"There will no thousands from Raidan. We're going to send those ships hotfoot after Heisham. Even if they don't overtake him they'll arrive so close behind that the Raidan authorities will have had no time to react."

"And what then?"

"A new binary will be born."

There was a brief silence, then Zalumar rasped with all the sarcasm he could muster, "So much for your well-beloved basic right."

"You've got hold of the correct stick—but at the wrong end," said Fox. "The right we recognize is that of every species to go *to hell after its own fashion.*"

"Eh?"

"So when you arrived we were willing to help. It was a cinch. One naturally expects the greedy and ruthless to behave greedily and ruthlessly. You ran true to type." Taking his gun from its holster, Fox carefully laid it in the center of the table. "This is further assistance."

With that they went out, Fox, McKenzie, Vitelli, and the guard named Milt. The door slammed shut. The lock clicked. Metal-shod boots commenced a monotonous patroling outside.

Zalumar and Lakin sat unmoving throughout the rest of the night and the whole of next day, staring blindly at the table and saying nothing. Toward dusk a tremendous bellowing sounded from the spaceport, screamed into the sky. Another and another, eight in all.

As the sun called Sol sank blood-red into the horizon, Zalumar walked ashen-faced to the table and picked up the gun.

A little later the patroling footsteps went away.

Thrilling, mind-expanding novels and stories by science fiction's most prestigious authors

The TEMPO Science Fiction Library